A Dark Champion

By Kinley MacGregor

A DARK CHAMPION
TAMING THE SCOTSMAN
BORN IN SIN
CLAIMING THE HIGHLANDER
MASTER OF DESIRE
MASTER OF SEDUCTION
A PIRATE OF HER OWN

If You've Enjoyed This Book,
Be Sure to Read These Other
AVON ROMANTIC TREASURES

ENGLAND'S PERFECT HERO *by Suzanne Enoch*
A GREEK GOD AT THE LADIES' CLUB *by Jenna McKnight*
GUILTY PLEASURES *by Laura Lee Guhrke*
IT TAKES A HERO *by Elizabeth Boyle*
MARRIED TO THE VISCOUNT *by Sabrina Jeffries*

Coming Soon

AN INVITATION TO SEDUCTION *by Lorraine Heath*

KINLEY MacGREGOR

A DARK CHAMPION

AVON BOOKS

An Imprint of HarperCollins*Publishers*

AVON BOOKS
An Imprint of HarperCollins*Publishers*
10 East 53rd Street
New York, New York 10022-5299

Copyright © 2004 by Sherrilyn Kenyon
ISBN: 0-7394-4269-4

For all my readers and for the support you give. Thank you! To the RBL women, who provide me with a daily laugh and a reminder that we can all pull together. For the women and men who play on my websites and who have waited so very patiently for the Brotherhood books to begin.

To my family, especially my husband, who never lets me forget that love really is the most important thing. To my friends who have supported me through everything (Janet, Brynna, Lo, Kim, Rebecca, and Cathy) and to Lyssa, May, and Nancy, who let me take chances. Most of all, for my family and friends who are no longer with me—I miss you much.

May the sun always shine on you all, and here's a big hug until next we meet!

BROTHERHOOD OF THE SWORD

Prologue

Come and sit with me a moment, friend and pilgrim, for I have a tale to tell that many of you have never heard before.

It is one of honor and friendship. One of bravery and nobility. One of strength and loyalty. It is a tale of boys who became men, not because they aged in years, but because they walked through the very fires of hell, arm in arm, back to back, defiant and bold with only one code of honor between them.

We all survive.

We all go home.

We are brothers unto the end.

It is said that the strongest steel is forged by Satan's fires. I have witnessed this myself. For I was once one of their number. Captured in a land known by many as Outremer or the Holy Land, and held as hostage by my enemies, it was there that I found these amazing men.

There were fifty of them in my cell. Cramped and cold, tired, beaten, and worn. But not defeated. Nay, these men could never be defeated.

Not by anything born of this earth.

Though I knew them for young men, and in some cases mere boys, they looked as haggard as any old beggar. Their faces were lined by horror and starvation, their clothes tattered and shredded, their bodies scarred and bleeding from old wounds and new. Still, they fought on with a strength of will that amazes me unto this day.

Out of fifty, five of them emerged as our leaders: the Wraith, who moved with stealth and secrecy while he ran interference with our guards; the Scot, who sacrificed himself for others so that they would not be punished; the Widowmaker, who watched over us and planned our escape; the Sorcerer, who was able to distract and steal whatever we needed; and the Abbot, whose scholarly ways and unending faith reminded us that we were still human even though we lived as animals in a filthy cage.

We named the five of them the *Quinfortis*, a Latin term that means the strength of five. They kept our spirits and hope alive every day as our captors sought to break us. Without them none of us would ever have made it home.

We would be dead now.

All of us.

It is in their honor that this chanson is written.

The Widowmaker

I met the man the Brotherhood termed the Widowmaker on the first day of my incarceration. His face had been so misshapen by a beating that he reminded me of some horrid monster. But it was his eyes that seared me.

Intelligent and sharp, they had seen right through me. He offered me his hand, as he had done the others who had been taken against their will, and told me that so long as he breathed, I would be protected.

He meant that.

On the night of our escape from hell, seven men stayed behind to cover our trail.

The Quinfortis, the Phantom, and the Pagan.

While we boarded a boat for home, the seven of them bravely faced our pursuers, alone with nothing more than their bare hands to protect them. Even now, years later, I can still clearly remember the sight of them in the moonlight as they fought like possessed champions while we ran at their behest.

The Wraith, the Scot, the Widowmaker, the Sorcerer, the Abbot, the Phantom, and the Pagan. Men who refused to use their God-given names while imprisoned since they had been reduced to animals forced to fight for bare sustenance.

Men who are bound by their scars and oaths to each other, and by the brand on their right hand that their enemies had placed there to remind them always of that time in the past when they were beasts.

But on the night of our escape, they weren't animals. They weren't men nor were they boys.

They were legends.

The kind of legends whose courage and selflessness should never be forgotten.

I have already told the tale of the Wraith in *Midsummer's Knight*, about the blessings that have since come upon Simon of Ravenswood.

It is time now that I write of another.

The Widowmaker who is best known to the world as Lord Stryder, earl of Blackmoor—a man of many secrets and strengths.

A man who has fought all his life and who has yet to realize the beauty that can be found off the battlefield.

And for those of you who are curious, my name, like those of the others, was hidden during my captivity. The Brotherhood gave me my own special moniker. I use my Christian name now, but for the purposes of introducing the world to the heroes I know, you may call me simply the Minstrel. I am a wandering bard, ever seeking my own peace from the past while I make sure that everyone knows of the personal sacrifices of the men who made up our company.

And now here begins the official tales of The Brotherhood of the Sword . . .

Chapter 1

"**T**est of arms, my bloody arse. They ought to call it the test of incompetent fools," Stryder of Blackmoor muttered as he made his way from the list toward his tent.

There hadn't been a single man on the field he had sparred against who had posed any contest to him at all. He might as well be fighting his brother Kit for all the skill the so-called knights showed.

It was a damn shame when a man couldn't find a decent opponent.

Of course, there were four men present at the yearly tournament who could challenge him—his own knights who traveled in his company: Raven, Will, Swan, and Val. But at this hour of the day, the only thing they would be fighting off was each other as they struggled to make it to the garderobe before their excesses of last night undignified them.

The five of them had been too long abroad, and the temptation of the English court and its decadence had been more than Stryder's men could deny. His four knights had spent all of last evening carousing and drinking.

The first to vanish had been Will, who had supped with a rich, voluptuous widow. After the meal and several tankards of mead, Will had discreetly made an exit with his lady in tow. Raven had collapsed from drink in the hall just after midnight, leaving Stryder and Swan to see him abed. Once they had the young man safely in his cot, Swan had left to meet with his latest paramour—a woman the knight had known all of an hour.

And Val . . .

Val had ended up in a drinking bout with several of the king's men. No doubt, Val's head would hurt for a week or more given how much beer and ale the man had consumed.

At half past three, Stryder had wished his friend well and sought his own bed. He hadn't seen Val since.

When Stryder had gone to break his fast before practice this morn, the hall had been clear of his men and none of them had been in their tents.

By now, surely they had risen from the dead and returned.

Then again, most likely not.

As Stryder left the practice list, he was mobbed by more than a score of maidens seeking his favor. They varied greatly in age and size. But one thing united them all.

Their desire to become the next countess of Blackmoor.

How he wished Simon of Ravenswood were here to help combat the shrill women who lauded his virtues as they elbowed and pranced trying to gain his notice.

Even his brother, Kit, would be of help.

But as usual, Kit was nowhere to be seen. No doubt he was off composing sappy, angst-filled songs with his mewling friends whose only thoughts were trivial and asinine.

Stryder deflected that thought quickly lest it test his temper even more.

"Lord Stryder, please choose me as the Lady of All Hearts!" one young woman screamed in his ear as she yanked at his black hair.

Stryder bit back a curse as he struggled to free himself of her demanding hand.

"Nay, I shall be the Lady, is that not correct, milord?"

Stryder couldn't answer due to other women shouting over him. The women each grabbed hold of him and pulled at his surcoat and limbs while others were busy ramming their tokens into his armor and helm.

Not to mention his chausses . . .

"I got a lock of Lord Stryder's hair!" one woman screamed as she fainted.

The other women stepped over her while one tried to swipe his hank of hair from the fallen woman's grasp. The "unconscious" woman quickly bit her and then ran off with her trophy.

That only started a frenzy as other women tried to get their own piece of his flesh.

Stryder didn't want to hurt any of the women, but disengaging them without violence was proving to be nearly impossible.

"Ladies, ladies!" a loud male voice boomed. "Please, a moment for his lordship who needs confess the multitude of sins he has committed."

Stryder gave a rare smile as he recognized the heavily accented voice of Christian of Acre. It had been nigh to three years since he last had the pleasure of seeing his old friend.

The women pouted in unison as they fell back and made room for the man who was dressed in a friar's homespun black habit.

But as they caught a look at Christian's tall, muscular form, their faces brightened considerably.

"'Tis a pity he's a monk," one of the women said rather loudly.

"Aye," another agreed.

Little did they know there was no holy oath binding the blond man in their midst. Christian wore a monk's clothes to keep his identity secret.

It was evidenced by the spurs that occasionally flashed from beneath the black hem that trailed on the ground and the black cowl that was drawn over his head to hide the fact that Christian lacked a tonsure. This was no cleric, but rather one of the finest swordsmen Stryder had ever beheld.

Not to mention that in his mother's homeland of Byzantium, Christian of Acre was a royal prince who was only one step away from the throne.

"Abbot," Stryder said in greeting as he shook Christian's proffered arm. "It's been too long."

"Aye," Christian agreed, gripping Stryder's arm tightly and patting him roughly on the shoulder. "It has indeed. But it appears little has changed with you." Christian's blue gaze swept through the women, who were still reluctant to leave them.

Stryder let out a tired breath. "True, very true."

"Brother?" one of the women asked Christian. She was a petite brunette with lush curves. The open invitation on her face said that if Christian agreed to it they would both be needing a priest to confess to by morning. "Might I give *my* confession later?"

A devilish look flashed in Christian's eyes. Stryder could see him weighing his answer carefully.

When he spoke, his words were what Stryder had expected. Christian might be a heathen in his current beliefs, but he still bore enough respect for the clergy who had raised him that he would never dishonor their reputation by accepting a woman's invitation while he wore a holy man's garb. "Aye, my lady. I am told the local priest here has quite a few openings."

Her face fell with disappointment.

"If you ladies will forgive us . . ." Christian led the way out of the group, toward the brightly colored tents that the knights had pitched on a hill outside the castle walls.

More than three hundred knights had ventured to Hexham for the monthlong games that were held every year in the fall. Unlike the other knights, Stryder hadn't come here seeking fame or fortune—he had more than his share of both. He was in Hexham at the king's command so that the king could keep an eye on Stryder, who had been having more than his fair share of "accidents" lately. Indeed, someone wanted him dead in the worst sort of way and until they found out who, Henry wanted to keep Stryder on home soil.

Stryder glanced over his shoulder to make sure none of the ladies were trailing after them. Though the women looked on their departure longingly, they had blessedly remained behind.

"What brings you here?" Stryder asked Christian.

Christian's expression was dark as they climbed the hill. "I come with bad tidings, I'm afraid. Lysander of Marseilles was killed."

Stryder stopped dead in his tracks at the news. Lysander of Marseilles had been one of the men who had been imprisoned in Outremer. Once the Brotherhood had freed the man, Stryder himself had sent Lysander to Scotland to serve in the household of a friend.

"How can that be?"

"He was tortured and murdered," Christian said, his voice carrying the full weight of anger that Stryder felt.

"Who would dare such?"

"An enemy to the Highland MacAllister clan," Christian said, his voice deepened by anger and grief. "After Lysander and Pagan helped Ewan MacAllister home, Lysander was captured and killed for the deed. I'm headed north now to help Pagan find and kill those responsible."

"You need another sword?"

Christian's face relaxed instantly. "I would say aye, but the mere fact that you are here in England and not on the continent tells me you are on king's business and not free to leave."

Stryder growled at that. "Aye. But it sits ill with me that one of our own was slain."

"Believe me, we all share that sentiment."

Stryder had no doubt. They hadn't survived the horrors of their captivity to return home to be tortured and murdered. The anger he felt at that thought swirled inside him, making him want blood. "Swear to me you'll make the culprit pay."

"You may have no fear on that count. Pagan wrote that he intended to show the one responsible how the Saracens treated their prisoners."

Stryder grimaced involuntarily at the reminder of some of their "lessons" at the hands of their captors. Those heathens knew well how to make anyone regret having been born, and when it came to bloody acts, he doubted if anyone could best Pagan. No one knew the man's real nationality, but they all knew Pagan's willingness to cut any handy throat. "Good."

Christian clapped him on the back and started up the hill again.

As they walked, Stryder began picking the ribbons and garters from his armor and helm where the women had placed them.

Christian gave a low deep laugh as he watched him. "Ever your curse to be pursued by the fairer sex, eh?"

Stryder gave him a droll stare. "Methinks I should tell them of Prince Christian. That should bide me a moment of peace from them and their machinations to wed me."

"That would help you not at all since I am already betrothed."

"Ahh," Stryder said, laughing darkly. "The mysterious princess you've never seen. Tell me, do you really think she still waits on your hoary hide to return to her?"

"I wish it were otherwise, but I receive enough letters from my uncle urging me to return home and marry her to know she is ever the dutiful maid who sits waiting patiently for my homecoming." Christian's voice was tinged with ire at that.

Stryder knew his friend well enough to know Christian wished the maid would find someone else to marry. Like him, Christian was most happy as a bachelor and had no desire to tie a woman to his side.

At least not for any longer than a single night.

Stryder led the way into his red and white–striped tent. He set his helm on the table and doffed his gauntlets. "Will you return home to marry her soon?"

Bitter anger flashed in Christian's eyes. "I've no desire to return home for many reasons. Prince I may be, but I owe them nothing. My loyalties are strictly to the Brotherhood now."

Stryder nodded in understanding. Christian's family had been the reason he was living in the monastery when it had been captured by Saracens in Acre. After the death of Christian's parents when he was six, Christian's uncle had sequestered the boy with the monks in hopes that Christian would learn his place so that he could return to Byzantium to be a puppet easily controlled.

That plan could not have gone more wrongly, since the man before Stryder was stronger than steel and would never be controlled by anyone or anything.

Stryder's squire, Druce, came running into the tent. At ten-and-four, the boy was gangly and uncoordinated. His curly black hair was cut short, but always managed to look unruly. The boy often ran about daydreaming and falling over things. Even so, Stryder never lost patience with him.

Like Stryder had been at that age, Druce was an orphan and a ward of the crown.

"I'm sorry I'm late, milord," Druce said as he grabbed a stool and dragged it toward Stryder. "There was a storyteller who came and she was fantastic. I could have listened to her all day as she spun stories of lovers betrayed by the Fates." Druce climbed onto the stool and reached to unlace the back of Stryder's armor.

Stryder grunted at that as he dipped lower so Druce could reach the fastenings more easily.

Stryder knew the instant Druce became aware of Christian's presence. The boy tumbled off the stool and almost knocked Stryder over as he went sprawling onto the floor.

The boy looked up, his entire face contrite. "I'm so sorry, Lord Stryder. Did I interrupt something?"

"Nay," Stryder said, helping him up. "Christian and I were only talking of inconsequential matters." Stryder introduced the lad to Christian. "Christian of Acre, meet Druce, my ward and squire."

"Greetings, Druce," Christian said before meeting Stryder's gaze. Christian's eyes were troubled even more than before. "Did something happen to Raven?"

"Nay. He was knighted a few months back and is sleeping off a night of misbegotten youth."

His face relaxing, Christian grunted at that as Druce returned to disarm Stryder.

Druce meanwhile prattled on about the woman he'd been listening to. "Have you ever heard of the Lady of Love, milord?"

"Nay," Stryder answered.

"I have," Christian said as he took a seat at the desk and poured himself a cup of ale. "She's just your type of lady, Stryder. A troubadour of great renown, she despises knights and writes only of courtly love and how needed it is in this day and age of great violence."

Stryder curled his lips at that. If there was one thing he hated above all, it was those who purveyed the virtues of courtly love. That so-called noble sentiment had cost more lives and strife than any sword ever had. "A pox to all of her ilk."

"Nay, milord," Druce said, his face dreamy. "She is more beautiful than Venus and holds the voice of the sweetest lark. Surely the lady has no equal. You should listen to her as she tells how the world could be if only we strove for peace with the same passion we use to pursue war."

Stryder exchanged a knowing look with Christian. "You are

young, Druce. One day you will realize that all women are the same. They want nothing more than a man to care for them so that they can pester and pick until a man is nigh mad with their nagging. They have but one use."

"And that is, milord?" Druce asked.

Christian's eyes danced with merriment. "That you will soon discover on your own, boy. But for now you are too young for it."

Druce's mouth formed a small O that said the boy already had an inkling of it as he gathered Stryder's mail pieces.

Stryder tossed his squire a bag of coins. "Drop the armor off with the armorer to be polished, and then take the rest of the day and enjoy it."

Druce beamed. Thanking him, he dashed off with the mail armor draped over his shoulder and the money cradled carefully in his hand.

"You spoil him," Christian said.

Stryder shrugged. "Children should be spoiled. Would that we had known such at his age."

Christian's gaze turned haunted at that and Stryder wondered if his own eyes showed the scars of his past so plainly.

Like him, Christian had been raised with the single principle of "spare the rod, spoil the child."

Stryder could fell a full-grown man with a single blow. The idea of striking someone so much smaller than he sat ill in his gullet. With one reckless strike, he could kill the boy. Indeed, Stryder's own lord had broken his jaw when he was Druce's age for nothing more than dropping the man's sword.

It was a chance he'd never take. He'd sooner cut off his arm than ever prey on someone weaker than he.

Stryder reached for a towel at the same time his tent flap was slung backward. He half expected to see a maid coming through it to offer herself to him and was a bit surprised to find his younger brother there, since Kit held no love of battle and often refused to come near Stryder's tent.

Like Druce before him, Kit paid no heed to Christian in the corner.

Dressed in a garish red and orange combination, Kit held a large basket in his hands that was overfilled with letters and various pieces of ladies' garb.

"What is this?" Stryder asked, as Kit set the whole of it at his feet.

Kit swept his orange hat from his head and wiped his sweaty brow with his arm. "Tokens from your admirers. I have been instructed to give you all of these personally and to make sure no other living human touches them."

Christian laughed.

Kit snapped around to see Christian leaning back in the chair with a stein of ale braced on his stomach while his long legs were stretched out before him and crossed at the ankles.

Kit's blue eyes widened considerably. "You're entertaining priests now?"

Stryder snorted at that. "Nay, Kit. Meet an old friend of mine, Christian. Christian, meet my younger brother, Kit."

Christian inclined his head to Stryder's brother.

Kit's gaze never wavered from Christian, and it turned speculative the instant he noticed Christian's spurs and mail-covered boots peeking out from the hem of his black robes.

Stryder cleared his throat to draw Kit's notice back toward him. Once he had his brother's attention, Stryder very subtlety shook his head nay and passed a censoring gaze toward Christian.

Kit immediately took the hint to ask no questions and turned his back to Christian. He leaned over and pulled from the bunch a bright red ribbon that had a key attached to it. "This one in particular said that I was to make sure you received her gift or else she would poison me while I eat. So in lieu of hiring a taster for my meals, I wanted to make sure it reached you."

Stryder rolled his eyes as Kit took it and broke the seal on the note that was also attached to the ribbon.

His brother read it aloud.

"Milord, 'tis with great honor I give you the key to my chastity belt. Meet me tonight in the rose courtyard.

Ever your lady,
Charity of York"

"A key to a chastity belt?" Christian asked in an amused tone.

"Aye," Stryder said, his voice thick with ill humor. "And an invitation to a forced wedding if ever I saw one."

Christian laughed again at that. "And you wonder why I prefer to wear the garb of a monk. It's the best shield I have found against conniving would-be brides, and even it isn't foolproof, as you have seen."

Stryder handed the key back to Kit. "Tell the lady I am previously engaged."

Kit arched a brow at that, then headed for one of Stryder's plate codpieces.

He frowned as he watched his brother place the codpiece inside his hose. "What is it you do?"

"The last time I told one of your would-be paramours nay on your behalf, she damn near unmanned me. This time I wish protection when I deliver the news."

Stryder joined Christian's laughter.

"'Tis not amusing," Kit said, his tone offended. "You think what you do is dangerous? I defy you to be in my boots for one moment when I face the great Ovarian Horde in your stead."

"And that is why I send you, my brother. I haven't the courage to face them."

"What?" Christian said in feigned shock. "Stryder of Blackmoor afraid? I never thought I would live to see the day a mere maid could send you craven."

"The day you doff your cleric's robes and don your crown, Your Highness, you may taunt me on that front. Until then, I know you for the coward you are as well."

Christian's eyes danced with mischief. "Women do make cowards of us all."

Kit opened his mouth to say something, then must have rethought it. Grabbing a shield, he headed for the door. "If I don't return by night's fall, please make sure I am buried on home soil."

Stryder shook his head at his brother's play, but then again . . .

Nay. None of the women would really hurt Kit.

As soon as they were alone, Stryder washed his face and chest in the wash basin, then toweled himself dry.

"How is it after all we have been through together that I never even knew you had a brother?" Christian asked as Stryder draped the towel over his shoulder and moved forward to pour himself a goblet of wine.

Stryder squelched the pain that innocent question conjured. Though he had shared much of his life with Christian, there were many things he had not shared with anyone. Things he would *never* share with anyone. "We are half brothers who grew up apart."

"Ah," Christian said as he watched his friend take a seat across from him.

Stryder looked tired. His blue eyes were troubled, but then Stryder had never been light of heart. His friend, much like him, had always been overly earnest.

Simon of Ravenswood used to refer to them as the Doomsday Duo. But then they had all seen far too much of the darker side of man's cruelty.

It had a way of robbing them of their optimism.

"Have you seen the Scot lately?" Stryder asked.

"It will be a year ago September."

"How does he?"

Christian sighed as he remembered their companion who had chosen to hide himself in the country of England as opposed to going home to his family in Scotland. "Same as before. He is reclusive and refuses to let any see his face. He barely spoke to me while I was there."

Stryder looked away, his brow even more troubled. Christian knew he blamed himself for what had happened to the Scot during their captivity. "It wasn't your fault."

Christian referred to the incident when one of their group had tried to escape. Barely ten-and-six in age, the boy's escape route had been discovered before any of them had had a chance to use it.

When the Saracens came for one of them to punish for it, the Scot had stepped forward to take the blame, knowing the one responsible would never have survived the punishment.

Their captors had tortured the Scot for a full fortnight. When he was returned to their cell, his eye had been taken and the man had been left horribly scarred.

The Scot had never been the same, and Stryder blamed himself to this day for not taking the blame himself.

"You can't carry the ills for the entire world, Stryder. Some things are just meant to be."

Stryder took a deep draught of wine, but said nothing.

He didn't have to. The two of them had known each other so long that Christian knew what was on his mind.

What they did was hard and never ending. They had more commitments than they could meet and both of them felt responsible for every member of their guard.

Theirs was a lonely life.

Aye, they could have any wench who took their fancy, maiden or experienced, but then what?

Neither of them needed or wanted the burden of a wife who would demand even more of their precious time.

Christian had the burden of a kingdom waiting one day to claim him, but Stryder . . . He had demons who commanded him. Demons that wouldn't give him peace.

Ever.

Christian only hoped that in the end, they wouldn't drive his friend mad the way they had driven Stryder's father insane.

It was well known by all that Geoffrey of Blackmoor had died by his own hand.

But not before he had tried to kill his own son.

Chapter 2

"**Y**ou should have been there, Rowena."

Rowena de Vitry plastered a patient smile on her face as her lady-in-waiting, Elizabeth, rambled on while their maids prepared their hair and veils for the coming supper. They each sat on wooden chairs before an open window.

"Lord Stryder just popped out of his tent as we headed for the castle. Barely three feet away from us, he hardly had a stitch on." Elizabeth sighed dreamily as she propped her elbow on the dressing table and stared into space.

Rowena did her best not to roll her eyes at her friend's adolescent behavior. She held little doubt that if left alone, Elizabeth would spend the next sennight doing nothing more than staring out her bower window, mooning over the earl.

"You've never seen a man so well shaped. His jet-black hair was wet and dripping down his muscles and . . ."

Elizabeth broke off into another sigh. "You should see his chest. I declare but you can see every tiny muscle flex when he breathes."

Rowena could feel her smile slipping away. "Yea, and I'm sure they flex well as they drive a sword into a man to take his life."

"Of course," Elizabeth agreed, sitting up straighter so that her maid could coil her braids about her head and pin them. "By all accounts he is the fiercest knight in all Christendom. Why else would he be named the king's champion?"

"Why else, indeed," Rowena whispered, then clenched her

teeth. Knights. How she despised them and all they signified. To her, there was nothing glorious about battle or death.

What real man could take pride in spreading misery and heartache?

Ever since she had received news at age eleven that her beloved father had fallen in battle, she had despised war and those who took part in it. Unlike her friends, she didn't swoon when she confronted a purveyor of death. Nay, she gave them a wide berth.

And she wished a pox on them all.

In her heart, it was a gentle man she sought. One who was kind to others and who could be compassionate without fear of it weakening him.

"Find the man who will love you, bit. One who is worthy of your devotion. Let no man have you because you are landed. Better I should give up all to Henry than have my girl miserable. Life's too short for all of us, and I want you to enjoy every day of yours."

Her father's words still echoed in her mind and, most importantly, in her heart. He had been a good man, and it was one such as he that she sought for husband.

Unfortunately, she had yet to find anyone even close to his decency. Instead, she was courted by men who saw nothing but lands and wealth whenever they looked at her.

At age ten-and-five, she had once come to sup at banquet dressed as a gold nugget and caused quite a stir amongst the nobles. Her unamused uncle had taken a strap to her and quickly forced her to change her clothes.

Though she had never repeated that experience, Rowena was still the same. She would never have a man who saw her as a means to an end. She would only marry a man who saw her as a woman.

"Do you think Lord Stryder might choose me as the Lady of All Hearts?" Elizabeth prattled on. "I know he'll be the knight who wins the tourney, and I should like so much to be picked." A blush crept over Elizabeth's cheeks. "I left him my handkerchief as a token when he helped us bring Joanne inside. Do you think he kept it?"

Rowena gave Elizabeth a genuine smile. Her friend couldn't help her infatuation for a barbarian. And though it pained her to listen to it, she loved Elizabeth enough not to crush her dreams. If being tossed over a man's shoulder and being treated like a possession made her friend happy, and it did, then Rowena wished her friend well and all the barbarians her friend could handle. "Why would he not keep a token from someone as beautiful as you?"

Elizabeth smiled. "You're so kind, Rowena. I hope you fill the hall at your recital."

Rowena glanced to her lute, which rested on the window sill. Music and poetry were her life. And it was the only life she wanted, if the truth were told. While her ladies-in-waiting dreamed of husbands, children, and titles, she dreamed of traveling from castle to castle, singing for her supper and seeing the world, or at the very least, opening a school so that she could train others to cherish music as much as she did.

But unlike her male minstrel counterparts, who wrote songs that glorified war and knights, she wrote only of love.

Her stance against the order of knighthood was often mocked by other troubadours and nobles who thought her foolish. However, she didn't care. She'd won enough awards and contests with her words of love that she didn't need the approval of the more traditional minstrels. She had faith in her music.

If only her father had lived to see her success. . . .

Rowena blinked away the mist in her eyes. Even after all this time, her heart still ached for the father she'd loved so dearly. But it wasn't in her nature to let others see her pain. She was a quiet sort who kept her feelings close to her breast.

As she turned her attention back to Elizabeth, a knock sounded on the door.

At Elizabeth's bidding, Joanne stuck her blond head in, slightly dislodging her yellow veil in the process. She wore a gown of watchet, and her green eyes twinkled merrily. Joanne was one of four ladies-in-waiting who were fostering in Rowena's household and who had come with her to Hexham for the tournament. "Are you two not ready?"

Elizabeth ignored the question and asked one of her own. "Is *he* in the hall yet?" The excitement in Elizabeth's voice told Rowena that the *he* she referred to must be the earl of Blackmoor.

The earl had arrived in Hexham two days before and so far Rowena had been spared his boorish company.

Something that was sure to change shortly.

Joanne's face beamed. "Aye, he just entered the hall."

Elizabeth overturned her chair in her haste to leave the room.

Sedately, Rowena rose to her feet and followed after her friends, who were rushing down the corridor in a most unladylike fashion as they giggled and recounted their earlier encounter with the earl.

"I can't believe he actually carried me," Joanne said in a breathless voice. "How I wish I'd been awake."

"How I wish I'd been the one who fainted," Elizabeth inserted. "Oh, to be carried by those strong arms!"

Rowena shook her head. In spite of her best efforts, a smile hovered at the edges of her lips. She loved her two friends, but there were times when they still acted as if they were children instead of women full grown.

Elizabeth and Joanne paused along the gallery where numerous other women were leaning over the low stone wall to spy on the men below. The hall was crowded with people and hounds and musicians as servants prepared the tables for the coming meal. Over and over, Rowena heard various women exclaiming over Lord Stryder, the earl of Blackmoor.

"Is his hair not as dark as a midnight sky?" a woman to her left breathed.

"Oh, aye. And his shoulders are by far the broadest of any below."

"You can tell by his walk that he's a man to satisfy a woman's needs. Oh, but for a chance to find out for myself."

Rowena plucked absently at her sleeve as she sought a way to block out the inane prattle. It was such an effort not to be sick in the midst of the hallway.

"I hear he's vowed to never marry."

Rowena quirked an eyebrow at the untoward comment. Perhaps the man had some intelligence after all.

"Why would he vow such?" Elizabeth asked.

"They say he's cursed."

"Cursed with the looks of a handsome devil, and the prowess

of Saint George. I wish someone would curse me with such a man!"

Unable to stand any more of their comments, Rowena pushed gently past the thronging women and slowly descended the stairs. Let them ogle if they must. She had other things to do, such as finding something bitter to remove the cloying sugary taste of their comments from her throat.

As she entered the foyer, a young page accidently ran into her in his haste to fetch more wine for his lord. Rowena tried to right herself, but just as she straightened a hound shot across her path and caught in the hem of her gown. Propelled forward, she felt herself falling.

She gasped, reaching out for a way to steady herself. Just as she was certain she would undignify herself with a sprawl in the center of the crowd, someone caught her.

Strong arms wrapped tightly around her, spinning her about before holding her close against a chest taut with muscles.

Rowena looked up and felt her jaw go slack.

Never in the whole of her life had she seen the like . . .

Never.

Blue eyes, fierce and piercing, stared out from a face of pure masculine heaven. It was all she could do to not reach out and run her hand along the sharp angle of that perfectly sculpted jaw, to let the telltale black stubble scrape her fingertip . . .

The man was utterly gorgeous.

Perfect.

He possessed that rare manly beauty that would be feminine on anyone who lacked his raw, earthy masculinity. Or on anyone who lacked the size of him.

He was huge! Tall and well muscled, he held her with ease. His unfashionably long hair spoke that this man didn't cater to current tastes, and the humor in his gaze said he possessed a good, tender nature.

As he continued to watch her with fascinated interest, her face burned with heat.

This was a most embarrassing embrace, if the truth were told. Her body was tilted backward so that she looked up at the stranger with only the strength of his arms supporting her. He surrounded her with warmth and security, and his handsome face bore a mixture of concern and amusement.

"Are you all right, milady?" he asked.

There was music in that masculine tone. A rich, deep bass that would no doubt resonate with beauty should he use it to sing.

An aura of danger surrounded him that said he followed no man's rules save his own. An aura that said he held a dark, sinister side to him that would have been frightening had it not been softened by an air of charming good humor. It was a strange dichotomy that held her enthralled.

His wavy black hair swept about his broad shoulders and as he smiled, she saw the dimples that cut deep moons into his cheeks.

Her heart pounded as chills went through her at the sight of those devilish dimples.

He had also asked her a question. She remembered it, but for her life she couldn't remember what he'd said.

Until he set her back on her feet.

Mortified that she hadn't moved, that she was acting every bit as childish as her friends, Rowena felt another wave of heat rush up over her cheeks.

In an effort to look away from the laughter in his blue mirthful eyes, her gaze dropped to his broad chest. He wore a tight red and black supertunic that slid sinuously over lean muscles, muscles she remembered feeling pressed against her all too well.

His body was truly a feast for her eyes.

Until she saw *it*. . . .

The sword he had strapped to his lean hips.

"You're a knight," she pronounced slowly, understanding now the dark side of him that she had glimpsed.

Knight. Murderer. They were synonymous, and she should have known he was one of their dreaded breed. She shouldn't be surprised by the knowledge. Most noblemen were knights, yet a wave of bitter disappointment claimed her.

How she wished he had been born another. 'Twas such a pity that so handsome a man would waste his time on such pointless, cruel endeavors.

"Aye, milady," he said again in that wonderful, melodic voice. "A knight ever at your service."

She supposed she should thank him for the quick reflexes that had kept her from falling, but then those reflexes had only been honed so that he could kill others. Rather she should sprawl upon the floor a thousand times than one man should perish in war.

"I appreciate your service, sir," she said, her voice carrying the full arctic impact of her mood.

She started away from him.

"Milady?"

Without thought, she paused and turned back toward him.

"Will you not give me your name?"

"Nay."

This time when she started away from him, he actually blocked her path.

"Nay?" he asked, his eyes showing his surprise, and yet they also managed to be charming and warm. 'Twas obvious he didn't hear that word often from a maid's lips.

"You have no need for my name, sir knight. I am sure there are plenty here who would gladly give you theirs, but I am not one of them."

One corner of his mouth quirked up, displaying a single dimple in his left cheek. In spite of her best intentions, she found his devilish air . . .

Entertaining?

Nay, that wasn't really the word, she found him . . . well . . . delightful, if she dare admit it. He really was too charming for words.

"Can I not claim mere curiosity, milady? After all, 'tis not often I find an unknown woman in my arms."

Rowena bit her bottom lip in an effort to suppress her smile which proved a treacherous beast against her will. "There is something about you, sir, that tells me that is not true."

His rich laughter rippled in her ears as he bestowed his full smile upon her. That smile did the strangest things to her body. It made her pulse race, her mind giddy.

"Then shall we say 'tis not often I find a maid in my arms who is reluctant?"

"Now that I believe most definitely." She took a step backward, more afraid of her sudden desire to stay with him than of his occupation.

Whatever was the matter with her? She'd never before wanted to be in the same country as such men, and now all of a sudden she actually wanted to take a moment to chat with this one.

She must have drunk too much wine.

You haven't had a sip, Rowena. You only just now entered the hall.

Oh, well, then it must be the excitement of the day's events. Aye, that was it.

That *must* be it.

"If you'll excuse me?" she asked.

He stepped back reluctantly. "This time only, milady. When next we meet, I'll be expecting a name for you."

"If that be the case, sir knight, then you shall again be disappointed."

Something akin to admiration glowed in those deep blue eyes. "Should I warn you, milady, I don't take disappointment well?"

Rowena smiled in spite of herself. She liked this verbal sparring with him. It wasn't often she found a man or woman who could match her so effortlessly. "Only if you allow me to warn you that I don't take warning well."

This time when she turned he didn't try to stop her, but she heard his laughter again.

Oh, she thought with a sigh. 'Twas terrible he was a knight. With such a voice and manner he would have made a fine troubadour indeed.

Halfway across the room Rowena did her best not to yield to a desire to turn around and see if he watched her still. Over and over she told herself she didn't care whether he watched her or not.

He was a dreaded, brutal knight.

And as she reached the side of a fellow minstrel, she did just happen to glance backward. Not that she was looking for him, she assured herself. It was Elizabeth, Bridget, or Marian she sought. And yet as her gaze skimmed the occupants and she saw no hint of her knight, she couldn't suppress her disappointment.

It's just as well. All a man such as that can offer is early widowhood and a broken heart as he traipses from bed to bed, ever careless of a woman's feelings.

Those words were ever so true, yet she did wonder at what his name might have been.

What name would fit a man of such charm and beauty? Certainly not Hugh, Henry, or Edward. Nay, he would have a name as unique as the man. . . .

Do stop thinking about it!

Putting the man out of her mind, she joined her friends and forced herself to enjoy the conversation.

Henry Plantagenet, king of England, ruler of Normandy, Anjou, and Aquitaine, undisputedly one of the most powerful men in the world, sat in the corner of his withdrawing room, holding a cool cloth to his head.

His temples throbbed, his heart raced with fury, and he was quite certain that in the next few minutes he might very well die from aggravation.

If one more knight, baron, earl, or other came through the doors of his room to beg him to force Stryder of Blackmoor to marry his daughter, he would kill them.

All of them.

He would go mad with anger and descend on the whole of his court like the Grim Reaper, seeking only peace from the locusts who were determined to kill him.

"Here," his wife Eleanor said as she brought him another cool cloth and placed it to his brow. She was an elegant queen. Tall, slender, and blonde, she was the envy of all Christendom, and at times such as this, Henry remembered why he had married her (aside from the fact that she held control of more French lands than the French king).

Henry handed her the old cloth and grimaced. "What am I to do, Nora?" he asked his wife. "Apparently no lady in the kingdom is willing to wed until Stryder chooses a bride. What foolishness has plagued these women?"

"If you were a woman, Henry, you would have no need to ask that. The man is quite pleasing to the eyes and has more wealth than even you."

He growled at her.

To his utter horror, another knock sounded. "If 'tis anyone other than my physician, send him away."

His guards opened the door to show him Lionel of Sussex. They were about to shove the man out when Henry stopped them. "Nay, he is one of the few people We are ever grateful to see. Unless he says the name Stryder of Blackmoor, that is."

Lionel frowned at that. He came forward and bowed low, his eyes never wavering from Henry's head where the cloth resided. "Have you an ache, my liege?"

"Aye, but We are trying to decide which one plagues Us most. The one in Our head or the one in Our—"

"Henry!" Eleanor snapped.

"Neck," he said gruffly. "I was going to say 'neck.'"

Eleanor gave him a disbelieving stare.

Lionel came forward to kiss the queen's hand before Eleanor sat down in the chair next to Henry.

Henry watched as his old friend took up pacing in the open area between his chair and the doors. He knew what vexed Lionel. "She won't decide?"

"Decide? Nay, Majesty. *She* won't agree to anyone at all. She has some foolish notion that she is a teacher and wants to set up a school."

Henry groaned at that. Lady Rowena was an heiress whose wealth was not so great in coin. Her desirability lay in the fact that she was heiress to practically the whole of southern England. Whoever married her would control the border of his kingdom and separate the northern part of England from his lands in France.

With all the trouble he was having with Phillip of France, the last thing he could afford was for that land to fall into the possession of anyone who was less than friendly toward him. In the wrong hands, that land would spell the end of his monarchy.

"What was wrong with Lord Ansley?"

"He, like the others, is knighted. She says she will not consider a knight."

"Then force her!" Henry snapped.

Lionel sighed. "I wish it were that simple, Majesty. The last time I tried to force her hand, she ran away to the continent and was gone until I agreed to forget my plans for her. I sent out more than two score men to find her and was unable to do so. She only returned because I signed a document swearing I would allow her the power to naysay any man I proposed to be her husband."

Eleanor laughed.

Both men glared at her.

"Forgive me, gentlemen," she said, smiling. "I have to say that I admire the girl's temerity and wherewithal."

"Will you admire it when Phillip sits upon Our throne?"

She sobered instantly. "Calm yourself, Henry."

Lionel raked a frustrated hand through his graying brown hair. "I fear I shall just have to live forever. I can't die and allow her lands to go to a man who can't protect them."

Henry snorted at that. "No offense, Lionel, even now We worry at your abilities to hold her inheritance. There are many men out there who grow impatient with her indecision. Sooner or later one of them is bound to pounce."

"No offense taken, Majesty. I have the same fear every time one of those greedy beasts comes calling for her hand. I know you speak the truth and I appreciate it."

The king pulled the cloth from his brow. "What is the matter with the youth of today?" Henry asked the ceiling above them as if addressing heaven itself. "In my day, we married when we were supposed to and we married who we were supposed to. Now I have an earl who refuses to take a bride and a strategically placed heiress who would sooner cut off her head than take a knight for husband. There has to be some solution to this."

Eleanor sat forward.

"Nay, Nora," Henry said as he noted the speculative look on her beautiful face. "Say not what I know is in your mind."

She waved his words away with her hand. "They would be perfect together. Who better to guard Our border than Stryder of Blackmoor? He is one of the few whose loyalty is above question."

"Aye, and look at what happened when I tried to marry him off to Kenna. The man still hasn't forgiven me."

"That's because you *ordered* him to, Henry, and need I remind you that he would have obeyed you."

"Aye, but an irate earl in Scotland is one thing. An irate earl sitting entrenched in lands that divide my kingdom in half is an entirely different matter."

She drummed her fingers on the arm of her chair and didn't appear to be listening to him. Typical. Eleanor only heard what she wanted to. "I have known Rowena since she was just a girl.

Like Stryder, if you tell her to go right, she will go left. Put them together and—"

"Rowena will geld your knight, Your Grace," Lionel said, interrupting her. "She despises all knights."

"But there is no woman whose heart is immune to Stryder of Blackmoor," she countered. "Rowena is a woman and he is not the usual knight. Put them together and I am sure they will suit."

Henry narrowed his eyes. "I'm not so sure I agree with you."

"You seldom do."

He ignored the venom in her voice. "But I would like to see the two of them married. What do you suggest?"

Eleanor thought it over. "Rowena wants her choice of husband. I say we give it to her."

"Are you mad?" Henry asked. "She'll pick one of those geldings who flock to your skirts. Those mewling minstrels who lack all masculinity."

She gave him a droll stare that warned him of her wrath should he continue to disparage those who curried her favor in nauseating droves. "Nay, she won't. Rowena prides herself on only one thing in life."

"Her music," Lionel said.

"Aye. As you said, she thinks to start a school."

Lionel nodded.

"Then let us cater to her desires, gentlemen. Tell her that if she can teach a knight to sing in the troubadour contest at the end of the tournament and win it that you will not only allow her the choice of husband, but that you will set up her school."

Henry frowned at the idea. "Are you suggesting she teach Stryder to sing?"

"Aye."

Henry shook his head. He knew Stryder well enough to know what the man would say to that. "Stryder will never do such. He despises minstrels even more than I do. The moment Rowena approaches him with the proposal, he will send her packing."

"Not if he is told that at the end of the tournament Rowena will wed the victor."

Oh, his queen was evil, and he loved her like this. The cold, cunning politician who was merciless. There were times when Henry thought that Eleanor should have been born a man.

The plan was brilliant. "Stryder is sure to win it."

"Aye, he is. His pride will never allow him to lose the tournament. The only way he can prevent his marriage to Rowena is to
sing. In order to sing, he will have to be around her to learn a
song and to practice. Once the two of them are together, I predict
love will follow its natural course between them."

There was only one flaw that Henry could see. "And what if
he wins this troubadour contest and Rowena doesn't choose him
as her husband?"

"I never said it wasn't a gamble, Henry. But I know I am right
and she will pick him at the end."

"And again, I say, what if you're wrong?"

"Then we kill off whoever she chooses," Lionel said merci-
lessly.

Eleanor made an exasperated noise as if his solution pained
her. "You won't have to. Trust me. I know men and I know
women."

Henry would certainly give her that. His queen did indeed
know how to manipulate people.

It was risky. If Rowena won, most likely she would never
choose a husband. Sooner or later he would have to force that
issue.

But if Eleanor was right . . .

"Very well then. Let us try this and see what happens."

Lionel crossed himself. "Let me go and deliver the news to
my niece."

Chapter 3

Rowena paused to the right of the crowd as she caught sight of the mysterious knight who had saved her.

He's a knight, he's a knight, he's a knight . . .

The litany went through her head, and though she should hate him for it, she couldn't quite muster so strong a negative emotion. Indeed, the only emotion filling her was a desire so potent that it made her very much aware of the fact that she was a woman full grown who had never known the taste of a man's lips.

It was something that had never bothered her before tonight.

But as she watched him talk and share a small grin with his companions, her curiosity swelled to gargantuan proportions.

What would it be like to hold so dark a champion in her arms? To let him kiss her on her lips as a man and not the quick, chaste kisses on her cheek she had known as a young girl from the boys who fostered at her uncle's.

A shiver went through her.

You're being a ninny.

And yet she couldn't take her gaze off him. He stood surrounded by a small group of men. Four of them were nice-looking gentlemen, and by their bearings, she would take them to be knights as well, who ranged in age from around a score of years to thirty. They stood with a monk whose dark blond handsomeness was only surpassed by that of her unknown knight.

How strange that they would speak to a cleric while the hall was filled with the highest members of society. Most knights were trying to reach the king or his direct advisors to curry his favor, and yet the small group of men stood off to the side as if completely unconcerned with politics and favor.

They reminded her of brothers, except none of them held any facial or even height similarities to mark them as family.

Her dark champion turned his head as a woman walked past in a red gown. She saw disappointment mar his brow as he focused on the woman's face. 'Twas obvious he sought another.

Glancing down at her own scarlet dress, she couldn't help but wonder if . . .

Nay, Rowena. He doesn't look for you and why would you care if he did?

She didn't care, she told herself. And to prove that, she was going to find her ladies and venture off to write more music.

Rowena was about to search out Elizabeth when her gaze fell to her lifelong friend, Christopher "Kit" de Montgomerie.

Kit saw her at about the same moment she saw him. His handsome face beamed as he crossed the room and drew to her side. He scooped her up in his arms and gave her a tremendous hug.

Oh, how she had missed him!

"Kit!" she breathed, looking up into his familiar green eyes that twinkled with love and respect. He barely stood a head taller than she, and as always his black hair was stylishly cut.

Thin of frame, he looked handsome tonight, dressed in orange and red, his cap tilted dangerously over his brow. It had been far too long since last they had seen each other.

Even though Kit was three years younger than she, they had more in common than she could count.

Good old Kit. He was her match in every way.

With a laugh, he kissed her lightly on the brow. She was so glad to see him much happier this time than he had been when last they met in Flanders, eighteen months ago. Then there had been an air of hopeless sadness about him.

He had looked haunted. Even terrified.

But there was none of that now. He reminded her of the boy she had loved in her childhood.

"Sweetest Rowena, 'tis so good to see you again. I have missed you terribly."

She squeezed his hand tightly. "I was so hoping you would be here for the tournament."

"So you could best me again with your words?"

"Aye, sir, you lose with such grace that it honors us both."

His smile beguiling, he offered her his arm. "Come, my dearest angel, and honor me with your presence while we sup. After being in my brother's company this past year, I find myself starving for some intelligent conversation that doesn't involve intrigue or politics."

She furrowed her brow as he led her through the crowded room. "Since when does Michael give a single fig for politics? I thought his attention was solely on his vineyards and lands."

"Not Michael, my sweet. 'Tis another brother of whom I speak. Well, half-brother, really, but blood nonetheless."

"And who is this mysterious brother of yours?" she asked as he led her across the room.

"Stryder of Blackmoor."

She stumbled in surprise. Dear heaven, was there anywhere she could go to escape the mention of that man's name? If she heard it once more this evening, she might very well become a raving lunatic from it.

"Are you all right?" Kit asked as he helped her catch her balance.

Her face flushing from embarrassment, she nodded. "Aye. That was just the last name I expected to hear from your lips."

And no wonder Kit was starved for intelligent conversation. From the stories she'd heard, his brother was no doubt the type of man who could barely speak of anything save war and his prowess on the field. She could just imagine Stryder posturing in his armor.

Why, I have the biggest sword in all the kingdom. Come, milady, and let me show it to you . . .

That was the most creative and crude seduction men of his kith could manage.

And if she heard it once more during her lifetime, she might very well take up swordsmanship on her own just to thrash them for it. How she hated listening to men who carried on and on about their glorious victories and derring-do.

Never mind the size of their . . .

Assets.

"Why not?" Kit asked, his voice laden in irony. "His name seems to be on the lips of everyone else here this evening."

"This is very true," she agreed. "But I must confess that I don't even know which of the men he is. Not that I care, mind you. I've heard his description enough these past hours that I swear I could draw a perfect sketch of him."

"Even if you couldn't, just look for the man with the largest amount of arrogance and you will undoubtedly be looking straight at him." Kit winked, then smiled teasingly at her.

Gracious, but he was handsome in a very pretty way. Like a dark angel. His features were so finely boned, his limbs long and willowy. A man of pure refinement and grace, Kit moved slow and gently.

He paused at a long trestle table and pulled a bench out for her.

Rowena swept before the bench, sat, then adjusted the skirt of her scarlet gown around her. Kit took the seat to her right, then motioned for a page to bring them wine.

"If his company is as oafish as the others of his kind," she asked, "why have you been traveling with him?"

Kit cleared his throat. "I never said his company was oafish, my love. Only that he has a single mind about his duties."

"Of killing people."

"Of protecting them."

She frowned at the strange note in his voice as he spoke that. "You defend a knight, Kit? When last we spoke you shared my view of them and of war."

"I still despise war and those who partake pleasure from it, but Stryder is my brother and I respect him and his decisions."

Rowena wrinkled her nose at his noble words, but then that was Kit. Loyal unto the end. "How is it you came to travel with him?"

Kit looked a bit sheepish. "I had nowhere else to go. Michael refuses to allow me entrance to his home. Even for a night."

The news surprised her. "Your own brother turned you out?"

"Aye, he never cared much for my bastard status or me personally. No sooner had I returned home from my travels abroad than he said he couldn't afford to feed a man who wouldn't fight to protect his lands. Since I know little of holding a sword, I found myself escorted off his lands and told never to return."

Anger welled up inside her. How dare anyone treat their brother that way! She had expected better than that from Michael de Montgomerie. "That onerous beast!"

"My thoughts were a great deal harsher than that, but 'twas along the same lines." Kit leaned back as a page appeared and reached for his goblet to fill it with wine.

Rowena waited while the page poured their cups. Once the boy left, she renewed her conversation. "What did you do?"

Kit took a sip of wine, then set the cup back on the table. "I did the only thing I knew how to, I started singing for my supper."

That sounded wonderful to her. Oh but to be a man who could do such . . .

Propping his arm on the table, Kit leaned his cheek against his fist and gave a bitter laugh. "However, I fear my talents were lacking, and I was practically starving to death. I never knew how many ears were so discriminating until my belly depended upon it."

She patted his arm in sympathy. "You don't look like you're starving now."

"I'm not, thanks to Stryder. I was playing in an inn down in Canterbury when several knights took issue with one of the serving women. I was trying to defend her, but with five of them and one of me, I was making a rather poor showing of it. As they were getting ready to thrash me soundly, Stryder intervened. He didn't even know who I was until after he'd sent them packing."

His words surprised her. From what she'd heard of the earl, she would have thought he'd be one of the men leading the thrashing.

Kit brushed his fingers over his chin. "Though it'd been more than a decade since we had last seen each other, Stryder recognized me and said that he had been looking for me for quite some time. Apparently, he'd been to Michael's and had learned of my banished status."

His gaze turned distant. "I still can't believe how angry he was on my behalf. I thought he might actually kill Michael over it." He offered her a timid smile. "Once I told him how I came to be in Canterbury, he insisted I join his household."

That was something she didn't find surprising. "As a knight, no doubt."

"Nay, as his brother. He told me he has strength aplenty to protect his lands, 'tis family he lacks."

How odd. Again, it wasn't something she would expect from a man of the earl's reputation.

Not that it mattered. She was irritated with Kit at the moment. No wonder he had looked so despondent the last time she had seen him. "Why did you not come to me? You know I would have—"

"I would never have imposed myself on your graciousness," he said, interrupting her. "I am a man, Rowena. Not a child needing shelter. Besides, I doubt your uncle would have cared for my presence. Even now he watches us like a lion guarding his cub."

Rowena glanced past her shoulder to see that Lord Lionel had finally returned to the hall and was indeed watching them from his corner on the far right.

Smiling, she waved at the man who had raised her since the death of her own father.

His face softened, until he looked to Kit and his sternness returned even sharper than before. She let out a tired breath at that. Her poor uncle was so afraid that she was going to elope with one of the troubadours she knew.

Unfortunately, she didn't want to marry any man. Even though Queen Eleanor often touted the pleasures that could be found in marriage, she saw enough of the queen's sadness over her husband's infidelities to know what heartbreak marriage held.

And Rowena had no desire to be made miserable by anything.

"I can tell he doesn't care for me."

"Oh, Kit, don't take it personally. He cares not for any man who sits too near me."

He scooted himself two inches further away.

Rowena laughed.

A servant placed a bread trencher down for them. Kit served Rowena a selection of roasted lamb, chicken, and venison while they chatted over nothing in particular.

She knew Kit watched her, and he grew very quiet as their meal progressed.

"Why do you look so sad all of a sudden, Kit?" she asked.

Kit glanced away from her as he picked at his roasted chicken. "I know not what you mean," he said in a low tone, trying to disguise the ache in his heart.

She placed her hand on his. That innocent caress set him on fire. "Is there something you wish to talk about?"

"Nay," he said, reluctantly removing his hand from hers. He didn't want to taint her. "I'm just a bit tired. Stryder keeps unholy hours."

"I'm quite sure he does."

By the tone of her voice, he could tell what she omitted. *And just who does he keep them with . . .*

"It's not what you think, Rowena."

She clucked her tongue in disbelief of that.

Kit opened his mouth to defend Stryder when a booming voice interrupted him.

"Ah, fairest Rowena, here you are."

Rowena went cold at the deep, gruff voice that belonged to Cyril Longshanks. She didn't bother to hide the distaste on her face as he grabbed Kit's arm and pushed him down the bench as if to give himself space so that he could sit between them.

"Make room, gelding. Why don't you go fetch wine for your betters."

Rowena was appalled by the knight and his manners. Her appetite gone, she rose to her feet and started away before he could sit beside her.

Cyril grabbed her arm.

"Let go of her," Kit growled, rising to his feet.

Without releasing her arm, Cyril shoved him backward. "Find me when you grow up, boy."

One minute Rowena was still attempting to extricate her arm; the next, she was completely free of Cyril as he went flying back several feet and crashed into the table.

Silence rang out in the hall.

Her jaw slack, Rowena realized another man had joined them. Tall and broad of shoulder, she knew him in an instant.

He was the one who had saved her from falling.

"You ever lay hand to my brother again," he snarled, "and I'll rip your arm off and beat you with it."

Cyril came to his feet with a fierce growl and ran for him.

The stranger caught him another blow that flipped Cyril up and over onto his back. Cyril lay on the floor dazed while the man put his foot on the center of Cyril's chest.

"Yield, Cyril. You know firsthand what I'm capable of doing to you."

To her amazement, Cyril nodded and held his hands up in surrender. "I yield."

The unknown knight removed his foot from Cyril's chest and turned toward Kit. "Are you all right?"

Kit nodded.

Cyril rose to his feet slowly. "Leave it to Stryder of Blackmoor to protect a gelding such as that one."

Stryder of Blackmoor.

Stunned Rowena looked at her mysterious knight to see the fury in his eyes over the insult Cyril had dealt Kit's manhood.

Before she could blink, Stryder had Cyril by the throat. He pulled the man up so that Cyril had to stand on his tiptoes to meet his gaze levelly. Cyril's eyes bulged as his face reddened.

"One more word," Stryder growled, "and I will silence you forever. Do you understand me?"

"Stryder!" Henry's voice rang out in the hall. "Release him."

Stryder hesitated before he obeyed his king.

Cyril coughed as he struggled to inhale air back into his lungs. "This isn't over," Cyril snarled.

The look on Stryder's face clearly contradicted him. "Aye, but it is. Cross me or mine again and it will be the final mistake of your life."

Rowena watched as Cyril passed an angry glare from Stryder to Kit, whose face was filled with embarrassed shame, and if she didn't know better . . . hatred.

Cyril's eyes widened for a second, then narrowed even more. Turning on his heel, he marched stiffly from the hall.

It was only after he was gone that Rowena realized her uncle was by her side.

"Are you all right, Rowena?" Lionel asked gently.

"Aye," she breathed, her gaze never wavering from Stryder who frowned at the mention of her name.

"Rowena de Vitry?" he asked, that deep voice sending a shiver through her.

"Aye."

He looked as ill at the mention of her name as she had felt at his. "So you're the ogress who writes those songs."

She would have felt complimented had he not insulted her first. "You know my work?"

" 'A plague to all who carry swords and a pox on their apish arms. May they all grow sterile and fat, and perish young.' Aye, milady, my squire informed me earlier this very day of your so-called work."

She stiffened at his open disdain. He wasn't the first to hate her or her work, but for some unfathomable reason she felt cut by his glare.

So she fought back the only way she could—with her words. "As I am aware of yours, milord. They say you have cleaved the heads off more than two hundred men and sliced five times as many in twain. I believe the Saracens refer to you as the English Butcher."

He curled his lip at her. "You have poisoned the mind of my squire."

She smiled in cold triumph at that. "I have liberated his mind."

Stryder took a step toward her.

Kit was immediately between them. "Rowena, Stryder," he said forcing more distance between them. "Remember yourselves."

Rowena felt her face flush as she recalled the fact that their "discussion" had an audience of the entire English court.

Stryder's icy gaze swept the room as well. He lowered his voice and when he spoke his deep voice resonated with powerful anger. "In the future, milady, I would appreciate it if you would refrain from liberating the mind of my impressionable squire. When someone comes at him with a sword, I would like to believe Druce will raise more than his tongue in defense of himself."

"If there were no swords about, milord, then he wouldn't have to live in fear of them, and neither would you."

He snorted at that. "I hold no fear of a sword, only of fools who refuse to see reason. 'Tis a pity no man in your life has ever sought to teach you your place."

The crowd as a whole sucked its collective breath in at that.

Rowena had never been angrier in her life. In that moment she well understood a man's desire to thrash another and she hated Stryder for making her feel such.

His gaze went to Kit. "If you have any further need of me, brother, just call." Those chilly eyes focused on her. "As for you, milady, I liked you much better when I didn't know who you were."

He turned and stalked off before she could respond.

The crowd actually applauded.

"Here, here, Stryder," one man shouted above the others. "You tell her, milord. 'Tis time someone took her down."

Rowena was horrified by the cheers that went up for Stryder. How dare they!

But more than that, she was hurt to learn just how many people scorned her feelings. Her beliefs.

Fine, let all of them perish and rot. How could they not see how wrong war and violence were?

Tears welled in her eyes, but she blinked them away. She would never let anyone in this crowd know how they wounded her.

Holding her head high, she headed the opposite direction, toward the door that led to the stairs.

Kit caught up with her. "Rowena?"

"Leave me, Kit. I wish to be alone."

"Don't be angry at my brother, Rowena."

She turned on him with hatred and anger burning furiously in her heart. "How can you defend him to me after what he just said?"

He countered with a question of his own. "How can you tolerate me and hate him? Do not fool yourself, love. If I were Stryder's size and possessed his skill and strength, I would have thrashed Cyril too."

She scoffed at that. "You could never hurt anyone, Kit. You're far too gentle."

"Trust me, life has a way of kicking that gentleness out of all of us. Stryder has been through much in his life. You shouldn't judge him so harshly."

"*I* judge *him*? Did you not hear what he said to me?"

"Aye, I did. But you know, milady, you could have said thank you to him. He did rid you of Cyril and save me from being hit.

Otherwise you would even now be with the oaf and I would be bleeding on the floor."

Maybe there was some truth to that.

Maybe.

"Rowena?"

She looked past Kit to see her uncle drawing near.

Kit excused himself and left them alone.

"Are you all right?" Lionel asked again.

"I shall survive it, no doubt. But I wish a plague of locusts would descend on Lord Stryder and follow him all the days of his life."

Her uncle stiffened. "I'm very sorry to hear that."

"Why?"

"Because at the end of the month, you shall marry him."

Chapter 4

Stryder had retired to his tent. Alone. After the confrontation in the hall with Rowena and Cyril, the last thing he wanted was anyone near him.

All he could do was hear Rowena's voice as she denounced his occupation. See the contempt in her eyes.

To the devil with her anyway. He had plenty of women who wanted him.

As for Cyril . . .

He'd never cared for the man. Even though Cyril was technically considered a member of the Brotherhood, he had never been one of them. In the hole that had been their home, more times than not they had been forced to fight him off their weaker members as he preyed on them for food and other things best not thought of.

Stryder had hated him from the moment they had first laid eyes on each other.

The world would be better off if men such as he were no longer in it.

Stryder pushed those thoughts away too. If he had to choose between people who rankled him, better he think of Rowena than Cyril.

At least she was fair and buxom. In a most irritating way. The kind that tended to haunt a man long after she was gone and make him wonder what her lips would taste like.

What her body would feel as he took her slowly and easily . . .

Stryder pushed those thoughts away as well. The last thing he needed was a woman who had no use for him when every other female in Christendom was doing everything she could to get into his bed.

He had stripped himself to his waist and was in the process of downing his tankard of ale when he heard the flap of his tent open.

Acting on instinct, he unsheathed his dagger and rose to face his intruder.

It was the devil herself.

Rowena gasped as soon as she came into the tent to find Lord Stryder virtually naked, holding a dagger in his hand as if ready to let it fly at her head.

"You can see every part of his muscles flex."

Elizabeth hadn't lied. Rowena really could. In fact, every muscle of that gorgeously virile body was plainly evident.

He was coiled to strike. Lethal.

She stiffened at the thought and cast him a chiding glare. "Put your weapon away."

He arched a daring brow at that. "Why should I when I have half a mind to make good use of it on you?"

"So you admit to having only half a mind, then?"

His eyes narrowed.

"I am but teasing, milord," she said, gentling her voice. "Put away your weapon, for I have serious business here with you."

"You have no business here with me, lady. None. Now hie yourself—"

"Nay," she said stubbornly. "I have just been told that the only chance I have for freedom is in your hands and by all that is holy, you will deliver me my freedom or I shall see to it that you live out the rest of your life in merciless misery."

He gaped at her. On any other man such an expression would have looked foolish, but to credit Lord Stryder, even when taken by surprise, he still managed to carry off an air of supreme authority and handsomeness. "I beg your pardon? Have you gone completely mad?"

"Not I, but rather the king you love so well. It appears he would see us marry."

"My hairy arse."

She gave him a droll stare. "That is much more information about your person, Lord Stryder, than I care to know."

He tossed the dagger with deadly precision into the table next to her. Thudding with its impact, it embedded in the top where it wobbled for a few seconds.

In spite of herself, she was impressed by his abilities.

"Henry knows better than to see me coerced into marriage . . . again."

"There you are wrong," she said primly. "You see, I have the grave misfortune of having been born the sole child to my father, Giles of Sussex."

Stryder's jaw went slack again as he understood her predicament.

Still, she explained it for him. "Henry wants a strong lord to marry me to control those lands, therefore whoever the fool is who wins this tournament is to be my husband."

His icy blue eyes flashed. "Then I shall withdraw immediately."

"The devil you say."

His gaze turned arctic. "I won't marry you."

As if she would have him!

"And I don't want to marry anyone at all," she snapped. "But, unlike a man, I'm not given much freedom in that regard. The only way I can have my choice of husband, it seems, is for you to win the singing contest at month's end."

He laughed aloud at that.

"'Tis not an amusing matter, milord."

"I will not sing for you or anyone else. Ever."

"Then you shall be my husband."

"As I said, I shall withdraw." He stepped away from her.

Rowena blocked his path. "Henry won't allow it, he told me so himself. And even if you do run, then I shall insist you be my husband just for spite. My uncle and the king will have you brought to the altar in chains if needs be."

He curled his lips at her. "Why? You despise me ever as much as I despise you."

"Because I want some degree of freedom, and my only hope lies in you. So you will either sing like a bird and win me my choice of husband or I shall see us both tied into wedded hell. Together."

Stryder cursed. "I don't believe you, milady. Either way of it, you win. Either way, I lose."

She was aghast at his logic. "How do you figure?"

"I either have to be a horse's ass before the entire court or you will make my future life miserable, while you on the other hand either get your freedom or you get marriage to me."

Her jaw dropped. "And you think I would relish marriage to you?"

"Aye. I know it for fact."

Rowena scowled at him and hoped the full disgust she felt was evident on her face. "Your arrogance knows no bound. This may come as a shock to you, Lord Stryder, but I do not find you attractive in the least."

He laughed in disbelief.

Rowena ground her teeth. "You are insufferable."

"And yet you would marry me. As I said, milady, *you* win either way."

Suddenly, all of this became more than she could stand. The mockery in the hall, her uncle and king's dictates, and now even Stryder the Horrible mocked her.

All she had ever wanted in her life was to make other people happy with her words and songs. To maybe show others that they could live without warfare. That peace was infinitely better than bloodshed.

And what did it get her?

Laughed at. Mocked. Ridiculed.

She knew what others called her behind her back. The Lady of Nonsense. But most oft they called her the Bitch of Sussex.

Someone needs teach her to heel and fetch. She'd be tolerable enough to bed, provided you gag her first.

She had always prided herself on being above their insults. But she wasn't. In spite of what they all thought, she was human and those words wounded her. Deeply.

Just as her uncle's betrayal this night hurt. Why couldn't she be left in peace?

Why did she have to conform to the dictates of men and be forced into marriage with a man who held no regard for her whatsoever?

Overwrought with it all, Rowena wanted to cry in frustration.

So this would be her life. Either she ran and kept running, never to see her home or uncle again, or she stayed and married some ruffian who would most likely beat her into submission.

She only hoped Stryder didn't rip her arm off and beat her with it as he had threatened to do with Cyril.

Why did she even care if these ruffians lived or died?

There was no hope to be found here. She'd been a fool to even think for one minute she could talk sense or threaten a man like Stryder.

So be it. She would go pack and leave behind all she knew. Better to run than be made a fool of any longer.

Tears stung her eyes as hopeless pain overwhelmed her.

"I'm sorry I disturbed you," she said before turning to leave.

She wouldn't give Stryder the satisfaction of seeing her cry. No doubt that would give him a great deal of pleasure.

With no real destination in mind, she left his tent and let her tears finally fall.

Stryder stood there for several heartbeats staring at the emptiness.

Had he seen tears in her eyes?

It seemed unlikely. Lady Rowena possessed a strong, powerful presence that even now left him feeling drained after having been around her.

Surely such a woman never wept.

And yet . . .

Before he could stop himself, he went after her.

She was already at the end of the line of tents. Quickening his steps, he caught up to her.

"Rowena," he said, gently taking her by the arm. "Wait."

She turned to face him and he felt his heart shrivel. Her cheeks were streaked with tears that she hastily wiped away.

"What is it now?" she snapped, her voice unsteady.

Stryder crumpled. He only had one weakness in life—tears. He'd never been able to stand to see any woman in pain. Let alone one who looked as vulnerable as Rowena did right now with the rushlights shining in her bright eyes.

"Here now," he said gently, brushing his hand over her icy cheek. "There's no need in this."

Rowena swallowed at the warmth of his hand on her flesh. Who would have thought that a barbarian such as this one could touch her so carefully? "No need? Why, sir, if not this, then what else would warrant them?"

"Am I really so horrid that I have reduced you to tears?"

He was teasing her and that surprised her even more than his presence here.

"Yea, you are."

To her surprise, he laughed. "I have to admit that you are the first woman I've ever met who cannot abide me."

"Perhaps you should get out more often."

He arched a brow at her. "Why is it you cannot utter anything other than insults for me and yet you would have my help?"

He was right about that.

"I'm sorry," she breathed. "I am so used to insulting those of your breed that it is most reflexive at this point." She looked up at him imploringly. "But if you would help me, milord, I swear I will not insult you again."

"Nay?"

"I swear it."

Stryder nodded. He'd spent three years of his life imprisoned. Three years where the will of others was forced upon him. He hadn't been allowed even the most basic need or want. The whims of his captors had always reigned over his own.

Those three years had seemed to last an eternity. Even now there were times when he thought he'd spent more of his life in shackles than free.

'Twould be a shame to see a lady, even one so abrasive, lose the rest of her life to someone else's whims. A woman such as this would never be happy in such a marriage. Like him, she would be imprisoned.

His Brotherhood oath went through him. He was sworn to help any who needed it.

All it would cost him was a song . . .

Stryder ground his teeth. Damn Henry for that. But then the king didn't know what such a thing would cost him. Why he despised troubadours and songs the way he did.

Damn them all for it.

He should turn her away, but he couldn't. She was a noble lady in need of a champion. And no matter how much he might wish otherwise, he couldn't find it within himself to turn her away.

"When is your contest, milady?"

Her eyes sparked with hope. "The day of your final match. There will be a panel of judges and you must woo them with your words and performance."

His stomach shrank. "Have you any idea how distasteful I find this?"

"Most likely as distasteful as I find having to ask this favor of you. It's not in my nature to ask aught of others when I can do for myself."

"And yet here we are, united in our misery."

At least his words succeeded in bringing a very small smile to her lips. A small smile that tugged at the edges of his heart. "I promise you, Lord Stryder, that so long as you make a good faith effort to win, I shall not add to your misery. Ever."

He inclined his head to her. "Then I bid you goodnight, milady."

As he started away from her, she stopped him. Before he realized what she was doing, she rose up on her tiptoes and laid a most gentle and chaste kiss to his cheek.

"Thank you for your kindness, rogue knight."

Stryder could barely muster a breath as she left him there in the stillness of the night air. He stared after her, his body afire with sudden heat. Never had he received so innocent a kiss and never had one played such havoc with his body.

He must be mad to feel such for a termagant.

And yet he couldn't take his gaze off her. Even after she was gone, he still stood outside like a simpkin staring at where she had vanished out of his sight.

"Are you all right?"

He turned at the sound of Christian's voice coming out of the darkness. "Aye," he said gruffly. "Why wouldn't I be?"

"I know not, only that you were standing there as if you'd just seen the face of heaven. You've a strange look about you."

Stryder shook himself mentally and moved toward his tent.

"Why are you out here?" Christian asked.

Grateful his friend hadn't seen Rowena, Stryder shrugged. "I felt the need for fresh air."

Christian looked a bit skeptical, but thankfully didn't question him more. Instead he led the way back into the tent.

"By the way," Christian said as Stryder joined him inside. "The color red definitely suits Lady Rowena, doesn't it?"

It was three hours past matins and all were abed. The cool breeze whispered through the tents as the lone figure crept stealthily through them.

There was no moon tonight, which was well, for such things were best done without the witness of Bella Luna.

Aquarius paused at the tent of Stryder of Blackmoor. He glanced down at his left arm, where the names of each of his targets were tattooed. It was an arm he kept covered at all times lest anyone see the shame of what he'd been.

The shame of what he'd become.

Stryder was the third name on the list.

He clutched the knife in his hand as he remembered his hatred for the one they called the Widowmaker.

"Thanks for the comfort, boy. Maybe one day you'll get out alive too . . ."

Those words whispered through his head now. But it wasn't Stryder who had said that to him.

It was Cyril. The one Stryder had sent to free him. Only Cyril had refused. Instead, he had abused Aquarius as the others before him had and then left him for dead.

The so-called Brotherhood that had sworn all of their camp would survive, that none would be left behind, had left this poor shattered soul in the hands of their enemies.

For more than a thousand days and nights, Aquarius had been abused and punished for the rest of them who had escaped.

Now it was his turn to punish them.

He brushed his hand over the front of Stryder's red and white tent.

Tonight, the earl would live.

The assassin had another name to cross off.

One who deserved his death even more than the earl of Black-moor.

Aquarius saluted the earl, then made his way to the other end of the hill.

Stryder came awake to someone rapping on the wooden post of his tent. He blinked open his eyes to see that it was still murky out. Most likely just past dawn.

Groaning, he rolled over to go back to sleep.

"Lord Stryder?"

The whispered call was soft and decidedly feminine.

"I'm asleep," he said gruffly.

To his dismay, the flap opened to show him Rowena.

Rowena stopped dead in her tracks as she caught sight of Stryder lying on his bed as bare as he'd been the day he entered the world. Why, she almost dropped the lute she held in her hands!

Never in her life had she beheld a naked man, but she had a thought that none could be more fair than the one in front of her now.

He was all sinewy, tanned flesh. A visual delight.

And against her will, her gaze fastened on the most private place of his body where he stood ramrod stiff.

Remembering herself, she spun about to give him her back. "Milord, would you please cover yourself?"

"Why should I?" he asked sullenly. "You've already seen all there is to me."

Heat burst across her face at that. "Are you always this crass?"

"When a woman awakens me from a sound sleep in the privacy of my own quarters, aye. I think I have a right to be rather upset. Don't you?"

"I thought you would be awake by now."

"And why would you think that?"

"No reason other than the fact that it is daylight, milord."

He huffed at that and, still completely bare, he got out of his bed and walked past her to look out the tent flap.

" 'Tis barely dawn. No one is up at this hour."

Clutching her lute to her, Rowena bit her lip at the sight of his bare posterior and the incredibly handsome sight he posed. She started to spin about as he looked at her over his shoulder, but forced herself not to.

He gave her a challenging stare.

"If you wish to flaunt yourself before me, milord, so be it. I am not a mouse to scurry at the approach of a cat."

He turned to face her.

Rowena couldn't breathe as her gaze took in his whole body from toe to head.

He was beautiful.

His broad shoulders tapered to narrow hips. Tawny skin glistened with vitality in the grayish light and his presence was mammoth. Commanding.

His manly body was lightly dusted with dark hairs that accentuated every muscle. His manhood was still stiff, rising high even in the chill of the moist, morning air.

She shivered at the fierce sight and wondered what it would be like to have a man such as this as a lover. Would he be tender? Or would he be true to his warrior's nature and take her roughly? Savagely . . .

"Careful, lady," he said with a note of warning in his voice. "There are those who would think you unchaste by such actions."

She shrugged. "If that is the least of what they call me, then I am truly fortunate. As it is, I know well what others think of me and I care not."

Stryder was amazed by her courage. What would it take to make such a woman tremble?

If not for the heated look in her innocent gaze, he would think she was one of those women who held no use for a man whatsoever.

But Rowena was not a follower of Sappho. She was all too aware of his nudity. And the blush on her face told him he was embarrassing her. Not to mention the fact that she gripped her instrument as if it were some kind of shield that could protect her from him.

He should cover himself, and yet he had to admit he liked the way she stared at him. The high color in her cheeks.

And he wondered what she would look like spread across his bed, her face wild in abandonment as he showed her exactly why troubadours wrote tributes to love. Or at least to the physical pleasures of it.

"Have you ever been kissed, milady?"

She frowned at his question. "I beg your pardon?"

He approached her slowly. Methodically. The last thing he wanted was to send her scurrying out of his tent. "Have you ever had a man press his lips to—"

"I know what a kiss is, milord."

"And?"

She stepped back from him. "My lips are no concern of yours. Nor is any other personal matter."

"Then why are you here?"

"I came to begin our lessons."

He was aghast at that. "At this hour?"

"We are least likely to be disturbed now."

"And I am least likely to agree to learn anything at this hour of day, milady. My sleep is hard won and too precious to be disturbed by something I find as distasteful as song."

Rowena hesitated at the catch in his voice as he spoke those words to her. "Hard won how?"

He didn't answer. Instead, he headed back for his bed. "Come back at midday, Rowena, and I will be more approachable."

"But—"

"No buts, milady. I am weary and wish to sleep."

His commanding tone sat ill with her, but what choice did she have?

She felt a childish urge to stamp her foot at him. Yet what good would that do?

None whatsoever. Sighing, she set her lute down for when she would return to teach him.

As she started for the opening, a cry rang out.

Lord Stryder was on his feet again in an instant, pulling on his breeches as chaos broke outside the tent.

Rowena left the tent with Stryder one step behind her. He held his sword in his hand as he brushed past her, rushing toward the tent where everyone else seemed to be gathering.

Half-dressed and half-asleep, knights were all stumbling past her.

At the top of the hill, men were gathered around a red and blue tent.

As soon as Stryder joined the men, they turned on him.

"You!" Lord Rupert, the elder brother of Cyril, snarled. "You killed my brother!"

Rowena wasn't sure which of them was more stunned by that accusation.

"We all heard your threats against him," Rupert snarled.

"I killed no one last night," Stryder said, tense and angry.

"Liar!"

"I saw him leave Cyril's tent myself just after matins," another knight said. "There's no mistaking the Blackmoor coat of arms."

Before she could blink, Stryder was seized by a group of knights as Henry made his way through the crowd.

Rupert repeated his accusation to Henry.

"What say you, Lord Stryder?" Henry asked.

"I am innocent."

One of Cyril's younger brothers came out of the tent, holding a bloodied medallion. He handed it over to the king.

Henry studied it carefully, before looking back at Stryder. "You were with Cyril in Outremer?"

"Aye, Sire."

"And where were you last night after you left the hall?"

"In my tent."

"Alone?"

"Aye."

"See," Rupert spat. "He has no alibi. He killed my brother and I demand justice."

"We shall investigate this matter further," the king said stoically. "Until then, the earl shall be held in the castle under royal custody."

Stryder's jaw went slack at the king's words. Indeed, even Rowena was stunned. Henry would arrest his own champion with no real evidence?

The royal guards seized Stryder's sword and made to tie his hands behind his back.

"Wait!"

All gazes turned to Eleanor, who came forward out of the

crowd. The queen passed a peeved glare from her husband to Rowena and finally to Stryder.

"Lord Stryder has an alibi."

Rowena had never seen more frowns or shifty gazes in her life as everyone glanced about the crowd.

"Please," Henry said, his voice tired as he looked at his queen. "Tell us not he was with you."

Eleanor's stare turned droll. "Nay, milord. The man was with Rowena last night per your royal dictate."

Rowena's eyes widened as she found herself the focal point of everyone. It was on the tip of her tongue to deny it, but no one called the queen of England a liar and kept said tongue for long.

"Is that not right, Lord Stryder?" Eleanor asked.

Stryder opened his mouth, then shot a look toward Rowena.

"Speak up, milord," Eleanor said. "We know you wish to protect the lady's reputation, but better she be compromised than you be hanged."

"Stryder with the Bitch of Sussex?" someone said from the crowd. "I don't believe it."

Laughter broke through the crowd. Rowena felt her face heat up immediately.

Holding her head high, she met Stryder's gaze and found an odd almost apologetic look there.

"And what were they doing, Your Grace?" Rupert asked. "Not to contradict your royal personage, but I find it hard to believe they would be romantically involved."

"And so they weren't," Eleanor said without missing a breath. "The lady was tutoring his lordship on the lute."

More laughter sounded.

Rowena began to panic. What was the queen thinking?

Henry looked at them skeptically. "The earl of Blackmoor spent his evening practicing music with the lady?"

"Is this not so, Rowena?" Eleanor asked.

All she could do was nod dutifully.

" 'Tis a lie the wench told you, my queen," Rupert said. "Everyone here knows the earl despises music."

"A lie?" Eleanor arched a royal, censorious brow. "Lady Rowena, where is your lute?"

"In Lord Stryder's tent," she answered honestly.

The queen sent a squire to fetch it.

When the lad returned, the guards released Stryder.

"Show them what you learned, my lord," the queen said quietly.

Stryder's gaze was locked to her own.

Rowena held her breath. Did the man even know how to hold a lute?

'Twas a terrible gamble the queen was taking with all their lives.

Stryder's gaze softened only a fraction of a degree before he held the lute in his hands. Astonished, she watched as his hands went straight to the correct positions, and then they fumbled a bit as he played a basic tune.

Silence rang out.

The man knew how to play . . .

Rowena's mind whirled with the knowledge of that.

Henry sighed and nodded. "Well then, it appears the earl has an alibi after all."

"Nay!" the knight who had accused him earlier said. "I saw him."

"Perhaps it was another you saw," Eleanor interjected. "One who favored the earl."

The man frowned, but his gaze said he was sure it was Stryder he had seen.

Henry took the lute from Stryder. His gaze was a bit suspicious as he handed the lute to Rowena, who was now fearful even more of a forced match.

"Relax, child," Henry said. "The two of you have a month as We promised. We pray you to make good use of it."

His words spoken, the king turned around and left them.

The crowd dispersed slowly. Rupert didn't move. He kept a gimlet eye on both of them.

By Stryder's face, she could tell how upset he was by all of this. Without a word, he headed back toward his tent.

Rowena followed. "Lord Stryder?"

"Leave me alone," he snarled without hesitating.

She hurried to catch up to him and pull him to a stop. "Milord, please . . ."

His gaze burned into her. "What is it you want of me now?"

"Who taught you to play?"

"What difference does it make?"

Rowena didn't know, but she was desperate for an answer. "Why do you disdain music so?"

"For the same reason you disdain knights, my lady. Music cost me the life of the one person I held dearest in this world and ever since her death, I hate not only it, but all who carry its sound."

Chapter 5

Rowena couldn't move as she watched the earl return to his tent. She took a step forward, but was stopped as someone took her by the arm.

"Give him some peace, Rowena."

She paused at the pleading look in Kit's eyes. "You heard?"

He nodded.

"He must have loved his lady greatly."

"Aye, he did. He still carries our mother's ring with him everywhere he goes."

"Your mother?"

He nodded. "She was murdered by Stryder's father when he learned of my bastard birth. They say his rage was such that no one dared go near him—no one but Stryder. In anger, his father accused him of being bastard born as well. He ran the boy through and then gashed Stryder's head." Kit made a mark on his neck where she knew Stryder carried a severe scar. "While Stryder lay on the floor of the hall, his father killed our mother before his eyes."

"Then his father took his own life," she breathed.

"That is what they say."

There was an odd note in his voice. "But?" she prompted.

Kit refused to say anything more. "Our mother was much like you. She loved nothing more than to play her lute and sing. My father was one of the noble-born minstrels who came to her hall while Stryder's father was away. I don't remember much of my mother, really, I was only five when she died. But I am told she birthed me at her sister's home and then sent me to my father so that her husband would never learn of my existence."

"She and Stryder came once to visit you while you fostered with us." Rowena vaguely recalled the event. It was the only time anyone had ever come to visit Kit.

"Aye. She did that as much as she dared. Unfortunately, it was such a visit to my father's home that caused her death. Stryder's father had come home early from a trip to find them gone. When they returned, one of her servants betrayed her."

Rowena felt for her friend deeply. "Oh Kit, I am so sorry."

His eyes sad, he swallowed. "I am not the one who needs your sympathy, Rowena. I grieve for her because she was my mother, but I knew her very little. 'Twas Stryder who was devastated. He worshiped her."

Rowena fought down her tears at the thought of the pain Stryder must feel.

"My brother's life has been most harsh and still he is honorable. I know of no other who could have survived what he has and remain so noble."

"Aye. He could have made both Eleanor and I out to be liars." He nodded.

"But what of Cyril?" she asked. "Do you think Lord Stryder—"

"Nay. I know better. If Stryder wished him dead, he would have faced him on the battlefield. Deception is not in my brother's nature."

She had thought as much. "Why would Lord Aubrey lie?"

"Perhaps he didn't. Anyone may don a cloak. In the dark, I should think one could look as guilty as any other."

Rowena bit her lip at the thought. Aye, but who would want Stryder blamed?

She excused herself and headed back toward the crowd that continued to gather around Cyril's tent.

"I still say the earl did this," one of the barons said to a small group outside the tent.

"Why would he sneak up on him and cut his throat while he slept? In all the years I've known Stryder, I've never known him to do such a thing."

Another baron snorted. "Madness possessed his father. Mayhap it has possessed him too."

Rowena ignored the men who continued to argue for and against Stryder. In truth, she felt very sorry for Cyril—more than she would have thought possible. Not even he had deserved a death such as this.

Her heart heavy, she had started toward the castle when something caught her gaze. It was a tiny slip of vellum poking out from underneath the canvas of Cyril's tent.

While the men continued to speculate, she bent over and retrieved it. The instant she opened it, her heart stopped.

It was written in Arabic.

We all did not go home.

We all did not survive.

Death to the Brotherhood. May you all burn in the fires of Lucifer's deepest pit.

At the bottom, stamped in blood, was a symbol she had seen just this morning while Stryder had stood naked before her . . .

Stryder was washing the sleep from his face when he heard someone enter his tent without preamble.

He spun to catch the culprit only to have her dodge and move quickly away, out of his grasp.

" 'Tis only I," a soft, feminine voice said.

Stryder growled low in his throat. "Can I not be free of you this morn?" he groused as he turned to face Rowena. Though to be honest, he did feel a bit of growing respect for the lady who had outmaneuvered him just now.

She straightened with a haughty stare at him. Instead of making one of her infamous remarks, she closed the distance between them and took his right hand into hers.

A small chill stole up his spine at the way she caressed the brand on the back of his hand. As always, the sight of that mark made his stomach shrink, his anger snap.

"What is this from?" she asked quietly.

"It's nothing," he said, trying to pull his hand away.

She wouldn't release it. "Why does this make you so angry?"

"Rowena—"

She didn't take the warning. Her fingers brushed over the

raised skin where the Saracens had seared their mark of a scimitar and moon on his flesh. He'd been only ten-and-five when they had branded him. Even after all these years, he could recall the pain of the wound. The degradation.

"Is this part of the Brotherhood of the Sword?"

He tensed at her question. "What do you know of the Brotherhood?"

"I travel with minstrels, milord. There are whispers of a group of men who were once political prisoners in the Holy Land. Men who saved others and brought them home. Noble and decent men who still fight to bring more home and see them safely to the bosoms of their families."

Pain racked Stryder, but his anger overshadowed that. No one was supposed to know of them. "Where have you heard this?"

"I told you, there are many who sing of such tales. The stories started about two years ago, and no one is certain who began them. The words and music show up anonymously at various tournaments where we gather, lauding the virtues and bravery of the Brotherhood's members." She narrowed her gaze on him as if she could read his very mind. "You are one of them, aren't you?"

Stryder had been hiding for so long that he couldn't bring himself to admit it to her. "Release me."

To his relief, she did. " 'They travel through the night on the wings of heavenly stallions bringing hope and new faith to those left behind. Even though they are free, they never forget their past and spend their lives trying to bring peace to others.' "

He frowned at her words. "What is that you quote?"

"One of the chansons that is written about the Brotherhood." She held the note out to Stryder. "This was on the ground just outside of Cyril's tent. I find it hard to believe that he was a member of your Brotherhood, but you . . ."

Stryder stared at the paper. He could read none of it, but he could see the bloody symbol. It was the same as the one on his hand. "What does this say?"

"Can you not read Arabic?"

"I can't read anything, Rowena."

He expected to see condemnation from her for his "uneducated" status. Instead, she merely nodded and then read the note for him.

Stryder's gaze darkened. "Are you sure this came from his tent?"

"Aye. It looked as if it had been blown free of wherever it had been placed." Her brow puckered. "What does the person mean that not everyone survived or went home?"

Stryder stood there, his soul screaming out at the letter and what it signified. Could one of their own have killed Cyril, or was this a Saracen playing havoc with them?

It didn't make sense. Nay, they had made certain no one was left behind the night they escaped.

No one.

It wasn't in his nature to trust anyone and yet he found himself confiding in Rowena. "It was a vow all of us made while we were prisoners that we all would survive and go home."

"Who was left behind?"

"No one out of our camp. We made sure of it. On the night we escaped, we sent groups to free the others while Christian and I led the youngest members out." He shook his head. "It can't be one of us. It's some Saracen playing with our heads. It has to be."

"Why?"

"To punish us for leaving and for helping others to escape. No doubt they have been hunting us all this time with no other purpose than to kill us off one by one."

"But why kill Cyril?" she asked as she folded up the note. "He didn't strike me as the kind to help anyone save himself."

It was true. Cyril had refused their cause once they were free and had gone home, ever forgetful of what they'd been through, of the promises they had made to each other.

"I don't know."

Her face lighted as if she'd had an epiphany. "Unless it was to frame you for it. Perhaps you were the target all along. Why else wear your cloak?"

"Those are points well taken." It could also explain why so many attempts had been made on his life. He and his men had been looking for someone who resented his friendship with the throne. Perhaps his enemy had nothing to do with Henry, but rather was his past coming back to claim him.

Stryder took the note from her and placed it on his desk. "Please don't mention this to anyone."

"You intend to keep your Brotherhood secret?"

"Aye. No one needs know who among us were there and what we were forced to do to survive. We've all struggled hard to regain the lives and dignity that were taken from us."

She inclined her head toward him as if she understood exactly what he meant. "I shall keep your secret, Stryder. Always."

She started for the door.

"Rowena?"

She paused at his voice.

"In the future, the best time to approach me for lessons is after we sup."

She nodded and offered him a small, almost fragile smile that played havoc with his insides . . . and his groin. "Then I shall see you tonight, milord. I prithee that you find no more trouble between now and then."

One corner of his mouth lifted in wry humor. "We shall see what the day holds, shall we not?"

Rowena nodded in agreement. They would indeed.

Gathering her skirts, she swept from his tent, past the four knights who traveled with Stryder. The small group of men paused outside the tent to stare in her wake while she made her way back to her rooms in the castle.

It didn't take long to return to her chambers inside the cool safety of the donjon's whitewashed walls.

The last thing Rowena expected was to find her women gathered together in her solar. Already word of Cyril's death and Stryder's possible part in it had reached them.

"What are we to do?" Bridget asked as Rowena's ladies-in-waiting huddled in the center of the room like a small flock of chickens. Bridget was a short woman who possessed jet-black hair and a small, willowy frame. "If Lord Stryder is convicted—"

"I shall never marry," Marian whined. Barely a year older than Rowena, Marian held light blond hair and a lush, round body that got the lady into plenty of compromising positions whenever a handsome man came near. "We'll all be forced back to Sussex!"

"Nay," Joanne said, her voice every bit as upset. "I cannot abide another milksop man coming to me and singing odes to my thighs and neck as if I'm nothing more than a succulent hen."

Bridget patted her comfortingly on her back. "Have no fear, Joanne. We will not go back to Sussex, nor will Lord Stryder perish. We shall find the one responsible and hang him ourselves."

"What is this?" Rowena asked.

Her ladies-in-waiting immediately broke apart. They looked about as if they were guilty of some crime.

"What is what, milady?" Joanne asked, feigning innocence.

Rowena looked at each one of them in turn. "What have you planned?"

"We're going to find Cyril's killer," Bridget announced proudly.

"We'll have to be devious," Marian chimed in. "Ply men with . . . drinks and our wiles. But I think we are up to the challenge."

The others nodded in ready agreement.

It was all Rowena could do to not roll her eyes as visions of her companions in trouble flashed through her mind. No wonder her uncle kept them secluded in Sussex. The whole lot of them, while tender-hearted, were ever ready to seduce any man who came near them. "You would do all this for Lord Stryder?"

Marian nodded. "Well, aye. He must be proven innocent."

"And why is that?" Rowena asked.

"So that you can marry him," Joanne said simply.

Rowena cocked her head at that. "I thought *you* wanted to marry him."

"Well, aye, I do, or did, but now that the king has chosen you for his bride we've been—"

Bridget cut her words off with a sharp elbow to her side.

"Ow!" Joanne snapped.

Rowena folded her arms over her chest as a bad feeling went through her. "You've been what?"

"You might as well tell her," Elizabeth spoke up from Joanne's right. "It's not like she won't figure it out."

Marian sighed. "Well, we've been talking. You and your uncle keep us sequestered in Sussex with your minstrel friends visiting and while we've been here, it has come to our attention that there is many a fine man to be had."

"Aye," Bridget agreed. "Have you seen Stephen of Nottingham? A finer man I've never beheld."

"He's a barbarian," Rowena said as she remembered the way the man had belched at dinner the night before. He had then slammed his goblet down and ordered more wine, which he had consumed faster than she could blink. It was followed by another belch.

"He's a man," Marian snapped. "No offense, milady, but we've all had it up to here"—she held her hand to her chin—"with those mewling knaves you have visiting Sussex. We're tired of having them sing odes to our eyes and juices while our juices are drying up. We want a real man."

"Aye!" they agreed in unison.

Bridget patted Rowena gently on the arm. "We understand and respect the fact that you're not inclined for a manly sort, milady. But for the rest of us, we rather like someone who can pick us up and not whine about it. Lord Stryder has many knights in his company."

Joanne nodded. "Knights from good families."

"Knights with strong muscles," Marian added.

"Aye," Bridget continued. "And to our way of thinking, you marry Lord Stryder and we can have our pick of them."

Rowena was aghast. "I can't believe this. You would sacrifice me to Stryder so that you can—"

"It's not a sacrifice," Joanne said, interrupting her. "Lord Stryder is the catch of all Christendom. You should be flattered."

If she heard that one more time . . .

Rowena sought peace from her women, but no matter where she tried to go, they dogged her steps, each one telling her of the plan she had to see Rowena united to Stryder forevermore.

This was turning out to be the longest day of her life.

Stryder paused in his tent as his men joined him.

Will stood even in height to him and held the same shoulder-length black hair. His demeanor was normally one of ill-natured surliness, but today his face was even stonier face than usual.

Two inches shorter, Swan stood to Will's right. Swan was the ladies' man out of their tight-knit group. A rogue charmer, he was seldom ever found without a woman near his side. His hair was a dark brown, falling just past his shoulders, and he wore a stylish goatee. His eyes were piercingly blue.

The man was fond of gambling equally with his life and with his coin.

To Swan's right was Raven, who was as dark as his name. At barely a score-and-one in age, he was still a bit gangly in frame, but would no doubt fill out in the next few years. He'd always been like a younger brother to Stryder, who had adopted the boy while they had been prisoners in Outremer.

Just behind the three of them was Val, who stood a good head and shoulders above them all. Named for St. Valentine, the man found very little amusing about his name and even less amusing about his giant height. But otherwise, he was without a doubt the best natured of the lot of them and was usually found laughing over the oddest things.

At the moment, though, his face would rival Will's for grave seriousness.

"Surely none of you think I killed Cyril," Stryder said as he faced them.

They passed a baffled look amongst themselves. "Nay, that never entered our minds," Will spoke for the group while he unsheathed his sword.

Stryder eyed him suspiciously. "What is it you do?"

"Remember when you told us you'd rather be dead than married?" Val asked.

Will stepped forward. "We're about to grant you your wish."

Stryder shook his head. "Put your sword away."

"Nay," Swan said. "I spent the night with a maid from Rowena's camp and she had much to say about their plans to see you two wed. You are doomed, Stryder. Run now while you're able."

Stryder scoffed. "Don't be a fool. Even if I wished to, which I don't, I can't. To do so would make me look guilty, and we need to find who really killed Cyril."

"Bah," Val said disgustedly. "He had enemies aplenty. Only a complete idiot would blame you for it."

"There are idiots aplenty at court," Swan interjected. "A man's reputation is at stake and the honor of all of us. Nay, it sits ill, but Stryder is right. We'll let him and Christian find the culprit while the rest of us keep the women occupied so that they cannot interfere and force a wedding."

Will snorted. "Leave it to you to come up with that suggestion."

"What?" Swan asked as if offended. "You find the idea of entertaining ladies distasteful? Why, Will, I had no idea you were a ganymede."

Will shoved Swan, hard.

"Enough," Stryder said, breaking them apart before their rough play escalated into violence. For full-grown knights, his men sometimes reminded him of children and he felt more like their father than overlord. "Shouldn't the lot of you be out in the list training?"

They looked at each other as if disgruntled by the idea.

"Why?" Will asked. " 'Tis not as if any of the lickspittles out there could best us. I'm thinking our time is best served elsewhere."

Stryder rubbed his brow as a vision of Will in the alehouse, with a goblet in one hand and a maid in the other went through his mind. He groaned at the image. " 'Tis a good thing I know where you were last night or else I might think you were the one who quarreled with Cyril and ended his life."

Will was ever threatening to tear men apart.

On second thought, it was seldom a threat, but more often an action they were forever pulling him back from. Yet for all of Will's willingness to kill others, Stryder doubted the man had really taken part in Cyril's demise.

Nay, there was another man who was guilty for the deed.

Stryder told them of Rowena's note and watched as one by one their faces turned grimmer.

"Our enemies haunt us," Will said.

"Aye," Stryder agreed. "I think we should set up sentries after this to ensure no more of us die."

"How many members of the Brotherhood are here?" Val asked.

"With Cyril dead, there's only us and Christian."

"Nay," Raven said quietly. "I saw Roger of Devonshire earlier this morn. He rode in late last eventide."

"Then there are seven of us," Stryder said. "Inform Roger of what has happened and have him bunk near us. I'll take the first shift tonight, then we can alternate watch."

They nodded in agreement.

"Just like old times," Swan said, reminding them all of the days in their youth when they had drawn straws to see who would be sentries against their enemies.

"Let us hope not," Raven said, his voice hoarse. "I've no desire to return to being frightened of my very shadow."

Val draped a long, brotherly arm over his shoulders. "Have no fear, whelp, I'll see you to manhood yet."

Swan grimaced. "Yet another gelding I'm forced with. Mayhap I should take up the first guard. I'm afraid with men such as these at my back."

Val swung at his head, but Swan ducked.

"Enough teasing," Stryder said sharply. "We need to be wary of everyone here. Remember, there is an enemy among us."

They nodded.

Inclining his head, Stryder made his way from his tent toward the castle.

Stryder's intent was to speak to Henry, but he'd no more entered the castle than he'd run headlong into Rowena who was simultaneously trying to dash out the door.

The impact of her soft curves against him was as exciting as it was shocking. Instinctively, he wrapped his arms about her to keep her from falling.

Her face was flush, her eyes bright and shining. But more than that, her breathlessness conjured images in his mind of what she would look like in the throes of passion.

Indeed, it was all he could do to not capture those parted lips with his own and see just how breathless he could make her.

"Milady, we must stop meeting like this."

Her face turned even redder. "It seems I am ever unbalanced in your lordship's presence."

He rumbled a low laugh at that. He felt much the same way around her.

She looked up at him with a searing gaze that made his groin tight and heavy. Aching. "But I am beginning to suspect my maids might be right about one thing."

"And that is?" he asked as he set her back on her feet.

"Strong arms do have their uses at such times."

Her unexpected words made him a bit nervous. Was that

truly a compliment from a woman who professed to hate all knights?

He looked about as if expecting the Second Coming.

"Are you all right, milord?"

"Aye, but a compliment from you makes me fear that my death may be imminent."

She laughed at that. "If your death is imminent 'tis from that sword you carry and not from my tongue."

He arched a brow at her, but before he could speak, she continued, "I promised you that I would insult you no more. Therefore, my claws are effectively sheathed."

Strange, but he rather missed the angry minx. She was easy to keep his guard against. He found this new side of her disturbing. Beguiling.

And the talk of her claws caused his gaze to drop to her hand where he noted she had her nails perfectly manicured. They were long and elegant.

A perfect set to have skimming down a man's spine. . . .

He stepped back as that unwanted thought went through him. He was beginning to think like Swan.

"Where were you off to in such a hurry?" he asked, trying to distract himself.

"Any place where none of my ladies-in-waiting can be found."

"And why is that?"

"They have this foolish notion that you and I should wed."

He let out a long, aggravated breath at that. "Then let us put them with my men, who are equally determined to see me bachelor."

"Truly?"

"Aye. They've no wish for our lives to change."

Her face turned speculative at that. "It might be interesting to let them loose on each other, just to see who wins, but in my experience, 'tis the man who invariably falls to the woman."

He arched a skeptical brow. "I wouldn't say that. The surrender seems to be mutual."

"How do you figure?"

"Man may take a bite of the apple, but afterward, the woman ends up following him wherever he leads."

"You think so?"

"You think not?"

She narrowed her eyes at him. "I think some lady needs to take that ego of yours down a notch or two."

Stryder gave her a hot once over. "And are you the lady to do it?"

A slow, seductive smile spread across her face. "Aye, Lord Charming. Unlike the others you have known, I am quite immune to your assets."

"My assets?" he asked, intrigued by the notion that she had attributed any to him after their confrontation in the hall on the night they met. "And what would those be?"

"I think you know well enough what most maids fawn over."

"But not you?"

"Nay," she said, raising her chin a degree. "I have never been swayed by bulging arms or a handsome face." She placed her hand against the center of his chest. "It's what a man has in here that matters to me."

Rowena had meant the words playfully, but the light in Stryder's eyes went out immediately. His face turned gravely earnest.

"Then we are truly ill suited, since I have nothing left in there."

His words surprised her. "Nothing?"

"Nay, lady. That part of me died long ago."

His heart beat fiercely under her hand. It was every bit as strong as the man who stood before her. "For something dead, it seems powerful enough to me. Indeed, you didn't hesitate to save Kit."

He withdrew from her.

"Stryder?" she said, stopping him as he headed away from her.

He paused and glanced back.

"Thank you, again, for your courtesy."

By his frown she could tell her words confused him. In truth, she didn't know why she was being so kind to a man she should hate and yet she didn't find it within her to hurt him. There was enough pain in his eyes.

"Ever at your service," he said almost tauntingly before he continued on his way.

A small smile hovered at the edges of her lips.

Rowena watched until he'd vanished. He did have a most masculine walk.

And a handsome backside.

He's a knight . . .

All humans had faults.

He kills people.

It was true and yet . . .

She shook her thoughts away. She wasn't like her friends who only wanted a man for his looks. Nor did she wish to lose herself to marriage. If she should ever choose a husband, she wanted a partnership. One built of mutual respect and friendship. Love would be a nice addition, but she didn't delude herself with that thought.

Only the extremely lucky ladies in her position ever found love, and most of them had found it outside of their marriages. Nay, unlike the other troubadours, she didn't believe in encouraging men and women into illicit affairs.

Rowena, like her parents before her, was an idealist. She imagined a world where everyone, rich and poor, married only for love.

But if she couldn't have that, then the least she would settle for was friendship.

Lost in thought, Rowena headed toward the orchard in the back of the castle, seeking a place where she could be alone.

She hadn't gone far into the area before a shadow caught her attention.

It moved quickly, like a phantom.

Frowning, she went toward it without thought.

Something that proved to be most unwise as she drew near enough to see what it was . . .

A large man.

He swung himself up to the top of the wall, but as he did so, the cowl of his cloak fell back.

Rowena gasped.

His hair was blacker than the midnight sky, his skin dark and tawny, and his eyes . . .

They were an eerie green that stood out from his dark skin.

The man was a Saracen!

And he had seen her as plainly as she had seen him.

Chapter 6

Part of Rowena wanted to scream and panic. The other, saner part made her run for her life.

She didn't know if the Saracen was after her or not, nor did she pause long enough to find out.

She had only one thought in her mind—escape.

Rounding the corner of the castle, she caught sight of Stryder with Kit and the monk.

Rowena headed straight for them and it wasn't until she had launched herself at Stryder that she dared look behind her.

Stryder stumbled sideways as someone propelled herself into his arms. Expecting it to be one of his many admirers, he couldn't have been more stunned to find Rowena there.

"Again, Rowena, we must stop meeting this way," he teased her.

Her eyes were wide and panic-filled, which immediately squelched his humor. "Is something amiss?"

"A Saracen," she gasped. "In the orchard."

His blood went cold at her words. Handing her over to his brother, he and Christian ran to check out the area.

Rowena watched the men run off while she struggled to control her pounding heart.

"Sh," Kit said, taking her by the hand and leading her off to sit on a bench near the water well. "Catch your breath."

She was ever grateful for her friend's consideration as her

heart still pounded and her limbs shook fretfully. That had been the most terrifying moment of her life. "Thank you, Kit."

He went to get her a cool sip of the water from the well while she watched the area where the other two men had vanished.

"Drink it slowly," he warned as he handed it to her.

Again, she thanked him.

"So, what did you see?" he asked after she had caught her breath.

She clutched the cold metal cup he had given her. "It was a man dressed in black Arab robes. He had eyes like a demon and moved like lightning. I'm still not sure he was quite human."

Kit's eyes showed he felt as much concern about this as she did.

"He must be the one who killed Cyril," she whispered. "But where could such a man hide?"

"People like that are always where you least expect them."

Perhaps that was true. . . .

She looked past Kit's shoulder to see Stryder and his friend returning.

Stryder approached her with a grim look. "We saw no one there."

Rowena didn't like the sound of that. "He must have run off when he saw me."

The monk nodded. "I think it best that I leave and—"

"Nay, Christian," Stryder said to the monk. "He's out to kill off our members. The last thing I want is you traveling alone."

Christian scoffed. "It would take more than a mere assassin to kill me, and well you know it."

"It's a chance I won't take," Stryder said emphatically. "Try to leave and I will shoot you in your leg with a bolt."

Christian looked offended. "You wouldn't dare."

"Test me."

The look that passed between them said that Christian didn't really doubt Stryder after all.

"Now then," Stryder said, facing her. "Tell me of this man you saw. What did he look like?"

"He was garbed all in black and I saw very little of his form. He was too well robed."

"Did he see you?" Christian asked.

"Aye."

All three men cursed.

Rowena swallowed nervously as she realized why. "He'll be coming for me, won't he?"

"Most likely," Christian said.

Stryder shoved at his friend. "Don't upset her any more."

"Would you have me lie?"

"Aye." Stryder turned back to her. "One of us will have to guard you."

She looked back and forth between Stryder, Kit, and Christian. Kit, while handsome and tall, wasn't the sort to wield a sword. Neither was the monk.

As for Lord Stryder . . .

"I can hire someone to guard me."

"Never trust a hired man," Stryder said. "If they'll serve you for one price, they'll gladly serve another for a higher one."

"Come to think of it," Kit snapped as he glared at Rowena, "why are you without an escort?"

"I'm on the castle's grounds," she snapped back. "There shouldn't be any danger within the walls."

Kit shook his head as if disgusted. "Your uncle gives you entirely too much freedom."

Rowena stiffened at Kit's tone. Never before had her friend spoken to her in such a manner.

Even Stryder looked surprised.

"What's done is done," Stryder said. "Our concern now is making sure our only witness remains alive to help us hunt down our killer."

"Very well," Christian said. "You guard her and I will notify your men what is happening. We'll do a search for our Saracen. He can't be too far away. Rather, I'm thinking he must be hiding amongst us."

"How so?" Kit asked. "Saracens are forbidden to wear our clothes."

Stryder gave his brother a fierce frown. "How do you know that?"

"Everyone knows that," Kit responded after a brief pause.

"We'll search the countryside," Christian said. "If there's a camp, we'll find him."

Stryder looked skeptical. "They vanish into the deserts for

days on end with nothing more than a knife to feed and protect them, and you think to find an assassin in the trees?"

Christian looked smug. "If he's there, I will find him."

"Don't take long."

Christian inclined his head, then left.

Kit looked as worried as Rowena felt. He excused himself and left her alone with Stryder, a man she should hate, and yet it had been him she had run to when she felt threatened. How very odd.

" 'Tis an evil thing that was done here," Rowena said quietly. "I hope we find this killer."

"Trust me, milady, we will."

He offered her his arm. "I'll take you back to the castle. You should make certain that you stay with other people at all times."

"So you won't be guarding me?"

"Aye, I shall. But something tells me you might take it upon yourself to escape my watchful eye."

"And something tells me that would prove a most difficult task."

He smiled respectfully at that. Glory, but the man was most handsome when his stern features softened.

Rowena felt suddenly feminine around him in a way she'd never felt feminine before. It was as if the woman in her was so beguiled by the male of him that she was more aware of herself and her needs than she had ever been before.

But the most disturbing thing of all was how much she wanted to know what a kiss from Stryder would feel like. What he would taste like.

Rowena!

She was shocked by that. And terrified. She wasn't like her friends, forever turned by a pretty face and yet as they walked along in silence, she found herself strangely curious about every facet of Stryder.

"They say you have no wish for children," she found herself saying. "Is that true?"

He nodded.

"Why? I should think a man in your position would be concerned about his lands."

"There are things in this life more important than lands."

She agreed, but she wondered what he treasured more. "Such as?"

"Brotherhood. Vows. My lands are only important to me because they allow me to put my money to good use. When I am dead, I am dead. The last thing I wish is to leave behind anyone to mourn my passing. I want no child left behind to weep over my grave."

She stopped as he spoke those soft words. But it wasn't the words she reacted to. It was the sound of his voice. The betrayed grief. "Not all children are left behind, milord. Some are fortunate enough to have their parents for a long while."

His eyes were so haunted that it made her chest ache for him. "But all too many are. And then they are slaves to that land that was their father's. Pawns to be used and for what? Even you are nothing more than an object in the eyes of Henry and your uncle. Would you want your daughter to be in your place?"

In that moment, she felt kinship to this stranger.

He understood her.

And that amazed her most of all. "Is that why you agreed to sing for me?"

He nodded. "I take my vows seriously, Rowena. And one of them was that I would do anything in my power to free those who are caught in situations that are harmful to them."

She would never have thought a mere knight capable of such compassion and introspection. "You are a man of surprising depth, Lord Stryder of Blackmoor."

"For a senseless knight, you mean?"

She felt her face flush. "Your squire told you of that too?"

"I believe his exact question was if all men had to abandon their senses to become soldiers."

She cringed at that. "I didn't mean *you*."

"Nay?"

"Well, I didn't know you then."

He laughed at that. "I have to admit that I rather like to see you flustered, milady. Your pinkened cheeks do marvels for your eyes."

"Are you complimenting me, sir?" she asked, amazed by this playful side of him.

"If I were?"

"I think I would be flattered."

"Then I am complimenting you."

Warmth flooded her. How noble and kind of her kn . . .

She swallowed as she realized the train of her thoughts. She'd almost considered him *her* knight. How untoward. She would never claim a man such as this. One who was known by how many men he'd killed.

It was unseemly and improper.

Wasn't it?

Clearing her throat, she headed toward the castle. "Are you planning on following me about for the rest of the day?" she asked as he walked beside her.

"Until we find out more about this Saracen you saw, I think it wise."

"And if I told you I was making it up, would you leave me in peace?"

"Nay, I would know you weren't being truthful."

"How so?"

His eyes were devilish and hot.

"You intentionally threw yourself into my arms, milady. Only the devil of a fright would have caused you to do such. Your terror was too real to be feigned."

"But surely in the castle—"

"Cyril was in the middle of a camp of knights. Some of us are most light sleepers and yet someone crept into his tent and killed him while we were all about. That took a great deal of nerve and skill to accomplish."

The dire tone of his voice raised the hairs on the back of her neck. "You're not telling me everything, are you?"

Again his eyes darkened. "If it is what we suspect, nay. I dare not."

A chill went over her.

He paused for a moment before he continued. "I know of a Saracen called El Sahaar."

She frowned as she recognized the term. "The Sorcerer?"

"How is it a lady of your standing knows Arabic?"

"My uncle's physician swears by their medicine. He spent much of his youth studying it in Jerusalem, where he collected many books. After a great deal of coercion, I convinced him to teach me to read some of their stories."

Stryder looked impressed. "You are quite remarkable."

She smiled at his compliment. "You were telling me of this man?"

"Aye. He was able to literally vanish into a cloud of smoke. Fast and lethal, he moved as if he were invisible and he told us stories of how his people trained assassins."

"I don't know that term."

"They are men trained to slay others silently. They come at you in the night, or even in the day, but always by surprise. Nassir . . . El Sahaar," he added, "said that he had known of some who would walk up to men in the bazaars and knife them so quickly that no one could even begin to guess who the murderer was."

That certainly sounded like the man she had seen in the orchard.

"So our Saracen could be anywhere?"

He nodded. "I would caution you to lock your window tonight. Hang a bell over the lock, just to be sure."

Rowena trembled at the thought. "Is there any way to stop them?"

"One can only fight fire with fire, milady. The only way to stop them is to be quicker than they are."

How she hated to hear that. It wasn't in her nature to return violence with more violence. Couldn't there be a peaceful solution?

Rowena led Stryder up the stairs to the ladies' solar, where numerous women were passing a lazy early afternoon gossiping in chairs that were all about the room.

At the sight of Lord Stryder, they immediately shrieked and rushed them.

Stryder pulled her back through the door so quickly that she stumbled. He slammed the door and held it while the women pounded and screamed from the other side.

"Lord Stryder!"

"Quick," he told Rowena, "grab that pole from the wall."

She did as he asked.

"Place it under the knob. Hurry."

Rowena hesitated. "They'll be trapped in there."

"Not for long. I shall send my squire back to unlock it. After, I'm gone."

She gave him a suspicious look before she agreed to it.

As soon as the pole was wedged to keep the door from opening, he released it and took a deep breath.

But not for long.

Another group of women were coming from the opposite end of the hall, no doubt to join the others.

They screamed and ran at them.

Stryder grabbed her hand and pulled her after him as he ran back for the stairs. Rowena would have laughed had one of the women not grabbed her braid and yanked.

"Ow!" she snapped.

Stryder didn't pause as he ran into the great hall. "Val!" he shouted at a man sitting in the corner. "Ten silver marks."

The man wasted no time cutting the women off from their pursuit as Stryder dashed back out the door and dodged to the small courtyard to the right.

Only when they were shielded from the yard by tall shrubs did he stop. His eyes panicked, he looked about as if expecting someone else to leap out at him.

"Does this happen to you often?" she asked as she tried to catch her breath.

"More than you'd believe," he said.

Rowena knew how women talked about the earl and their attempts to claim him, but she had never before witnessed them actually attacking him. "You're serious, aren't you?"

"I told you, Rowena, you alone seem immune to whatever it is that makes every woman I meet want to throw herself at me." His eyes twinkled at that. "Then again—"

"Don't say it," she said, placing her hand over his lips. "I have never intentionally thrown myself at you."

He arched a brow.

"Except when faced with near death."

She felt his lips curl under her hand and it was then she became aware of the fact that her flesh was touching his. That his lips, unlike the rest of him which was rock hard and steely, were soft. Tender.

Swallowing, she dropped her hand.

Stryder's breath caught as he watched the uncertain look on her face. The lass was beautiful with her veil askew while tendrils of her hair curled around her face. Her skin was mottled by their run and her eyes light.

Her lips slightly parted. . . .

It was those succulent lips that he focused on. Lips that begged for a taste. A nibble.

And before he could stop himself, he pulled her closer to him. Closer. Close enough so that her curves were pressed up against the hardness of his chest.

Aye, he wanted her.

Wanted her insanely. Before he could think better of it, he dipped his head and took possession of that mouth. Stryder moaned the instant he tasted her. The instant her ever vexing tongue swept into his mouth where she hesitantly tasted him in turn. The innocence of that kiss made his head spin.

Rowena was completely breathless as the strength of the earl overwhelmed her. The last thing she had expected was this over-load of sensation that electrified her entire body.

The strength of his hands pressing against her . . . the feel of his hard, muscled body.

It was truly divine.

No wonder women chased him down! He cupped her face with his hands as he deepened their kiss. Would she swoon? Surely no mere woman could feel this and not pass out.

An image of him naked flashed in her mind and for the first time in her life, she understood desire. Physical attraction. Most of all, she understood lust.

What she felt for him made a mockery of what she had ever felt for one of the troubadours who had come calling in Sussex. Lord Stryder was exceptional.

He pulled back slowly and looked down at her.

"Do all men kiss like that?" she asked quietly.

One corner of his mouth lifted up. "I know not since I have never kissed a man."

She laughed in spite of herself. Lord Stryder was so unex-pected. Who would have thought that a man like this could be funny and warm?

Compassionate?

"Would you do me a favor, milord?" she asked as she stepped back. "Be a boorish ass again."

He looked baffled by her request. "I beg your pardon?"

"You're much easier to hate when you're being arrogant rather than charming."

He tilted his head to study her. "Do you wish to hate me?"

"I would much rather hate you than be attracted to you."

"Why?"

"Because I don't want to bury another man I care for when some lunatic takes it upon himself to attack him from behind and cut his throat. If, God forbid, I am to marry, I would rather it be to someone who has no enemies. Someone who never feels the lure of battle and all its dangers."

Stryder's blue eyes were gentle as he took her hand into his. "Men die, Rowena. I am just as likely to trip and break my neck while walking across this yard as I am to fall in battle."

"Nay," she said, her voice thick with pain and sorrow that not even all the past years could diminish. "There's no real danger here. No one is running at you with an ax, trying to take your head from your shoulders."

"And Cyril was asleep in his bed. Far from the battlefield."

"But he was killed because he was a knight. Just as my father was. Nay, I want no more fear or strife. I want only to feel safe in my heart. To know that when I close my eyes, my husband will be by my side and not off to foreign lands to fight and die. I have no wish to live my mother's hellish life."

"Your mother's life was hellish?"

Rowena found herself confiding in him. "Aye. My father was a good man. But they were placed together by their parents and had nothing in common. Ever. My father all but ignored my mother whenever he was home. He spent most of his time away from us." Tears welled as she recalled the day of his death. "When my uncle came to tell us he had died, I shall never forget the look on my mother's face. It was empty. My world was shattered and hers. . . . It was as if my uncle had told her a neighbor had died."

"Perhaps she hid her pain."

"Nay," she said, remembering it all clearly. "She told me that she only wished he had stayed home and lived long enough to give her a son so that I wouldn't be forced to marry a man I didn't love. Even now, my mother is still locked into another loveless marriage with a man who ignores her."

"You were lucky," he said quietly. "My father loved my mother more than anything else on this earth. He always hated to leave her side and would rush home to be with her as soon as he could. I remember most the way he would stare at her, watching everything she did. Every move she made. It was as if he were looking at paradise."

"I don't understand," she said, thinking of Christopher who had been their mother's illegitimate son. "Kit?"

An angry tic started in Stryder's jaw. "My father loved my mother, but she never loved him." His gaze snapped at her. "He was just a stupid, ill-bred knight while my mother dreamed of a poet. She wanted a man whose tender words could woo her and my father knew nothing save warfare. But he knew his heart. And she was it." He shook his head. "My father had come rushing home to be with her, only to find his home vacant."

"You had gone to visit your brother?"

Stryder frowned. "How do you know that?"

"Kit told me that she had been betrayed by a servant."

He nodded. "Aye. My mother had gone to visit his father. Again. I knew she was unfaithful, but I had never betrayed her. I had given her my word."

Rowena's heart ached as she recalled the death of Stryder's parents. It was common knowledge that his father had slain his mother and tried to kill Stryder before the man took his own life. Until now, no one had known why. Stryder alone knew the reason and to her knowledge, he had never told a soul.

"I don't know if I can sing for you, Rowena. Ever."

Her heart ached at the anguish she saw in his deep blue eyes.

"And I could never take you for wife," he said, his voice carefully measured. "I refuse to have a wife who cannot love me for what I am. You are so like my mother and I am my father's son. There will never be a woman born I would trust to keep faith with me in my absence."

She nodded in understanding. "And I am my mother's

daughter. I could no more love a man of the sword than either of our mothers. So, tell me, Stryder. How do we get out of this?"

"I don't know. Murder?"

She gave him a droll stare. "I am not amused, milord."

"Lord Stryder!"

They both turned as another group of women spotted their hiding place.

Stryder groaned.

Rowena was beginning to understand just why the man was so arrogant. "Leave me," she said, urging him to run.

"I can't, Rowena. Your Saracen could return."

Before she could argue, he tossed her over his shoulder and ran with her.

Rowena was horrified, not to mention in a good deal of pain. No one had ever held her in so degrading a position, let alone ran pell-mell through the crowded inner bailey. With every step he took, he bounced her middle against his hard shoulder. It was all she could do not to cry out.

Everyone not chasing them turned to stare.

"Put me down, Stryder," she snapped.

He ignored her as he made his way to the stable. No sooner had he entered it than the door behind them slammed shut and was bolted.

Stryder skidded to a halt and turned to look at who had penned them inside.

Rowena strained to see herself and then wished she hadn't.

There were two shadows who had placed a brace over the door.

Both of them were Arabs.

Chapter 7

Rowena couldn't breathe as she saw the shadowed pair. The taller one with vibrant green eyes she recalled only too well.

" 'Tis him," she whispered to Stryder. "The demon in the orchard."

Stryder set her on her feet. Slowly. He put his body between her and the Saracens, then placed one hand on his sword hilt.

"You motherless excuse for a dung dealer," Stryder snarled. "How dare you show your face here."

Rowena frowned. Both of the Saracens' faces were covered by an opaque black veil.

The Saracen's eyes darkened. "Careful, infidel, I've been known to slice the tongues of your ilk and turn them into harmless asps to be butchered."

The other Saracen appeared every bit as confused by the exchange as Rowena was.

"I dare you to try it."

The Saracen arched his brow. "You would challenge me? You who have the stench of a rat and the brains to match?"

Why wasn't Stryder doing something?

Rowena wasted no time while Stryder approached their enemies slowly. She ran for a pitchfork in one of the stalls.

Grabbing it up, she rushed back toward them.

"Stryder!" the shorter Saracen snapped, startling Rowena.

Stryder spun about and caught her pitchfork from her hands.

"Whoa, lady," he said, taking it from her. "The last thing I would see is my friend skewered by you."

Rowena widened her eyes. "Friend?"

The taller Saracen pulled the veil from his head. Rowena hesitated. He was one of the most handsome men she'd ever beheld. His disheveled, jet-black hair curled becomingly around his face and shoulders. With the veil off, his eyes appeared even greener in contrast to his light tawny skin and thick black lashes.

"Nassir," Stryder explained, using the name of the man he had spoken of earlier. "And our friend, Zenobia."

The shorter one uncovered her head as well to show Rowena the face of an exotically beautiful woman. Like Nassir, Zenobia wore her hair to her shoulders, but it wasn't nearly as dark. Instead, it was a rich reddish brown. Her skin was a pale olive and she held topaz-colored eyes.

"What are you two doing here?" Stryder asked.

"Hiding from the Abbot," Zenobia explained. "The man is still part bloodhound. He almost captured Nassir earlier."

"Hardly," Nassir snapped, as if offended by her implication. "He was nowhere near me and I won't reveal myself to him until at least nightfall. Let him chase his tail for a bit."

Zenobia rolled her eyes. "We intercepted a messenger from Persia who was on his way to England with orders for an assassin."

"We tried to get here before the assassin," Nassir added, "but it appears we came too late."

"You heard about Cyril?" Stryder asked.

Nassir nodded. "I thought if we made our presence known to certain people"—his gaze went to Rowena—"that the assassin might think we were sent here as the messenger and make contact with one of us. Instead, your woman called out all of you and rather than have you waste your time guarding her from me, I thought it best to let you know we're here."

"You could have let me know this morning."

"You haven't been still once this morning," Nassir said, humor evident in his voice. "I particularly find the women in the garden amusing."

Stryder shook his head. "I'm delighted to know someone does."

"If you wish it, I could pretend to be your wife again," Zenobia offered.

Stryder snorted. "The last time we tried that, I almost got my throat cut."

Both Nassir and Zenobia laughed.

A sudden banging on the door commenced. "Lord Stryder!" the women outside screamed as they demanded entrance.

Nassir sighed wearily, then looked to Stryder. "Doff your clothes."

Stryder started disrobing without question.

"Excuse me," Rowena choked as the earl bared his tawny chest to her. And the earl had a fine chest too. One that she really didn't need to see any more of if she were to not think indecent thoughts of the man. He was haunting her thoughts all too much as it was. "What are you doing?"

"Nassir is going to ride out of here dressed as me," he explained, "to get the women to leave me in peace while Zenobia catches me up on what they've been up to."

Rowena's face heated as Nassir started pulling his own clothes off.

Smiling, Zenobia led her toward the rear of the stable. "You have to understand, milady. They lived for quite a few years in a hole where modesty was quickly sacrificed."

"But how did he know what Nassir had planned?"

"Again, they lived together for so long, fought side by side, that even now I can tell you what each of them is thinking. Many times, we need no words between us to understand each other."

Proving her point, Zenobia led her to the stall where Stryder's horse was kept and saddled it while the men exchanged clothes. That the Saracen lady knew which horse was Stryder's spoke much of her relationship with the earl.

"Greetings, Goliath," Zenobia said, patting the horse's neck. "It's been awhile, hasn't it, old friend?"

She let the horse sniff her before she saddled him.

Nassir joined them, wearing Stryder's clothes.

"You look nothing like him," Rowena said.

Nassir smiled. "They won't even notice. All they'll see is the black hair and clothes."

Once he was mounted, Stryder hid behind a stack of hay while she and Zenobia opened the stable door.

Nassir kicked the horse forward, tearing out the stable.

Shrieking, the women scurried in all directions.

"Lord Stryder, come back!" several screamed.

Realizing the man was gone, the group huffed and groused. Some cast a feral glare at Rowena before they dispersed.

Rowena was amazed it had worked, and it wasn't until all of them were gone that she realized Zenobia had rushed to hiding after they opened the door.

"Finally," Stryder breathed. "A moment of peace."

Rowena frowned at him in the black Saracen garb. He looked so strange and yet handsome in it.

"Have you any other clothes?" he asked Zenobia.

She shook her head. "There wasn't time."

"Rowena, would you have anything she could borrow?"

She nodded. Zenobia was a full head and shoulders taller than her, but then so was Elizabeth. She doubted if her friend would mind loaning out a few gowns to Zenobia.

"Thank you," Stryder said. "You collect her clothes while the two of us make our way back to my tent unseen. Would you meet us there as soon as possible?"

"Aye." She watched as they headed out and hoped that no one saw them. It would truly bode evil for Stryder if he were caught dressed like that when half the court still suspected him of Cyril's murder.

But what she liked was the way he moved like a silent wind. Quickly. Surely. All man and yet he was something more.

Something that made her feel a tenderness for him that she didn't want to feel. Lord Stryder would be an easy man to love. Unfortunately, he would never be an easy man to tame.

Aquarius watched from the shadows as the two Saracens made their way from the stable.

They had come for him just as they had promised.

Kill or be killed.

It was the one oath his captors had made to him when they had allowed him to go free. They had given him two years to complete his task. If all the men on his arm were dead within that time, they would allow him to live.

If not, another would be sent to kill him.

His two years had ended a month past and since then there had been no sign of his captors.

Aquarius had thought that he would be safe. No one knew he'd ever been in Outremer. No one could get close to him.

Apparently he was wrong.

Unlike the others, he knew the Saracens hadn't killed Cyril. But they *would* kill him.

There was no place to hide from such devils. They would find him.

Panic swelled inside his heart. There was no one he could trust. No one who could help him. If any of the Brotherhood learned of his presence, they would kill him just as quickly as the assassins.

And if Henry ever learned of the men he'd slain . . .

No one would care that those men had deserved their fate. Aquarius had killed in cold blood. That was all that would matter. His own degradations at their hands would be dismissed.

Worse, he would be exposed.

Nay, he refused to suffer any more humiliation.

His only choice would be to expose the Saracens before they found him or to complete the murders he was assigned.

There was only one name left on his arm.

Just one . . .

The Widowmaker.

Stryder cursed as he entered his tent and ducked the sword stroke aimed for his head.

Spinning around, Stryder caught his young assailant about his middle.

"Halt, Raven," he snarled as his knight went to attack him again. " 'Tis I."

Raven hesitated. "Stryder?"

Zenobia laughed from behind him. "Little Raven? Is that you?"

Raven frowned. "Zenobia?"

Once more she removed her hadji and smiled at him. He rushed to embrace her while Stryder began changing his clothes. "It's good to see you, scamp," Zenobia said affectionately. "I see Stryder hasn't killed you yet for aggravating him."

"Nay, and you . . ." Raven ran his gaze over her. The youth had always held a tenderness for the Ayasheen she-warrior. "You look wonderful, as always."

She smiled warmly.

"So why are the two of you dressed like that?" Raven asked.

Zenobia explained how she and Nassir had left immediately from the Holy Land to intercept the murderer while Stryder finished changing his clothes.

Once Stryder rejoined them, she gave him a teasing look. "Mayhap you should marry," Zenobia said. "At least then you could have a moment of peace from your adoring crowd."

He scoffed while Raven looked horrified. "We can't have Stryder married," he said defensively. "Who then would lead us?"

"There are more important things than direct leadership, scamp," she said affectionately. "A king may leave a country without losing his authority or without the country falling to pieces."

Stryder snorted. "And he who leaves Rome loses it."

Zenobia shook her head at him. "I'll remind you of that when you're old and alone with only mice to keep you company."

Stryder dismissed her words easily enough. "I don't see you rushing to the altar."

Her gaze turned sad. "My heart is already claimed, but the one who owns it thinks too much like you."

Stryder felt for his friend. He hadn't known she'd already fallen in love. "Nassir?"

She laughed aloud at that. "Nay. I would be blessed indeed if I could be with the one I love. But alas, he has his own path to follow and I have no place there."

Poor Zenobia. The daughter of their jailor, she had joined ranks with them just weeks before their escape. Indeed, she had been key to the success of their escape. She had given up everything to help them. It was something none of them had ever forgotten.

"When did you lose your heart?" he asked her.

"Long ago." Her eyes were filled with restrained anguish. "Trust me, Stryder, there is no greater pain than to let the one you love leave your side. Knowing they are out there, alone, and always wondering if they are healthy and happy."

He frowned at her words. It wasn't like Zenobia to be so candid with her feelings. "Why are you telling me this?"

"Because too many of us let our minds deafen our hearts." She went to the tent and opened the flap as Rowena approached.

Stryder's frown deepened. Zenobia was gifted with second sight, and there were times when her abilities were frightening.

She took the gown from Rowena and thanked her for it.

Stryder and Raven went to stand outside while she changed.

"Will you help me, milady?" Zenobia asked Rowena as she moved to join the men.

Rowena hesitated, then agreed. She didn't know why she felt a strange jealousy towards the Saracen woman, but she did.

"I'm no threat to you, *kateena*," Zenobia said gently.

"*Kateena?*"

"It means 'little precious one.' A term my people often apply to friends."

Rowena offered her a smile at the endearment as she helped Zenobia into Elizabeth's pale blue gown. "I don't think of you as a threat."

"Aye, but you do. You envy my friendship with Stryder."

"Hardly."

Zenobia gave her a knowing look. "Shh, *kateena*, you can't hide those thoughts from me. You fear what you feel for him."

"How do you know that?"

"Your feelings are so strong that they speak even when you don't."

Before Rowena could respond, Zenobia turned pale. "Falsworth," she breathed.

Her dress unlaced, Zenobia ran to the tent flap and pulled Stryder back inside. Her face was panicked, her eyes unfocused as she grabbed a handful of Stryder's tunic.

"Falsworth is next to die," Zenobia breathed. "Tonight or tomorrow."

"He's not here," Stryder said with a scowl. "He was supposed to come, but he hasn't arrived. Is he dead already?"

Zenobia tilted her head as if she were listening to something no one else could hear. "Nay. He lives. But there is evil all around him. He must be found."

"I'll send Raven and Will to his lands."

"It won't save him," she breathed as if she heard something else. Zenobia clenched her eyes shut and winced as if she felt some inner pain. "The hand of Fate can never be altered. He will die, and you . . ."

She looked up at Stryder as if something terrified her.

"What?" Stryder asked. "Zenobia. Tell me what you see."

"I can't," she whispered. "It's all shadows and darkness. I can't tell what it is."

"Raven," he snapped at his young knight. "Fetch Will. I want the two of you to head to York to warn Falsworth."

The youth nodded, then ran to obey.

Stryder started out of the tent.

"It won't save him, Stryder," Zenobia warned.

"Maybe not, but I have to try."

He left the two women alone again.

Rather skittish of the woman now, Rowena let the awkward silence stand between them.

"Could you lace my back?" Zenobia asked, turning around.

Rowena quietly assisted her.

"You don't have to be afraid of me," Zenobia said while Rowena tied her gown.

"I'm not afraid of you . . . exactly."

"You know not what to make of me."

"You are rather odd."

Zenobia laughed. "But you appreciate oddity in others."

"To a degree."

Zenobia faced her with a smile. Dressed in one of Elizabeth's gowns, the woman could easily pass for a European, even though she held an exotic look to her.

"You know, milady," she said as she adjusted her sleeves, "my people believe women are even stronger than men."

"Really?" Rowena asked, amazed by that fact. She'd always been under the misconception that Arab women were held in even less esteem than their European counterparts.

"Aye. The strongest woman of our tribe is chosen to lead our men into battle. She is called the *Darina*. My mother was *Darina* and had I stayed with our people, I would have taken the place of her successor."

"Why do you tell me this?"

"Because there is a time for all things. My people, like you, believe in peace. But sometimes, the only way to have peace is to fight for it."

Rowena shook her head in denial. "The only way to peace is to lay aside weapons."

"And the bloodiest of wars are often fought not with weapons, but rather with tongues. A man can heal an external wound a thousand times faster than he can heal even a small one dealt to his heart."

Rowena stood back as Zenobia's words sank in.

"You are a warrior, milady," Zenobia spoke softly. "You just choose a different forum for your battles, but you battle nonetheless. Like the men you hate so much, you hurt and wound. Have you given thought to why you fight the wars you do?"

Before she could answer, Zenobia swept out of the tent and left her there to silently contemplate her words.

It was hours later that Rowena found herself walking through the castle grounds. She looked around at the people who were milling and working. The servants either ignored her, or nodded in courtesy. She knew only a few of them by face. At home in Sussex, she would have known them all by name.

But it was the nobles who glared at her while Zenobia's words haunted her.

For an obvious reason, Rowena had purposefully surrounded herself only with minstrels who felt as she did. Those who glorified war had been sent packing as soon as they reached her home. The few times a year when she traveled with her uncle, she had noticed the way people mocked her, but paid them little heed.

Now she saw every one of them.

They were people, just as she was. Had she really wounded them with her words?

The thought made her ill.

She wanted to speak with someone she trusted. She'd been to Lord Stryder's tent only to find it empty. Her maids had all thought her foolish to doubt herself, but as her friends, their loyalty was to her.

She wanted to talk to someone else.

Nay, it was Stryder alone she wished to speak to. He would be honest with her. But since he was absent, she chose another to confide in.

Heading for the chapel, she decided that the priest would provide good counsel. Yet as she opened the door, she was floored by what she found.

Lord Stryder was there, on his knees before the votive stand, praying. He looked so incredibly sad, as if the full weight of the world rested on his shoulders alone.

Thinking to comfort him, she started for him only to find Kit cutting her off. Silently, he shook his head nay and escorted her back outside.

"I wanted to—"

"I know, Rowena," Kit said quietly once they were back in the courtyard. "But Stryder is best left alone when he prays like this."

Understanding dawned on her. "He prays for your mother."

"Nay," Kit said, his voice thick with emotion. "He prays for others. A little boy in particular."

"A boy?" she asked. "A son?"

Kit took a deep, ragged breath as if he felt Stryder's pain every bit as deeply as the earl did. "Nay, love. Long ago, my brother was held prisoner by the Saracens. While there, he befriended a young boy. Stryder had promised the child every night while the boy wept in hopeless despair that he would get him home, safe and sound. But on the night they escaped, he was told the boy had died earlier that day. 'Tis something that has haunted him since. He blames himself for not saving the boy as he promised. It was on this very day seven years past that the boy perished, so now my brother prays for the boy's lost soul and for all the others yet to be freed." Kit looked back at the chapel. "He never forgets that day. Not even for a moment."

"Oh, Kit," she breathed, her heart aching for Stryder.

Kit's face was every bit as haunted as Stryder's. "So bother him not, Rowena, about anything trivial."

She nodded, her throat far too tight to speak.

She left Kit and returned inside where Stryder still prayed. The light of the candles played in his dark hair while he held himself as still as any statue.

She realized as she glanced about that two more of his knights were there praying as well. The only ones missing were Nassir, Zenobia, and Christian.

No doubt they were off trying to find Cyril's killer before he could kill again while Raven and Will traveled to forewarn Falsworth.

Rowena offered up her own prayer that they all succeed.

Stryder slowly became aware of someone watching him. He opened his eyes to see Rowena just on the edge of his peripheral vision. His heart heavy over the one promise in his life that he had made and broken, he crossed himself and rose slowly to his feet.

As he approached Rowena, he realized her eyes were filled with unshed tears. "Are you all right, milady?"

To his utter shock, she pulled him into her arms and held him tightly. He felt her tears fall against his neck as she clutched him to her.

Stryder couldn't have been more stunned had she slapped him. Indeed, that he would have almost expected.

But he needed this warmth from her at the moment. Wrapping his own arms around her, he held her and let the pain inside him lessen a degree.

If he lived an eternity, he would never forget the boy whose face he never saw. He could hear only the child's voice through the walls of their prison. Hear the sounds of his cries as their captors tormented and abused the boy.

"*Swear to me, Widowmaker. Swear you won't leave me here for them.*"

"*I swear it. I will get you out of here and take you someplace where no one will ever hurt you again.*"

He had missed that promise by one day. One single day. If they had left just one night sooner the child would have lived.

Someone cleared his throat.

Stryder became aware of the fact that he and Rowena were

embracing in the midst of a church. Reluctantly, he withdrew from Rowena to see Val indicating a priest who was glaring at them.

Taking her hand, Stryder led her from the chapel, back outside. Val and Swan walked on past them, in the direction of the training list, while he hesitated outside the chapel door with Rowena.

He wiped the cold tears from her cheeks as he watched her closely. "What has you so upset?"

She sniffed delicately. "Nothing. I fear I didn't get enough sleep last night."

He arched a brow at that.

"I had something in my eye?" she tried again.

Now he frowned.

Rowena rubbed a hand over her brow as if every bit as bemused as he was. "Forget my actions, milord. You just looked as if you needed comfort and I felt the peculiar urge to give it."

"Do you do this often with men you've just met?"

She laughed nervously. "Nay. I'm hardly the sort to do such and yet . . . I suspect you're a good man beneath your armor."

"For a brutal killer, you mean?"

She nodded. "You've never really killed in cold blood, have you?"

"Nay, but I have felt the urge a time or two in my life."

"As have I." Her confession surprised him. "If ever I found the man who killed my father, I think I could kill him gladly."

He took her hand into his and studied the delicate bones of it. Her hand was soft, well tapered. The gentle hand of a lady. "It's not easy to kill someone, Rowena. To stare at them, face to face, that moment when you both realize you've dealt them a mortal blow. There is something that passes between you. My father once told me it's a part of their soul that creeps into you. A part that will haunt you all of your life."

"And yet you're a knight."

"Because I have seen the great evil that is done on this earth to those who can't fight for themselves. The meek only inherit the grave while the strong go on until someone stronger stops them."

Rowena had never thought of it that way. "Is that why you fight?"

His eyes turned dark, brooding. "Aye. I fight for the ghost of a boy who cried because he was weak. A ghost I cannot exorcize no matter how hard I try."

Rowena reached up and touched the scar to the side of his neck where his father had cut him during his last fit of madness. It was only barely visible through his long hair.

Stryder closed his eyes, savoring the comfort of her gentle touch. Unlike other women, she wanted nothing from him. She was merely giving.

And that meant more to him than any amount of words.

Before he could stop himself, he bent his head down and captured her lips with his. The kiss was brief, but so needed that it surprised him more than her acquiescence to it.

He pulled back to watch her stare up at him.

Her smile weakened him instantly. "Careful, milord," she said quietly, "else I might mistake you for a friend."

He returned her smile. "I already consider you one, Rowena."

Rowena felt a strange chill rush over her at those words. "Even though I don't agree with you?"

"Most of my friends don't. Indeed, Christian and Nassir have turned arguing with me into an art form."

Her light smile made his body ache with desire. "Then I shall consider you my friend as well. Even though you find me maddening."

"Never maddening, milady. Just mad."

She laughed at his teasing. He took her hand in his and placed a gentle kiss across her knuckles.

She watched as he took his leave of her.

"Lord Stryder?" she called after him.

He turned to look at her and his pose took her breath.

"Shall we practice tonight?"

He grimaced. "If you insist on the torture."

"Indeed, I do."

He sighed heavily. "Then pick your device well. I shall be waiting on the rack for you just after supper. I will meet you in the hall."

She inclined her head to him. "Then I shall choose my thumbscrews wisely."

He turned and left her.

Rowena stood, her gaze never wavering as he walked away.

Lord Stryder was a man to woo a woman's heart. No wonder the others chased after him. . . .

Rowena hesitated as a realization struck her. The women who chased after him knew nothing of the man—no more than the men who pursued her hand knew of her.

Lord Stryder had very few friends.

And she was one of them.

She shook her head. Friend to a knight. Who would have ever thought such, and yet there was no denying what she felt toward him.

It most certainly wasn't hatred any longer or contempt.

Nay, she respected him.

"What are you doing, Rowena?" she asked herself aloud. "You want nothing to do with a knight. 'Tis a minstrel you seek."

Aye, it was true. Lord Stryder might be appealing, but at the end of the day, he wasn't the kind of man to stay at home while she built her school. He had his own calling in life.

One far nobler than hers.

Leashing her wayward heart, she headed toward the hall, where she hoped to put Stryder out of her thoughts.

But even so, she knew better. A man like him could never be driven out. Especially not by her heart, which couldn't really deny what she was beginning to feel for him.

Chapter 8

I t was well into the evening before supper began. Rowena sat with Kit at a lower table while the king, queen, and her uncle held court at the high table along with the Lord of Hexham and other prominent nobles.

The true festivities of the tournament were scheduled to begin tomorrow with a squire's melee and joust.

Those who were to participate wore scarlet tunics emblazoned with their lord's coat of arms. Druce sat in the midst of the youths who continued to brag that though their lords might not be able to best Lord Stryder, the boys could certainly best his squire.

Rowena felt badly for the boy who was being teased, and she hoped on the morrow Druce trounced them all.

Not that she should have such thoughts. Still, she hated to see the fear and uncertainty on the boy's handsome face.

"Where is your brother?" she asked Kit. Neither Stryder, his men, nor his "friends" had been there all night.

Kit shrugged. "I haven't seen him since I left the two of you at the chapel."

Rowena frowned, wondering what kept the man from eating, while her gaze drifted around the other nobles present. Surely he would be here, and yet as the meal progressed, it became obvious he had no intention of joining her.

As soon as the meals were finished, the tables were cleared and moved for dancing.

Elizabeth and Joanne joined them in one corner, where they waited, but not for long. They quickly went off to find partners for the coming dance.

Still there was no sign of Stryder. Rowena fought down her disappointment.

"He won't come at this point," Kit told her as he led her toward the floor so that they could dance. "Once he hears music, he retires for the night."

"But we were to meet for lessons."

Kit frowned at that. "I know how much you want your freedom to choose a husband you can tolerate, Rowena, but I beg you not to press him on the issue."

"I haven't."

He nodded in approval as he led her to the center of the room to start a lively dance.

Stryder ground his teeth as he heard the music coming from the hall. He hadn't meant for his meeting with Nassir, Christian, and Zenobia to last so long. But he had promised Rowena they could practice.

He had hoped to make it to the hall before the revelry began. How he hated to watch dancers and hear music.

Even now he could hear his mother mocking his father whenever his father was gone. *"The man is as clumsy as a plow. I know not how he can be so uncoordinated off the battlefield while he is so successful on it."*

His father had never known of her mockery and though he hated to dance, his father had done so in hopes of making Stryder's mother happy.

The only time she'd ever been happy was when she visited Kit's father.

Banishing the memories, he forced himself into the hall. He had given his word and above all else, he would not breech it. The crowd was thick with nobles surrounding the dancers. Stryder made his way through them, seeking the petite blonde who haunted him.

He froze the instant he saw Rowena in his brother's arms. Something painful shot through him so unexpectedly that it took his breath.

She was beautiful. Her cheeks reddened by her exercise.

Desire tore through him as he ached with want. The dance ended. She and Kit stayed on the dance floor while the group made ready for the masketelle.

All the women present drew straws to be the first lady to wear the mask. The idea of the dance was for the masked lady to be twirled around and then set free to find her dance partner for the rest of the night. They would lead the next dance and on the morrow, they would reign as the "king and queen" of the squire's tournament.

The lady chosen would remain the tournament lady until the knights held their tournament, and the victor named the Lady of All Hearts, who would then bestow the prizes on the victors and be the guest of honor at the banquet held on the final night of the tournament. Personally, Stryder thought it a foolish game, but the ladies considered it quite an honor.

Under the supervision of a matron, the straws were quickly drawn and compared. One by one, faces fell as the women realized they weren't the winner.

Until one face went pale. "Rowena de Vitry is our first queen," the matron pronounced.

The sudden silence was deafening. Normally when a lady was chosen, a cheer went up for her. There was no such celebration for Rowena.

The black feathered mask was brought forward and secured to Rowena's head while the minstrels began to play. The women twirled Rowena around.

Custom dictated that the men surround her so that they could elbow and shove for a chance to be picked.

None moved.

Indeed, many stepped back. Rowena stumbled about with her arms held out while the men began to elbow and prod one another.

"You brave her tongue," one man said to another.

"I can do without a shrew. Not even her lands are worth her prattle."

Laughter rang out as they took to insulting her.

Rowena froze.

But in her honor, she didn't cry or run. She merely stood there in the center of their mockery with her head held high.

Kit started forward.

"Aye, you take her, Christopher. She can't unman you."

Stryder's vision turned dark. Deadly.

Rowena wanted to die in shame. It was all she could do not to tear the mask off and run from the hall. But she wouldn't give them the satisfaction.

Worst of all, she felt for poor Kit, who had tried to help her. The last thing he deserved was to be mocked for his kind heart.

The laughter of the crowd died as she felt someone near her. Expecting it to be Kit, she was completely startled when strong arms pulled her close to a large, hard body.

The minstrels began playing again. There was no sound now from anyone in the hall as her unknown champion led her through a dance. His steps were flawless and commanding.

"Stryder?" she whispered, knowing the feel of him. His warm scent.

"Aye, milady."

Her heart shattered at the sound of his deep voice. And that succeeded in loosening a single tear from her eye. She was thankful for the mask that absorbed it.

"Thank you," she said quietly.

He paused in the dance to pull the mask from her. She shivered at the sight of him standing there, looking down at her with a passionate gaze that scorched her. "Ever at your service."

She smiled as he pulled her back into his arms and finished the dance.

Once it was over, he led her toward the door. Stryder paused beside a group of men. Handing her the mask, he turned to one knight and slammed his fist straight into the man's jaw.

"My brother is ten times the man you are, Hugh," he snarled at the knight on the ground. "And the next time you question that, I'll make sure you leave the tournament field with nothing but skin upon your back."

Turning on his heel, Stryder captured her hand and led her from the hall.

Rowena's eyes were wide from what he'd just done.

"I know," Stryder said in a tired tone. "I am ever the barbarian."

Rowena offered him a chiding smile. "Nay, you are not. I only wish you had punched him harder."

Stryder arched a brow at her words. "Can it be I am converting you?"

She shrugged. "Mayhap, but then you were the one who just danced with me in a hall full of people."

He grimaced at that. "Be grateful you wore the mask. This way you weren't able to witness the horror of my inability."

She pulled him to a stop. "Why did you come? Kit said you wouldn't show if you heard music."

"I made you a promise, Rowena."

"And so you came for me?"

He nodded.

Rowena bit her lip as she stared up at him. His face was shadowed by rushlights, but still she knew every mark of his features. Every dimple and whisker. "Thank you. I have a feeling that before this month ends I shall owe you more than can ever be repaid."

"Nay, milady. Think nothing of it. I've never been the kind of person to tolerate cruelty of any sort. There's no need in it. Life is ever hard enough."

"Aye, it is."

She took his hand into hers and noted the blood on his knuckles. "You're hurt!"

He shrugged it off. "Hugh has a hard head."

She frowned at his light tone. "Come, this needs be tended."

Stryder led her back to his tent, where he kept his supplies. He pulled out the small chest that contained bandages and salves for his injuries.

Rowena took it from his hand and made him sit in a chair so that she could tend his bleeding hand.

He watched as she gathered his wash basin, pitcher and ale skin. "I'm still confused by your acceptance of my actions when I know how much you loathe violence."

Rowena paused. In truth, she was as well. But for some reason she couldn't find anything appalling about his behavior tonight. For once, she did feel it was justified.

"We are friends," she said as she held his hand in hers and poured water over the cut. "Is that not what you said?"

"Aye."

"Well then, friends accept each other's shortcomings and their differences of opinions. Tonight, however, our differences were not as wide as they would have been yesterday."

He chuckled at that.

Rowena swallowed at the sensation of his hand in hers. His fingers were lean and dark compared to hers. Strong. She poured ale over them to cleanse the wound. Stryder hissed.

"Don't be a baby," she chided.

He took it good-naturedly.

Rowena reached for a small pot of white salve to rub over the injury. "Why do the men mock Kit so?" she asked. "He's not the only minstrel who doesn't fight."

Stryder looked away from her. "There are some who think he is more woman than man."

Rowena scoffed at what he was implying. "Kit is certainly not the kind of man inclined to be with other men."

"I agree, but he has never been found in the company of a woman, if you understand what I mean. Nor does he make it his habit to seek out any woman other than you. But he is often found in the company of men. I personally don't care what his tastes are. We are brothers and no man living will ever hurt him without answering to me for it."

Without thought, Rowena reached out and touched Stryder's face. "They should make more brothers such as you."

To her surprise, he turned his face into her hand and kissed her lightly on the palm.

Rowena's entire body grew warm. But what disturbed her most was the tenderness she felt toward him. The tenderness she saw in him. He was such an unexpected treasure.

Stryder watched her carefully. What he wanted more than anything was to pull her against him and taste the sweetness of her mouth. But if he did that, he doubted he would be able to let her go, and the last thing either of them needed was a tryst in his tent.

Not to mention he had a bad feeling that one taste of her would never sate him. Rather it would only whet his appetite for more of her.

She stepped back and wrapped his hand carefully. This was

such an odd moment. He'd had women aplenty who had volunteered to see to his wounds, but none of them had made him feel the way Rowena did.

"Thank you, milady," he said as she tucked the edges of the cloth in, then set about returning his items to their box.

"My pleasure." As she returned the box to its case, she paused. "I didn't bring my lute."

Stryder's gaze drifted to the large trunk by his bed. It was where he kept his personal items and inside, tucked away in its case, was the lute he hadn't seen since the death of his mother.

It had been silenced the same day she had.

"I have one." The words were out before he could stop them.

Rowena's face showed the same surprise he felt. He didn't know why he had offered her his mother's most treasured prize.

Stryder got up slowly and walked to his trunk. He opened the lid to find his family sword, his clothes, and other items he touched almost every day.

But the case in the bottom . . .

It was still as pristine as the day he had placed it there, where it was shielded by his clothes.

Rowena came forward and watched Stryder closely. There was such an air of sadness around him as he pulled a shiny black case from the bottom of his trunk.

In an instant, she understood. "It's your mother's?"

He only nodded.

"I can go get mine. It'll only—"

"Nay, Rowena. We all have to face our pasts at some point. If I am forced to conjure up her ghost, then let us not shirk."

She frowned, not sure of what he meant.

He took a deep breath as he opened the case to display one of the finest crafted lutes she had ever beheld. " 'Tis beautiful."

Stryder nodded. "My father's gift to her when she told him she was pregnant with me. He sent to Paris for it."

To her amazement, Stryder handed it to her. Rowena held it with respect. There was no single scratch or mar on its surface. It was obvious his mother had treasured it greatly.

"Why do you keep it with you?"

"It and her ring are all I have of her. She might not have been a good wife, but she was a wonderful mother. A beautiful lady who believed in the love poetry of Eleanor's court that says true love can never be found inside of marriage."

His gaze met hers and the coldness there sent a shiver over her.

"I don't believe that," she said honestly. "I think love is found where we least expect it. My father's greatest wish was for me to only marry the man I loved. He oft said that no marriage should ever be made for any other reason. Indeed, Andre the Chaplain, who sometimes travels with Eleanor, says the same. He believes that love should only be within the confines of marriage."

"Do your songs say as much?"

"Aye. I write of people who come together against great odds so that they can live their lives out in bliss."

"Then sing to me, Rowena. Let me hear a song of a happy couple who live within the confines of their vows. I want nothing of deceit or treachery."

Stryder spoke from his heart and it touched hers in a way she wouldn't have thought possible.

Nodding, she took his lute to a chair by his desk and sat down to tune it.

Stryder listened to her as she brought his mother's lute back to life. He would have thought by now the strings would have rotted, but it was a testament to Rowena's skill and gentle touch that they didn't break as she strummed them.

Instead, she made a gentle tune with it. And when she sang, her voice held all the music of heaven. Druce had been right. Surely there was no divine choir that could surpass her skill.

And she did sing to him of a falconer and a dairy maid who were star-crossed, and yet they found love and married.

When she had finished, they sat in silence.

"A falconer," he said quietly, thinking over her tale as he sat in a chair across from her. "So you don't believe nobility can marry for love?"

"I do. I just have never witnessed it."

Stryder's thoughts turned to his friend Simon of Ravenswood and Simon's wife, Kenna. "I have. 'Tis a beautiful thing to see two people come together when they would rather die than live apart."

Rowena sighed wistfully. "I would give all I have to feel such."

Stryder nodded and found it strange that they were discussing this when he had never spoken aloud of such things. "And what sort of man would you fall in love with, Rowena?"

She strummed an idle chord as she thought it over. "One of gentle touch. Honorable, of course. And he must make me laugh."

Her list surprised him. "You have no physical requirements?"

"Nay, not really. 'Tis what a man is inside that matters to me." She looked at him. "And what of you? What kind of woman could win the heart of the earl of Blackmoor?"

"None," he said, his voice thick as he took a draught of ale. "My heart is dead and completely incapable of beating for a woman."

"Completely?"

"Aye. A woman would only distract me from my duties, and I would ever fear to leave her lest her head be turned by another in my absence."

She gave him an arched look. "Women are no more faithless than men, milord. It takes two to commit adultery."

"Aye, it does indeed."

She came forward and set the lute in his lap. "Do you need me to show you the chords?"

He shook his head.

Rowena was startled the instant he placed his hands on the lute and began plucking an old ballad. He made a few mistakes, but overall his technique and skill were impressive.

This was a man who had once played often. Obviously his mother had taught him well.

"You're remarkable."

"My mother's doing. She oft said that the only way to woo a woman's heart was with poetry and song."

"You don't agree?"

He gave her a droll stare. "I have yet to meet a minstrel who is chased more than I am, Rowena. I haven't noticed you having to hide in the shrubs with one of your mewling troubadours."

She laughed in spite of herself. "Truer words were never spoken."

"What is this?"

Stryder looked up to see Swan entering his tent. The man's

face was horrified as he caught sight of Rowena and the lute in Stryder's hands.

"Nay, nay, nay!" the man snapped, rushing forward to pull the instrument away. "I thought we had this discussion. You and Rowena hate each other while we keep her maids occupied so that they cannot play matchmaker. Yet I turn my back and find the two of you in here . . . alone. Nay, this I cannot allow."

Rowena exchanged a puzzled frown with Stryder. "You told your men to occupy my maids?"

"Nay," Stryder said quickly. "They took that duty upon themselves. I honestly had nothing to do with their machinations." He glared at his knight. "Truly, they have gone mad."

"Nay, we are not mad, Stryder. We're only looking out for everyone's best interest." Swan handed the lute to Rowena and urged her for the door.

"This isn't mine," she said, whirling from his grasp, toward Stryder.

Swan's features were appalled. "Already she's taken root. You purchased one of these for your own?"

"Calm yourself," Stryder snapped. "It belonged to my mother."

"Ah," Swan said. He took the lute from Rowena and handed it to Stryder. "In that case, return it to hiding while I escort the lady back to the castle."

"And if I wish to stay?" Rowena asked.

Swan didn't hesitate with an answer. "I shall drug you."

Her face was aghast. "Is your man serious?"

"Most likely." Stryder handed the lute to Swan. "Put this away and I shall escort her back."

"That rather defeats the purpose of keeping the two of you apart."

"Enough foolishness, Swan. Rowena and I are only friends."

"And hell is just a balmy isle. Nay, I think it—"

"Put the lute away," Stryder said firmly, cutting off his words. "I shall be back shortly."

"If you're not, I shall send Val after you . . . with his sword drawn."

Stryder shook his head as he offered Rowena his arm.

"I want a full yard between you two."

Stryder ignored him. "Mayhap I should hire him out as a nurse."

Rowena placed her hand into the crook of his arm. "Mmmm, he might prove a most good one. My own nurse is seldom so censoring."

Stryder's features lightened.

"I'm not an old woman," Swan called after them as he watched them from the tent's flap. "And I know well how long it takes to walk to the castle and back. If you haven't returned, I shall make sure you are fetched."

"Is he always so protective?" Rowena asked as they walked toward the castle.

"Nay. In fact, I find him ever absent whenever women are after me."

"Then he doesn't like me."

"Not you personally. Rather he doesn't like the prospect of our forced marriage. He lives in fear of being penned down anywhere."

Swan's comments were muffled now. Unintelligible.

"I would think all men yearn for a home," Rowena said.

"Some, perhaps, but not us. We spent three years locked away. It's hard for us to be indoors now. 'Tis why I prefer my tent when I could easily request quarters in the castle. Like Swan, I don't care for stone walls around me."

Rowena ached for him and what he must have suffered as a prisoner. "It must have been horrible."

Stryder grew quiet.

By his face she could tell he was reliving the past and she wanted to make him laugh again. Rowena tried to think of something witty to say, but could think of nothing.

So she did something she hadn't done in years. She reached over and tickled him.

Stryder jumped as Rowena ran her hand over his ribs.

"Are you not ticklish?" she asked.

Before he could answer, she assaulted him. He laughed in spite of himself. "Have you lost your mind?" he asked as he dodged away from her.

"Most likely. But I could think of no other way to amuse you."

Completely bemused by her, Stryder merely shook his head

as he avoided her questing hands. "Do you often reach out and tickle people?"

"Honestly? I haven't done such since I was a girl. But then I haven't felt the urge since then, either."

He captured her hands. "In the future, I would appreciate your ignoring said urges."

She responded by freeing her hands and tickling him even more.

Stryder quickly retaliated against her. She squealed, running away from him.

"Ho, nay!" he said, chasing after her. "You don't start this and then flee, milady."

"Only a true knave would tickle a lady!" she said between peals of laughter.

"And you have called me far worse than that."

"Not you personally." She dodged around the rushlight.

Stryder caught her, then froze as the full softness of her body contacted with his. Her laughter caressed his skin.

Before he even realized it, he was kissing her.

Rowena moaned at the taste of him. He was like touching a dream.

And as she tasted him, wicked images went through her mind. The sight of him naked in his tent. The thought of lying beside him as she allowed him to touch her in ways no man ever had.

Aye, he would be incredible in her bed. Even though she was a virgin, she knew instinctively he would treat her kindly there and a part of her was desperate with curiosity.

Stryder pulled back from her lips before he buried his face against her neck and inhaled the warm fragrance of her skin and perfume. "Rowena," he breathed. "Be grateful I'm not a knave."

"Why?"

"Because if I were, you would be mine this night."

She trembled at the deepness of his voice.

He pulled away and looked down at her. "I'd best get you back to the others before my lust overrides my common sense and I do something we shall both regret come morning."

Would she?

Rowena bit her lip at the disturbing thought. In truth, she wasn't sure if she would regret lying with him.

Before she could speak, he took her hand and led her to the donjon, where the other nobles were still caught in the throes of their celebration.

She looked about for her ladies-in-waiting, but could find neither them nor Kit.

Her uncle, however, came instantly to her side. "Where have the two of you been?" he asked.

"I was teaching Lord Stryder to play," she answered honestly.

Her uncle arched a brow at that. "So you intend to partake of this lunacy?" he asked Stryder.

Stryder drew a deep breath. "It would appear so."

"Then you are a braver man than I am." Passing a look between them, her uncle drifted off into the crowd.

Rowena hesitated at leaving Stryder. She didn't want him to go. And that shocked her most of all. "Sleep well, milord," she said.

He nodded and took a step away, then came back to her side.

"Thank you for making me laugh, Rowena," he said before placing a chaste kiss to her cheek.

For a moment, she thought she might actually swoon from the tenderness of that gesture. "Any time you need a good tickling, milord, just call out for me."

He laughed again and she fought the urge to place her fingertips to his dimples.

There were several women nearby who cast murderous glares at her, but Rowena didn't care. They might covet Stryder's attention, however they knew nothing of the man.

She had seen sides to him she was sure he shared with very few people.

And she was honored to be one of them.

He kissed her hand and then left her there.

She didn't move again until he was gone from her sight. But he wasn't gone from her thoughts. There he stayed for the rest of the night.

Stryder made his way back to his tent relatively unmolested. There were a few women he had to dodge.

If only Rowena had chased after him . . .

He smiled at the thought. Aye, his little minx could be charming and fun once she dropped her frigid formality.

And waspish comments.

Who could have guessed that she could be so warm and charming?

By the time he reached his tent, he found Swan sitting inside with Nassir and Zenobia.

"Any luck?" he asked the two Saracens.

They shook their heads. "If the assassin is here, he's not looking to make contact," Nassir said quietly.

"Have you any feelings on the matter?" Stryder asked Zenobia.

"None whatsoever. I wish I could channel my sight better, but unfortunately I can't."

"Any word from Christian, then?"

"Again, none."

"I shall return to the hall," Zenobia said, rising to her feet. "Men often speak more easily when they're into their cups and a woman smiles at them. Perhaps one of them will let something slip."

"I'll escort you," Swan said, rising also.

Nassir didn't move or speak until they were alone.

"What's on your mind?" Stryder asked.

"I'm thinking our assassin isn't one of my people, but rather that he's one of yours."

Stryder frowned at that. "How so?"

Nassir held his hands out to show them to Stryder. "I do not pass among your kind."

Stryder scoffed at that as he looked at his friend dressed as a European noble. "You blend more than you know. Your skin is no darker than mine."

"Perhaps but there are other things that I do that are ingrained in me that your people don't. I think our assassin was once one of yours who was trained by my people and then set loose on you."

Stryder considered that. He'd met Sin MacAllister on more than one occasion. As Nassir had pointed out, Sin had been trained by the Saracens to kill his fellow Europeans. "It does make sense. So how do we find him?"

"You."

"Me?"

"If he is after Brotherhood members, who better to attack than the man who leads us?"

"I'm not the leader."

"We all deferred to you in the camp and well you know it. If they are after us, it only stands to reason that you are on the list of men to be killed."

Nassir rose to his feet. "I will leave you and hopefully he will make his presence known to you soon enough."

"Wish me dead, eh?"

Nassir's face turned deadly earnest. "Nay, my friend. Never that. I wish you the speed of a cobra."

Stryder inclined his head as Nassir took his leave. Alone, he grabbed a goblet of ale and took it to his bed, where he prepared himself to sleep.

It was early for him, but if Nassir was correct, it would be best that he give the assassin ample time to make his move.

As he removed his clothes, his thoughts turned to Rowena, and he smiled as he remembered the look on her face when she'd seen him naked.

He so loved to tease her.

And as he got into bed, he realized just how much he wished he hadn't released her in the hall. How much he wished her here in his bed with him.

Would she be as playful between his sheets?

Aye, without a doubt. And as he let his thoughts wander, he could almost swear he heard her laughter on the wind.

Rolling over, Stryder stared at the wall and imagined her face.

'Twas a shame that he picked that moment to turn. Had he not, he might have seen the shadow that drifted past the right side of his tent. . . .

Chapter 9

Rowena came awake to the sounds of a riot occurring outside her windows. Before she could sit up in her bed to investigate, her door was flung wide by Joanne and Elizabeth, who rushed across the room to throw open the shutters and look below.

Dressed only in their chemises, neither of them had taken time to even brush their hair. The two of them stood on bare tiptoes, peering outside.

"Rowena," Elizabeth said over her shoulder, "come quickly and look. They have arrested Lord Stryder!"

Rowena sat up immediately. "They what?"

Leaving the warmth of her bed, Rowena joined them there at the window to see the chaos where more than three score of people were gathered in the courtyard. They were shouting and screaming all manner of insults and accusations.

In their midst was Stryder surrounded by royal guards who struggled to get him safely through the ravenous crowd that demanded his blood. The earl's face betrayed every bit of his anger.

Her heart hammering, Rowena moved away from the window, pulled a gown from her coffer and donned it, then ran below.

She vaguely heard Joanne calling out for her return, but she paid no attention to it. She had to find out exactly what had happened and why everyone wanted Stryder's head.

Struggling to tie the gown laces behind her, she pushed her

way through the crowd until she stood outside on the stoop with a dozen other people.

Henry and Eleanor stood off to the side of the crowd wearing dour expressions.

"I didn't do this, Sire," Stryder snarled as the king's guards struggled to bring him inside the castle. "You know I didn't."

By Henry's face, she could tell the king believed him. "Go quietly, Stryder. 'Tis best for everyone."

Stryder fought even harder. It took ten men to drag him up the stairs.

The earl fought them until he caught sight of her.

Rowena trembled. Their gazes locked and it was there she saw the most shocking thing of all.

Stryder's panic.

And if she didn't know better, she'd swear she saw a glimmer of fear in those celestial blue eyes.

One of the guards shoved Stryder through the door.

Rowena's heart pounded as she made her way to Eleanor, who was still beside Henry.

"Majesty? What has happened?"

The queen looked ill. "Another noble was murdered last night. Roger of Devonshire."

Rowena crossed herself as she felt pity for a man she knew only by name. He was the youngest son of a baron and rumored to be a fair enough sort of fellow. "But Your Majesties can't honestly believe Lord Stryder—"

"There was proof, Rowena," Eleanor said, her tone sharp and brittle. "A fragment of Lord Stryder's tunic was found in the dead hand of Roger as if they had fought." The queen handed Rowena a tunic where the collar was ripped. "That was taken from Stryder's tent this morning after another knight said he had seen the earl leaving Roger's tent late last night."

Rowena stared at the crimson cloth and what it signified.

Nay. Rowena couldn't believe Stryder would do such a thing. Could he?

But why Roger? At least she understood the motivation for Cyril's murder. He was part animal and had insulted Kit. But Roger . . .

To her knowledge no one had ever complained of the man. Why would Stryder wish him dead, let alone kill him?

It made no sense whatsoever.

Eleanor looked around as the men surrounded the king and demanded Stryder's life for the deed.

"Close your mouth, dearest," Eleanor said beneath her breath as she took her hand and shut Rowena's gape. "Between us, I believe him innocent. Lord Stryder is too intelligent a man to leave something so damning behind. This reeks of treachery, and the men, God bless their souls, are too consumed with bloodlust to see the truth of it."

"But who would wish to blame the earl for this?"

Eleanor sighed. "The earl has many enemies. Apparently one has found a most effective way of dealing with him." She looked back at her husband and glared intently. "I shall talk to Henry when we are alone and see what can be done. But for the time being, I agree with him. If Stryder is locked up, then the ones calling for his death can't get to him. He can't keep his eyes open all the time for an attack and believe me, one of them will attack at his back. With any luck our killer will strike again."

"And if he doesn't?"

"Then let us hope Lord Stryder survives his trial."

Rowena stepped back as terror washed over her. Stryder was a noble, but Henry could choose any trial he wished for the earl. One that could leave him maimed or worse, dead. Nay, she couldn't allow that to happen.

Stryder was innocent. She knew it.

The queen returned to Henry's side while Rowena struggled to make sense of this. She saw Kit standing to the side of the crowd with Stryder's men. Every one of them looked as if they were ready to kill the devil himself to get Stryder free.

Leaving the queen's side, Rowena made her way over to them.

"I say we tear down the walls to reach him," Swan snarled.

Val shook his head. "Better we hope the assassin kills someone else, and soon."

Zenobia elbowed the giant in the ribs. "That's a terrible thing to wish."

Terrible or not, 'twas truth. "The queen said herself that if no one else turns up dead, they'll most likely try Lord Stryder," Rowena said as she joined them.

"Then I vote we kill Kit as a sacrifice to prove Stryder innocent," Swan said.

Zenobia groaned out loud.

"What?" Swan asked innocently. "He's the least useful of all of us."

"I take issue with that," Kit said, his tone greatly offended. "I'm far from worthless. I say we cut your throat as sacrifice."

"Cease!" Nassir said, cutting them all off. "We'll deal with finding the culprit later, but first we are forgetting that right now Stryder is being locked into a stone cell."

Rowena watched as one by one their faces went pale with the realization.

For years they had all been locked inside such a place and tortured.

"I'll go to him," Rowena said without hesitation.

"He needs his men," Swan said sharply.

She gave him a droll stare. "They won't let one of his *men* in to see him," she reminded the knight. She looked at Nassir and Zenobia. "Nor are they likely to let him have unknown visitors. I can get the queen to force the guards to let me see him."

"She has a point," Nassir said. "The queen does seem to dote upon her."

Rowena noted the instant respect on Zenobia's face.

"Aye," Christian agreed, "she can stay with him while we continue to search for the killer."

Rowena left them and headed back toward Eleanor, who looked as if she were ready to knock a few heads together herself.

"Majesty?" she asked, drawing the queen's attention toward her. "Might I go and see to Lord Stryder's care while he is in custody?"

Eleanor cocked her head as if she were measuring Rowena's rationale. "Why would you wish to do such?"

"I am concerned for him and doubt if the guards will take his care under consideration."

A knowing smile curved the queen's lips. She appeared quite

pleased by Rowena's devotion to her friend. "Aye, child. Come and let us see how he fares."

Rowena followed behind the queen as Eleanor led the way into and through the castle. They headed down the narrow, spiraling staircase that led below the donjon, deep into the foundation. It was dark and dreary down here. The walls were unpainted and reflected dimly under the torch lights and candles. They threw evil, distorted shadows along the walls. Shadows that made her shiver.

It was very much like being led into the devil's abyss. No wonder Stryder had fought so hard against being taken.

"He's guilty," a man was saying as they made their way down to the lower level. His voice echoed eerily in the stillness. "I say that mob will hang him before Henry has a—"

Another knight made a rude, echoing noise of disagreement. "Henry will never allow one of his favorites to swing. He'll find someway to liberate him. Mark my words."

"Not if Cyril's brother has his way," the first guard spoke again. "I've heard he'll pay one hundred marks to the man who'll slip a dagger between the earl's ribs."

Rowena was horrified by their almost gleeful exchange.

"What goes here?" Eleanor snapped as they entered the small room where the guards were gathered. The men ranged from medium size to large and reminded Rowena of the looming gargoyles she had seen on French cathedrals during her visit to Paris three years back.

"Majesty!" they jerked upright in unison, then bowed before Eleanor.

"Forgive us, your grace," the one who appeared to be in charge said. "We meant no harm."

Eleanor narrowed her regal gaze on them. 'Twas obvious the queen wasn't fooled even a tiny bit by their obsequiousness. She turned back toward Rowena and indicated her with a royal wave of her hand. "The Lady Rowena wishes a word with Lord Stryder. Open the door and let her in."

The captain spoke up. "He's to have no—"

"Are you deaf?" Eleanor asked with a cold, haughty glare that defied the man to speak another word.

The guard snapped his mouth shut and shook his head. He rushed to carry out Eleanor's wishes.

Rowena breathed a sigh of relief.

"Do you wish for anything?" Eleanor asked as Rowena started after the guard.

She paused as she considered Stryder and what condition they were most likely keeping him in. She'd never been inside a cell before, but judging from what she had seen thus far, it must be less than welcoming. "I would like for someone to bring my lute, Majesty. As well as blankets and pillows to make his lordship more comfortable."

"I shall see to it."

Rowena curtsied and gave her gratitude before she followed after the guard who led her to a solid door at the end of the short corridor.

He unlocked the door, opened it quickly, then shoved her inside.

Rowena jumped as it slammed shut behind her. The room was indeed small and cramped. Probably no more than eight feet squared. There was an old, dilapidated cot in one corner with a tattered blanket and the only light came from a window set high above the floor that let in a modicum of sunshine. No doubt Stryder would be in total darkness come nightfall. There was no place on the wall for a torch, nor were there any signs of a candle or stand.

The cell was truly dreary and no place for a man such as Stryder of Blackmoor.

Lord Stryder stood in the far corner, his eyes haunted. He was still ruggedly handsome, but for the first time since she had met him, there was an air of vulnerability to him. He reminded her more of a lost boy than the fierce knight she knew him to be.

"Stryder?" she asked gently.

He didn't appear to see her.

"Stryder!" she said more forcefully as she neared him. She was beginning to fear for his sanity.

"You should leave here, Rowena," he said, his tone low, his gaze glazed by churning emotions.

"Why?"

He moved away from her so that all she had of him was his rigid back. "I don't want you to see me like this."

"Like what?" she asked with a frown, trying to understand why he would wish to be alone when it was obvious he didn't want solitude. "Afraid?"

His breathing was ragged. "I would rather be hanged than locked in here."

Her heart clenched at his words and tenderness spread through her. Poor Stryder. For him, this was his worst nightmare. She closed the distance between them, but refrained from touching him as she longed to do. She wasn't sure if her touch would help or only cause him more grief.

"All will be well, Stryder. I'm here with you."

He raked his hand over his face as if he were fighting images in his mind. As if he were reliving a hell so unimaginable that at any moment he would die from it. She wanted to soothe him so badly that she ached from her inability to make things better for him.

"You can't be in here because of me," he snarled at her. He turned around and urged her toward the closed door. "Don't you understand? I need you to leave."

"Why?"

"Because!" Stryder shouted, then he lowered his voice and spoke to her between clenched teeth. "Because I was responsible for Simon and Raven. I was supposed to protect them. Instead, I let an idiot divide our number and then I led them all into captivity. I was stupid and arrogant and . . . You have to leave. Please."

Rowena cupped his face in her hands and tried to make him understand something she didn't really understand herself. She didn't know why she was here other than the fact that leaving him alone hurt her. She couldn't stand the thought of it. "I won't leave you alone in this horrid place, Stryder. All will be well. You shall see."

Stryder wanted to believe that. He needed to, but right now the past was swirling through his mind with vicious clarity. He could smell the stench of decay and hell. Hear the screams of his friends, their prayers that they would die rather than suffer another day.

'Twas more than he could stand.

"You're not in Outremer," Rowena breathed as she reached out and touched his arm. "You are with me here in England."

He focused on her gentle face. On her light green eyes that showed him compassion and warmth. Not hatred. Nay, there was no hatred or scorn there. Only concern.

Her face and her emotions helped to drive away the horrors of his past. Her eyes, her hair, her touch . . .

She was the present. She wasn't part of his past.

He focused on that and held tightly to it.

Rowena took a breath as she realized she had reached him. His eyes were no longer glazed. They were sharp and focused, and they stared at her with a heat that made her entire body burn. Made her shivery and instantly needful. God love this man, but there was something about him that was undeniably irresistible to a woman's senses.

Seeking to distract them both, she released him and said, "Tell me what happened this morning. Why did they accuse you of murder?"

He took a deep breath as if to draw in strength and to combat the sudden anger she saw flash into his eyes. "I know not. One moment I was asleep and in the next, Henry was there with his guards. They said I had been seen again in the middle of the night leaving Roger's tent. I tried to argue, but one of Henry's men saw my tunic over a chair and told Henry it matched the fragment they had found in Roger's hand."

"Who would want to blame you for such a crime?"

He shrugged. "I know not. I can't even imagine why someone would do something like this." His face hardened and turned into the visage of the knight she'd glimpsed that evening when Cyril had insulted Kit. This was the Stryder of legend. The one who made grown men flee in terror of his wrath. "But whoever is responsible had best give his final confession. Once I'm away from here, I swear I shall murder whoever did this."

She couldn't blame him for that. He didn't deserve to be locked away in this wretched place. "Your men are looking into the matter. They will find the assassin."

"Nay," he said, his voice thick with doubt. "He's too clever for that. Whoever went to such lengths as to steal into my tent and rip my tunic for an incriminating piece of fabric wouldn't be so foolish. He won't attack while I'm locked up."

"But why frame you and not another?"

"He's after the Brotherhood. I'm sure of it. What better way to get back at us than to frame me for murdering my brethren?"

She frowned at his words. "Roger was one of you?"

"Aye. He wasn't an active participant. He kept to himself both in prison and once we were out of there. I can't imagine why anyone would do him harm."

Apparently their killer wasn't that discriminating with his executions. It appeared one Brotherhood member was just as good as another. "But how did he get your tunic without you or one of your men seeing him?"

"Anyone could have ventured into my tent."

"Without being seen?" she insisted.

He scowled at her. "What are you saying?"

"Is it possible the assassin could be one of the men you trust?"

Stryder paused as the thought played across his mind. He quickly disregarded it as he considered every one of his company. "Nay. My men would never do such a thing."

"How do you know?"

"Nassir and Zenobia said they had found a messenger who knew of other deaths. Apparently the assassin has been working for some time now. There are bodies in Rouen, Nice, Hamburg, Flanders—"

"Tournament cities?"

Stryder hesitated. "Aye. I hadn't thought of that connection." Now he felt foolish that he hadn't realized that as soon as Nassir told him of the deaths.

"Were the murders during tournaments?"

"I know not. I didn't ask at the time, but Nassir would know." Stryder's thoughts whirled as he remembered Nassir's speculations about who would want all of them dead and who the Saracens would send to execute them. "Nassir might be right. The killer could very well be a European knight sent at their behest."

Rowena nodded in agreement. "Someone the others trust. Someone who could enter their tents on friendly terms."

It was truly a sobering thought that someone could be out there even now moving amongst the crowd. One of their own and yet one bent on murder in the name of their enemies . . .

The door opened to show the guard, who held his sword out as if expecting Stryder to attack him.

Bemused, Stryder was stunned by what he saw next. Several servants came in bearing a variety of comforts. Blankets, pillows, new linens, a change of clothes, a basket of food, pitchers of water and ale, small toiletries and even a polished lute.

They set the items down near the cot.

Rowena thanked them before they left them alone once more.

"What is all this?" he asked incredulously as he went over to inspect the items.

Rowena came up behind him, her presence electrifying and warming. "I didn't want an innocent man to suffer, and Eleanor agreed." She went to the baskets and pulled out fresh blankets and pillows, then placed them on his cot.

Stryder was aghast at her thoughtfulness. No one had ever gone to such a length on his behalf. His men seldom gave any thoughts to his comfort and as for Kit . . . he complained like an old mewling woman if Stryder asked him to so much as cock an eyebrow.

He was overwhelmed by her kindness. "You shouldn't have done all this."

She straightened up from dressing his bed. "What was I supposed to do? Leave you here to suffer unnecessarily when we both know you didn't kill Roger or Cyril?"

He didn't know what surprised him more, her conviction or her presence. "How do you know I'm innocent? You barely know me at all."

She took his hand into hers. Stryder swallowed at the soft sensation of her flesh on his, at the fire it sent through his body, straight to his groin.

"You're right, milord. I don't know you well enough to say for certain. But I trust my instincts, and they tell me that you are not the monster those people outside would claim. If you were, I would never be here." She gave him a heartfelt stare. "I believe in you and your men. So here I am."

"It's not proper for you to be with me."

Her grip tightened on his hand, sending another wave of desire through him as he imagined what that hand would feel like sliding down his back, holding him close to a body he wanted only to taste.

"I know," she said in a low tone.

"The court will be scandalized," he warned, needing the words said for his benefit as much as for hers.

She shrugged nonchalantly as she released his hand and returned to dressing his bed. "They despise me anyway. Let them gossip if they must. If I'm fortunate, they shall brand me such a whore that no man will have me."

Stryder sucked his breath in sharply at her words as anger swept away his desire. He pulled her away from the bed to face him. "Don't ever tease about that."

Rowena bit her lip in uncertainty. The anger in his tone surprised her. It was easy to forget while talking to him that he was a fierce knight capable of killing. "I'm sorry, Stryder, I was only trying to lighten your mood."

His features relaxed along with his grip on her arm. "You did that the moment you stepped through yon door."

Rowena smiled up at him as his words set her heart to pounding.

The next thing she knew, he pulled her close and kissed her soundly on the lips. She surrendered her weight to him as her body erupted with desire.

His strength. His power. It was unlike anything she had ever known. If decadence had a taste, it would be Stryder's lips. No man should ever be so tempting. No wonder women mobbed him so.

He took his time exploring her mouth, teasing her senses with his tongue while she held him in her arms.

And in the back of her mind, she wondered what it would be like to biblically know this man who kissed her so tenderly . . .

Aquarius pulled his dagger out of the heart of the messenger, then wiped the blade clean against the dead man's tunic. It was a good thing he had seen the messenger skulking in the shadows toward the castle. Any other man would have dismissed him for a servant, but Aquarius knew a Saracen spy when he saw one. They had a distinguishable walk they could never hide.

So, there was another assassin here. Damn. The Saracens had warned him that they would be keeping an eye on him, that he would never be free of them until he fulfilled his pact. But after all this time, he had lured himself into a false sense of security.

More fool he for thinking even for a minute that he was free of the past. That he would *ever* be free of his past.

They were here. No doubt they intended to kill him.

Very well. He couldn't run forever.

And when cornered, the fox always attacked. It was time he taught his masters exactly what he had learned at their hands.

Carefully, he wrapped the Saracen body in a rug and tied it closed. It wouldn't do for anyone to find another dead body while Stryder was locked up.

Especially not a Saracen's. It would raise too many questions and suspicions.

Aquarius carefully hid the body in his own tent, making sure no one saw him. He placed it under his cot and made certain no one could see it should they venture into his quarters. Not that anyone would.

The court avoided him like a plagued beggar. Which was a good thing, since it made his kills all the easier to accomplish.

He would rid himself of the body after nightfall. After all, getting rid of such evidence was one of the many things he had learned well at Saracen hands.

Too bad they hadn't considered what would happen once the fox was released back into the wild. He wasn't about to be recalled or silenced. Ever.

Retrieving the parchment from the dead man's satchel, he sat down and reread it.

It was addressed to another assassin here in the midst of the tournament festivities with orders to kill off Aquarius and someone called the Jackal. So be it. The way to stop the viper was to cut off its head.

All he knew was that the letter was addressed to the Scorpion. According to the letter the Scorpion was one of their own sent home to kill just as Aquarius had been.

Too bad the messenger had impaled himself on Aquarius's dagger before he'd gotten a description of the Jackal or the Scorpion.

No matter. He would find the Scorpion and he would kill him.

Sighing, Aquarius hid the satchel with the body, pasted a false smile on his face, and headed out to join the rest of Henry's court to find the Scorpion.

Rowena sat on the pallet Stryder had made for them on the floor and leaned back against his hard chest while they drank wine and shared secrets with each other.

"Are you sure this school will make you happy?" Stryder asked as she lay nestled against him. It was the most joyous sensation Rowena had ever known.

He was comfortable and warm. More than just a friend, he felt safe and soothing, things she shouldn't experience while in the company of a knight. Yet he gave her such a feeling of elation that she wanted nothing more than to kiss him again and again and again, until they were both numb from it.

Stop thinking of his lips . . .

So she lowered her gaze to his muscled thigh and answered his question. "Aye. Better than being slave to a man who has no regard for me other than a broodmare for his children."

"True," he said, his words a bit slurred. "I should hate to be a broodmare for a man."

Rowena laughed at the ludicrous image. She leaned her head back to look up at him. "Are you drunk, milord?"

"Aye," he confessed with a smile while he caressed her cheek with his callused hand, "but only a little."

She *tsked* at him and pulled his goblet away.

He scoffed at her gesture. "Why are you bothering, Rowena? I have nowhere to go and nothing better to do than drink myself to a stupor."

For some reason that angered her. Granted she wasn't one to desire battle or to urge anyone to fight, but something about the defeatist nature of his words set off her ire. "Is that what you do whenever you are bested."

His eyes sparked like blue fire. Even his cheeks mottled with the heat of his wrath. "I have *never* been bested. Nor will I," he said earnestly. Then he relaxed ever so slightly. "I am merely biding time."

"For what?"

"For the moment when I am out of this cell and am able to wreak havoc on the one who put me here. I'm going to pull out his innards through his nostrils and dance around his entrails."

Rowena screwed up her face at the grisly image. She cringed at the very thought. "Please, Stryder. I pray you jest and are speaking from desire and not actual experience."

He blinked at her. "Nay, I have never danced on anyone's entrails. But I should like to just once." He pulled his goblet back before he continued. "It bothers me beyond endurance whenever I see injustice. I can't bear to think that out there is the killer, just waiting to strike at his next victim."

He took another drink.

"Is that why the Brotherhood is so important to you?"

"Aye," he breathed, setting the goblet aside. "Every person I save is another victory against the evil that festers in this world and I will not rest until every captive is free."

It was quite a goal her knight had set for himself. "So you will never rest? Never know marriage or family?"

"Marriage." He spat the word as if it were poison on his tongue. " 'Tis an unholy union between two people, and for what purpose? To make them both miserable."

Rowena was taken back by his hostility. True, she had often said similar things, but deep down she didn't mean it. Nay, marriage could and should be a wonderful union.

"I don't believe it has to be that way," she said, confessing her true thoughts to him. "Imagine a marriage where the man and woman respect each other. Where they are partners and allies."

He snorted at her. "You are sober and speak more foolishness than I do while drunk." He pulled his hair away from his neck where a vicious scar curled around to his back. It must have been truly painful to receive it. "See you this?"

"Aye," she said, tracing the raised, whitened skin with her fingertip. She watched as chills spread over Stryder's neck, but they did nothing to dull the fury in his eyes.

"My father gave me that when I tried to keep him from killing my mother. He turned on me and said I wasn't his son." Stryder's voice was hollow as if he told her of someone else and yet as she stared into his eyes, she saw the torment he concealed. The grief. "I can still see the hatred on his face as he denounced me for a faithless, worthless bastard." His crystal gaze locked with hers and it burned her with its intense sincerity. "I am, you know. Kit isn't my half brother. We are full brothers."

His declaration stunned her. "Does he know?"

Stryder shook his head. "I swore to my mother that I would never breathe a word of it to anyone. And I haven't until now. It's why the Blackmoor lands and title mean nothing to me. They're not really mine."

Rowena sat in silence as she realized Stryder had just entrusted her with a secret that could ruin him. If she so much as breathed a word of his bastard status, he would lose his title and lands.

Not that she would. How could she betray this man when he had just bared his soul to her?

She reached up and placed her hand against his stubbled cheek. "You are more entitled to your noble status than any man I know," she said sincerely. "You're the only knight who is decent. Honest."

He grunted at that. "Perhaps you need to get out more often."

She smiled as he used her words against her. "I get out quite enough to know the truth."

He dipped his head down and kissed her gently on her lips. The taste of Stryder and wine invaded her head and set it reeling. His kiss was fierce, demanding.

Breathless, Rowena didn't protest as he laid her back against the floor. Her body burned at the intimate contact of his body pressed against hers while his weight pressed her down, trapping her.

It was the most wondrous thing she'd ever experienced. His lean, hard body lay fully against hers. His chest to her breast, his legs to hers.

A deep-seated fire started inside her, making her hot and aching.

Stryder licked and teased her mouth, wanting to taste more of her. Nay, he *needed* to have more of her.

Her taste and scent were all he could think of. And the feel of her beneath him was more than a mere mortal man could take.

He had to have her. . . .

Stryder pulled back with a deep groan borne of great pain and effort. "You should leave now, Rowena."

She frowned up at him with an innocent and open gaze. "Why?"

"Because I want you too badly to be a gentleman, and I've had far too much to drink. If you don't leave me now, I'm going to take you and show you the physical side to those songs you write about."

Rowena swallowed at his deep, husky voice. At the promise he was giving her and the choice.

She could see the need in his eyes as he watched her closely. See his naked desire for her.

Go.

She didn't. In truth, she'd always wondered what it would feel like to take a man into her body. Elizabeth and Joanne had long ago lost their virginity. Late at night, after all were abed, they had often told her what men were like.

Rowena had always been too afraid of herself and her position to try what they had.

But for the first time since Joanne had returned from her first tryst all rosy-cheeked and filled with details, Rowena felt her courage swell.

She wanted to know this man. It didn't make sense. She had spent her lifetime trying to convince men to lay aside their swords and yet here she was about to hand her most prized possession over to a knight.

But he wasn't just any knight.

He was Stryder of Blackmoor.

"Will you hurt me?" she asked, remembering how Bridget had cried the night she'd first been with a man. Even though he had been a minstrel, he'd been less than gentle with her friend.

Stryder looked offended by her question. "How could I ever hurt you?"

Taking a deep breath for courage, she cupped his face in her hands and forced herself to speak her heart. "Then I am yours, milord."

Stryder couldn't breathe as her words played havoc with his foggy senses. Surely she wasn't really going to let him . . .

"Do you not understand what I'm telling you?"

"Virgins aren't daft milord," she said as she laced her fingers in his silken black hair, sending chills down the length of his whole body. "I'm a woman full grown and I understand completely what it is you're wanting from me. And I'm willing to give it to you."

He returned to her lips then and let the full weight of his desire course through him. For so long he'd been numb to the world. Numb to the appeal of a woman's caresses.

How ironic that now with his senses dulled by wine, he was strangely lucid and fully aware.

He felt so deep inside for her that his body actually ached. He didn't know what it was about her, but she touched something in him. Some alien part he'd never known before.

Right now, he needed a physical connection to her. Needed to feel her wrapped around him as he lost himself to the softness of her woman's body.

Rowena was nervous and even a little scared as Stryder reached to loosen the stays on her gown. This moment was irreversible. Once she let him inside her body, there was no way back.

She would be forever changed.

She would know things about the world and most especially about the man in her arms that she had never known before.

But then she already knew things about Stryder no one else did.

She moaned as he buried his lips against her throat and teased her skin with his tongue, his teeth. Though her friends had described the physical act, they had never mentioned the overwhelming chills she felt now. The way her body was on fire from his touch. The uncertain fear that made her breathless and weak even while her desire and curiosity consumed her.

Stryder moved away from her and pulled his surcoat over his head.

Rowena reached up and ran her hand over his sculpted shoulders. They were hard and filled with strength. And the way they rippled when he moved . . .

It was more than she could stand.

He lay himself down between her spread thighs. The material of her gown trapped her legs while he loosened her undertunic.

"Are you afraid of me, Rowena?" he asked. His breath tickled the skin of her cheek.

"I'm not afraid of you, Stryder." It was herself that scared her. These reeling feelings that made her tender toward him.

He smiled those dimples down at her before brushing her top aside and bearing her right breast. Heat stung her cheeks as he dipped his head down and took her taut peak into his mouth.

Hissing in pleasure, she cupped his head to her and held him there while he tasted her. She felt every flick of his tongue deep inside her body, all the way to her stomach that contracted with each nibble.

Stryder growled at the taste of Rowena. Her hands were buried deep in his hair. The velvet of her gown caressed his skin, but was nowhere near as soft as her pale, tender skin.

Suddenly, he hated the gown that kept her body from him. Kissing her nipple, he moved back enough so that he could pull her gown lower on her body.

His breath caught at the sight of her upper body bare.

She was scared, he knew that. Could sense it and yet she didn't say anything as he slid her gown lower and lower until he finally could see the part of her he wanted most.

Rowena was mortified to be lying naked before him. She'd dressed so quickly, she hadn't even thought to put on stockings or shoes.

She was completely bare to him both physically and emotionally. He pulled her up to sit and kissed her lightly on the lips.

"You are beautiful," he whispered. "Definitely worth a few milksop words of dribble."

She was aghast at him. "Should I be flattered by that?"

But the devilish, charming air about him told her that no harm was intended. He was only teasing her.

She watched quietly while Stryder disrobed. There was something odd about lying naked with him in his cell. But at least there were no windows on the door. The only one was set high in the wall far over their heads. No one could see them.

And they spoke low enough so that no one could hear them either.

"Have you ever touched a man, Rowena?"

She shook her head.

He took her hand in his and kissed her open palm, then moved it slowly toward his erection. She bit her lip in expectation before he placed her hand on him.

He closed his eyes and hissed in pleasure as she gently explored his rigid shaft. It was so strangely soft and yet rock hard. She couldn't imagine what it would be like to take that into her.

But soon, she would know.

She lowered her hand down the velvety length of him until she could cup him.

Stryder dipped his head to tease her breast while she explored the part of his body that was so incredibly different from hers.

He sat up on his knees and framed her face in his hands. "You've no idea of how I want to take you, Rowena. How badly I want to ride you."

"Ride me how?"

"In shocking ways." His eyes tender, he kissed the corner of her mouth. Then he moved lower. This time he barely flicked his tongue over her breast before he moved down toward her stomach.

He pushed her back on her arms while he trailed his lips lower and lower.

"Stryder?"

He didn't answer her as he nudged her legs apart, then buried his lips against her.

Rowena fell back at the incredible feeling of him there. She swore she could see stars as his tongue did the most incredible things to her.

Stryder took his time teasing and tasting her body. He'd dreamed of claiming her since the first moment they had met and she had thrown herself into his arms. Now that he had her, he wanted to take his time with her. To explore every inch of her body until they were both sated and exhausted.

And when she came for him, he smiled, but still he didn't stop. He refused to. He wanted her to know the full sensation of her first orgasm.

Growling, he looked up to see the pleasure on her face as she writhed and moaned.

It was a beautiful sight.

Stryder waited until the last tremor shook her and she begged him for clemency. Kissing his way up her body, he was more than ready to show her the rest of her womanhood.

He spread her legs gently and placed his body there carefully so that he would cause as little pain as possible with his breech.

Rowena tensed as she felt the tip of his manhood against her. Stryder took her hand in his and held it tight an instant before he slid himself into her body.

She cried out the instant he filled her. The foreign fullness was shocking and yet strangely gratifying.

So this was carnality, she thought, as he held himself still while her body adjusted to the size of him.

This was what it felt like for a man to claim her.

She'd wondered many times, but no dream could compare to this feeling of sharing herself with him. Aye, there was pain, but more than that there was a special closeness she felt to Stryder.

Stryder held his breath as he fought down the urge inside him to ride her hard and fast. The male animal part of him didn't want to be gentle, but he wouldn't hurt her.

She had given him what no other lady ever had. He'd purposefully avoided virgins for fear of the wedding noose.

Rowena wasn't out to trap him for a husband. Nor was she out to claim him as a trophy. She was sharing herself with him. Offering him comfort and warmth.

He'd never felt anything like this.

She was special to him in a way no woman had ever been. He doubted if any woman could ever mean as much to him as she did right now.

Rowena almost wept from her overwhelming emotions as Stryder tenderly kissed her hand that was joined with his while his gaze never wavered from hers. Slow and easy, he started to thrust against her hips.

She wrapped her body around his as she felt his restrained strength. He was incredible. He could fell a man with a single blow and yet here he was with her even more gentle than a noble minstrel.

It was the fact that she knew what he was capable of that made his tenderness all the more touching.

She listened to his breathlessness that matched hers as she arched her hips to draw him in deeper.

Stryder tried to wait for her, but it wasn't possible. All too soon, he felt his pleasure build until he could hold back no longer. Growling deep in his throat, he buried his face in her neck and inhaled her sweet scent before he released himself inside her.

Rowena lay still as he clutched her. His heart pounded against her breastbone while his ragged breathing caressed her ear.

"Thank you, *ma petite*," he whispered.

Rowena squeezed him tight. " 'Twas my pleasure, my lord."

Stryder kissed her as he withdrew. She was amazing. He'd been told that virgins most often cried during their first time, and yet there were no tears in Rowena's eyes.

Instead, she looked up at him like a woman. Sated. Pleased and welcoming.

And it was then he knew he would have to do the right thing by her. No matter his convictions on the subject.

No matter his common sense.

He was honor-bound to this.

Taking a deep breath, he forced himself to utter the very words he had sworn to himself that he would never speak. "Will you marry me, Rowena?"

She looked up at him, blinked twice, then burst out laughing.

Chapter 10

Rowena was quite certain Stryder had to be jesting. Surely he didn't really expect her to marry him now? What madness that would be.

But the offended look on his face told her his question had been an earnest one.

Suddenly, she felt quite guilty for laughing at his offer. She wasn't the kind of woman to ever intentionally hurt another's feelings, least of all those of Stryder. "You're serious?" she asked as she reached for her chemise and pulled it on over her head.

Some things were best done dressed, and confronting a man about an unwanted marriage proposal was one of them. She adjusted the linen around her while she sat on the floor, watching him as his offer echoed in her ears. If she were sane, she would take it. But in her heart she knew neither of them would ever be happy. Not if they married simply for this. She wanted more than Stryder's body. She wanted his heart.

Stryder made no moves to dress himself. Instead he lay there in all his naked glory, completely bare and enticing. "Of course I am."

"But why?" she asked, as she gathered her waist-length blond hair and pulled it over one shoulder to keep it from knotting any further. The ends of it pooled in her lap. "Why would you consent to marriage . . . with me?"

He looked as baffled by her question as she was by his. "I took your maidenhead."

"I gave it to you, Stryder. That doesn't require a marriage proposal. Indeed, I have friends aplenty who meet with their lovers enough to know better."

"But you are a lady."

"As are they, and you are a lord. What has that to do with anything?"

He sat up with a stern frown on his face. "What if you're pregnant with my child?"

"What if I'm not? Will you be content in nine months if no child is born and you feel trapped by my actions?"

His frown deepened as did his stern tone. "Rowena, be reasonable."

"You be reasonable," she said, brushing back a lock of his hair from his face. "I am sure that I'm not the first woman you have been with. In fact, I know I'm not and yet I doubt you have ever proposed to the others."

"They were different."

"I'm certainly glad to hear that," she said as a strange wave of satisfaction went through her. It was nice to know that he hadn't just tupped her without thought. Perhaps he even held some true feelings for her. That thought made her much warmer than it should. "But it changes naught. I do not wish to marry."

She gave him a hard, meaningful stare. "And neither do you."

"But—"

She placed her hand over his lips to stop his words. "Answer me honestly, Stryder. Do you truly, deeply wish to marry me, or are you only asking because you think it is the right thing to do?"

He looked away and she had her answer, even though it stung a bit.

" 'Tis as I thought," she said, letting her hand fall away from the softness of his mouth, a mouth she could remember tasting only too well. If marriage ever did appeal to her, she couldn't imagine having it with anyone more handsome or gentle than Stryder of Blackmoor.

His taste and feel would haunt her forever.

But that was no reason to rush headlong into a lifetime commitment that could destroy the deep feelings they shared. Eleanor had once loved Henry, and now look at them. They were both miserable in their marriage.

Rowena desired more than that in her life. The last thing she wanted was to come to hate the man she was forced, by the laws of nature and man, to submit to. As insane a notion as it was, she wanted a man she could love for all her life. One who respected her and who took her wishes into account whenever he made a decision that regarded her, her children, and their life together.

"You wouldn't be happy married to me, Stryder," she said gently. "Any more than I would be happy married to you. What we shared today was wonderful—incredible—and I thank you for being my first, and for being so considerate with my body. But it shouldn't make either one of us do something we will both regret one day. I want to be a troubadour and you are on a quest to save the world. What kind of marriage could we have?"

Lying on his back while he watched her, Stryder took her hand in his and held it over the center of his chest where she felt his heart beat a slow and steady rhythm. His grip was firm and binding, her hand pale against the darker tone of his skin. His hard, muscled body was taut with his masculine strength and power. Even naked, he was a force to be reckoned with. One she found almost impossible to deny.

But she must for both their sakes.

"And if you carry my child?"

"We will deal with that when the time comes. There are plenty of women who have survived the birth of illegitimate children, and when a lady has as much standing as I do, the scandal is far from debilitating. For now, let us not rush headlong into disaster."

Stryder was amazed by her as he watched her honest and open stare. Never in his life had he met her equal when it came to courage and conviction. He kept her hand in his and reached with his other hand to tease a lock of her hair that was nestled in her lap. "You are truly remarkable."

Her light green eyes teased him with mirth. "You say that only because you are drunk."

"Nay, I think I'm rather sober now."

Her smile dazzled him.

Not once in his life had he thought to meet a woman who could tempt him to marriage. Yet he felt that temptation now.

What would it be like to have a wife this strong at his side?

Someone who wouldn't just submit docilely, but who would question and speak her mind regardless of consequence?

Unlike the others of her species, Rowena wasn't turned by his looks. While other women crawled naked into his bed just to boast later that they had been with him, he knew Rowena would never tell anyone else of what they had shared.

And it was a sharing. Unlike anything he'd ever experienced before.

He felt his body stirring again at the memory of what she had been like under him.

Rowena's eyes widened as she noticed it herself. "Does it do that a lot?"

He shook his head and pulled her closer to him. "Only when I think of you."

Rowena moaned as he captured her lips. He released her hand so that he could bury his hand in her hair. She felt his fingers splay against her scalp as he held her tightly to him.

Oh, this was heaven. She inhaled the crisp, manly scent of him, letting the warmth of his body seep into every part of hers. She could just melt into him.

Skimming her hand down his lean, hard body, she delighted in the rugged male terrain. She loved the sensation of the short hairs that dusted every part of him, especially the thick thatch of hair that nestled his maleness.

He growled and deepened their kiss as she raked her fingers through that most private area until she could cup him in her hand. His shaft turned rigid once more as she explored it from the very bottom to the tip.

Stryder hissed as he pulled away from her. "Oh how you tempt me, Rowena." He covered her hand with his and showed her how to stroke him before he pulled her hand away.

"You'd best stop doing that."

"Why?"

"Because if you don't, I shall make love to you again, and you're far too new at this to take me into you again so soon. It'll make you even more sore."

She didn't feel sore, but then as he said, she knew very little about this physical side of love. "Have you taken many virgins?"

she asked before she lost her courage. "You seem to know much about us."

"Nay, love. I've only had you. But I've heard other men talk enough to know."

She smiled at his confession. Though why it pleased her, she couldn't imagine. "Who was your first lover?"

He looked a bit startled by her question. "Do you truly wish to know?"

"You know who mine is."

He gave an odd half laugh at that as he reached for his clothes and dressed himself. "She was a lady in France where I was sent to foster. She'd come to the count's domain with her father that winter."

"She was experienced?"

"Aye. She and her ladies had come out to the list to watch the knights train. She said that she had seen me assisting my lord and was enchanted by me."

Rowena couldn't fault the woman for that, and she wished she had known Stryder then. Had he been as handsome as a young man as he was now? "Was she older?"

"By four years."

"And how old were you?"

"I had just turned ten-and-five."

Rowena was stunned by his words. "You were far too young for her."

"She thought not."

She rolled her eyes at the arrogant boast of those words. How ever true to male form. "Do you ever see her now?"

"Nay. She died from illness while I was in the Holy Land."

Rowena felt a pang of sadness for the woman's fate. "I'm sorry."

"As was I. She seemed too kind a lady to have such a young death."

Something in his voice caught her heart. "Would you have married her?"

"Nay, I barely knew her in truth. We were together that once and then I never saw her again. It was only by coincidence that I learned what had befallen her."

Stryder sat up and helped her dress while Rowena reflected on what she had done with him and everything she had learned.

Surely she wasn't pregnant. Her ladies were ever after men, and none of them had ever become pregnant.

Even so, the prospect of having Stryder's baby wasn't quite as repugnant to her as it should be.

Instead, a part of her almost hoped for it. What would it be like to have a child growing inside her? To watch Stryder play father to their son or daughter?

He would be a good, kind father, she was certain, like her own father had been.

But with that thought came the bitter reminder of what had happened to her father. Stryder had even more enemies who would like as not relish the idea of sticking a knife between his ribs while his back was turned. The guard's words echoed in her ears.

Instinctively, she flinched away from him.

"Rowena?"

"Forgive me," she said, forcing those thoughts out of her mind.

"What is it?"

"Nothing."

He tilted her chin until she looked up at him. "Tell me."

"I just remembered my father dying. One of his own men had been paid by an enemy to stab him from behind."

Stryder frowned.

"My father was a good friend to Henry," she said quietly. "As you well know, there are nobles who don't like anyone who is closer to the king than they are, and they are willing to pay quite a lot to rid themselves of the competition."

He looked around the stone walls as if his enemies were here with them now. Indeed, it was most likely one of them who had caused Stryder to be blamed for last night's murder. "Aye. Evil does abound."

"I'm afraid one day that such a thing will happen to you."

Stryder's thoughts turned to the last time he was in England with Simon. It was true, someone had tried to kill him.

Just how many assassins were there? Until now he'd never given much thought to the attempts on his life. As Rowena had pointed out, jealous courtiers abounded. He'd never equated the attempts on his life with his position in the Brotherhood.

But now that he thought it over, the attempts hadn't started until he'd been free for three years. Of course, it had taken him that long to become the king's champion. . . .

Coincidence?

Or had it taken the Saracens that long to train and dispatch their assassins?

That thought chilled him, but he didn't want to think about it at present.

He had Rowena with him. Her soft, delicate scent. Her warm touch. It was all he wanted to think about.

He sat down on the pallet and leaned his back against the wall. Holding his hand out to Rowena, he pulled her into his lap the instant she took it.

Rowena laid her head on his chest as they snuggled in the cell. He held her quietly, letting her scent and softness wash over him. He brushed his hand through her hair while she looked up at him with those trusting green eyes.

This was such a peaceful moment. One of the very few in his life. Who would have imagined that it would be a woman renowned for her hatred of knights who would give it to him.

It was almost laughable.

"I hope you get your freedom, Rowena," he breathed quietly.

"I hope you don't get hanged."

He gave a half laugh at that. "Have no fear on that quarter. My men will never allow it."

"What can they do?"

"We have taken an oath to watch each other's backs. If all else fails, they will break me out of here."

Her gaze turned dreamy at the thought of his escape. "Where will you go?"

"I have no idea. Back to the continent. We'll live as gypsies, making our fortunes at the tournaments as free lances."

She sighed wistfully. "Ah, true freedom. I should like to know of it one day."

"Then come with us."

She looked up at him. Her heart and hopes swam in her gaze. "You are tempting me to even greater folly, Stryder, Lord of

Blackmoor. But I can't leave my home, no matter how much I might wish to. My uncle would be crushed if I vanished. He still hasn't recovered from my last escape venture, and I only went to stay with my cousin Camilla in Normandy." She shook her head. "Even if I did find the nerve to leave again, what would you do with the likes of me?"

He gave her a wicked, charming smile. "I can think of many things I should like to do with you."

Her face turned bright red. "I was being serious."

"As was I."

She sat there in thought for several heartbeats and he watched as her face turned troubled. "It should be easy to leave, shouldn't it? To just take my lute and pack a few belongings, then venture off. But it isn't. My uncle has no heirs, and I am certain Henry would confiscate our lands and hand them over to another noble."

"Aye, he would."

She sighed. "So there really is no escape for me, is there? I shall have to marry eventually."

"Perhaps there is. We could give Henry what he wants. A marriage between us that would set us both free."

She gave him a peeved glare. "Again, you propose the impossible."

"Aye, but it would make perfect sense. You would be free to pursue your music and I would have at least some of my admirers thwarted by my marriage. After all, why pursue me to be the countess of Blackmoor when I already have one safely entrenched on my lands?"

"Is this truly what you desire? A bride to be left alone while you travel the world?"

"We both have to marry someone, Rowena. That fate seems every bit as inescapable for me as it is for you."

Rowena considered his words for a bit. It would get her uncle to leave her in peace and it would allow her to build her school.

"But what of love?" she asked quietly.

"What of it?"

"Do you not wish to be in love? To feel the ecstasy of Cupid's bow piercing your heart with hope and promise? To ache with want every time you think of your wife waiting for your return?"

Stryder made a disgusted noise. "You are speaking foolishness now. Love like that doesn't exist. Love is merely a title given to responsibilities to make them easier to bear."

She frowned at his words. Did he truly mean that? "Is that all Kit is to you? Your Brotherhood?"

He looked away from her. "I treasure them all, aye, but in the end I would treasure my vow to you just as deeply."

"Nay, Stryder," she said, reaching up to take his chin into her hand. She forced him to look at her. "I'm not speaking of treasuring a vow. Not like that. I mean the fierce *passion* that love can bring. I want from my husband that same heartfelt devotion that causes you to pound any man who questions Kit's manhood into the ground. I want more than my husband's loyalty. I want his heart. I want him to burn for me in my absence just as I burn for him. I want my heart to ache with pain at the thought of being without him."

He scoffed at that. "There is enough pain in life, why would you wish for more?"

"Because true love isn't pain. It's beautiful. It makes all of us better people. Makes us strive to improve and become more than what we are."

"Bah! If love is so great why then have you never felt it? Why haven't I? There is no love like you describe. It's a fabrication made up by men who seek only to get other men's wives to betray their lords for them."

Perhaps some men played on women's hearts. But not all. She believed it existed. "Your father loved your mother beyond all reason. You said it yourself."

"My father was a fool. One who killed himself and her. If that is love, then you can have it. I've no desire to run my sword through you, let alone myself."

"And what of your friend Simon of Ravenswood? Did he not find love?"

He hesitated before he spoke. "They are newly wedded. 'Tis too soon to see if their love is real or merely infatuation."

Rowena ground her teeth in frustration. She shoved lightly at his shoulder. "Stryder of Blackmoor, love does exist, and I will marry for nothing less."

"And if the king commands otherwise?"

She paused at that. Henry could be most capricious at times, and he could very well recant his oath to her. It was a king's prerogative to make marriages that benefitted his crown.

She would die if Henry forced her to marry someone like Cyril.

"Marry me, Rowena," Stryder insisted. "I can't offer you a great love, but I can make sure that Henry doesn't tie you to another who will have no respect or regard for you whatsoever."

Oh, it was tempting. But even though she adored Stryder, they were so very different. He hated the things she held dear and she hated the warring nature that he lived for.

"What of my songs you despise so?" she asked him. "Will you tolerate them?"

"Grudgingly so, aye."

She shook her head at that. "At least you're honest."

"At the end of the day, honesty is all I can offer you, Rowena. I can't give you what I don't feel, but I can give you truthfulness and respect."

Rowena sighed as she sat there contemplating his words. It would solve much to be married to Stryder. He could shelter her and as this morning had shown, he was a kind and considerate lover. One who might not make her heart burn, but he did her body. Even now his touch was seared into her memory.

"And if I one day find the great love that I seek?" she asked quietly. "Or you for that matter. What then?"

He curled his lips in disgust. "You are a child questing for rainbows."

His words set her anger off. "Am I? There is nothing childish in wanting to be loved."

Stryder wanted to strangle her for her inability to see reason. Their marriage was the only sensible thing to do. They were compatible enough and he doubted if he would ever find a woman who appealed to him more. She would be a fine and sensible bride if she would give up this current madness that had her seeking the impossible.

Rowena placed her hand to his cheek. "I appreciate what you're offering me, Stryder. Really, I do. But I want a dream, and I won't settle for anything less than that."

"And if Henry forces you?"

Her eyes turned dark and sad. "I shall be miserable all the rest of my life. But until then, I will stand by my convictions and believe that there is something better for me than the shallow marriage my parents shared."

He stamped down his impatience with her and admired her again for the fact that she wasn't so easily swayed by anyone's arguments. If he respected anything in life, it was someone who could stand behind their beliefs and defend them. "Then I hope you find this great love you seek and that it comes to you before it's too late."

The door opened to show them a chancellor who stood there glaring at them. "Come, my lady," he said sternly. " 'Tis unseemly for you to be here without chaperone."

Rowena went stiff in his arms. "But the queen—"

"My orders are from the king himself. You must leave."

Rowena bit her lip at the thought of leaving Stryder alone in his cell. She recalled the panic on his face when she'd first entered.

"Go, milady," Stryder said, urging her toward the chancellor.

"I can't leave you here."

His gaze softened as he traced the line of her jaw with his rough fingers. "I'm a man full grown. I shall be fine alone. Believe me, I lived a nightmare for years. This little cell is nothing."

Even so, she saw the uncertainty in his crystal blue eyes.

"I will return to you as soon as I speak to Henry."

Stryder took her hand into his and placed a most gentle kiss on her hand. "Thank you, Rowena. For your comfort."

She inclined her head to him and reluctantly withdrew her hand. Stryder gave her hand one lingering squeeze before he released her.

"I will be back, Stryder."

Stryder nodded as the chancellor took her arm and escorted her out of his cell.

His heart was lodged in his throat as the door slammed shut, enclosing him in the small space alone again. Only the comfort of Rowena's scent on his skin kept him sane and whole.

The image of her face gave him the strength and courage he needed to bear the terror of the four stone walls that imprisoned him. The strength he needed to fight the demons of the past that tried to tear him down.

Stryder looked up at the window far above his head. His men would find the assassin. He had faith in them.

Just as he had faith in Rowena. She would be back. And until then he would focus on her and not let the past defeat him.

"What do you mean, I can't see him again, Majesty?" Rowena asked. Her entire body shook with the weight of her anger at King Henry's denial of her request to stay with Stryder.

Against her normal custom, she had taken a full hour to dress appropriately before she sought an audience with the king. Henry never looked favorably on people who didn't show him respect and so she had taken great care with her appearance.

Not to mention she had wasted another three hours waiting outside his quarters in a small room packed with other nobles wanting to speak with him.

In all that time, Stryder had been waiting, alone, in his cell. It was enough to make her want to trounce the king fully for his cruelty.

"We have told you, Lady Rowena, 'tis unseemly for you to visit with a man while he is locked inside a prison cell under suspicion of murder."

"But he is innocent!" she said, trying to mitigate some of the fury out of her tone.

Henry's eyes turned dark in warning. "We do not know this. There are two witnesses now that have seen him leaving the scene of both murders, not to mention the evidence of his tunic in the hand of the dead man."

Rowena looked at Eleanor, but the queen refused to meet her gaze.

How could they do this to Stryder? Did they not understand the extent of their cruelty? "But Majesty, Lord Stryder will die in that cell alone. You can't imprison him."

"He will not die, Rowena," Henry said as if she were an idiotic child who knew nothing of the world. "You may have faith in that. Now if you'll excuse Us, We have other more pressing business."

Rowena wanted to argue, but didn't dare. No one argued with the king. At least not for long.

Sighing, she gathered her skirts and headed out of the king's receiving chambers with no real destination in mind.

What was she going to do now?

She had given her word, and it pained her greatly that she couldn't keep it. More than that, it pained her that there was no one there with Stryder. No one to give him comfort and keep him distracted.

Damn the king and his blindness!

As she walked through the halls of the castle, everyone was gossiping about Stryder's arrest. His guilt.

"He is his father's son. . . ."

The words were repeated over and over again by more people than she could count. Only she knew the truth. He wasn't his father's son. But that knowledge would only damage him more.

Seeking peace from their inane speculations and cruelty, she headed toward the one place she knew she wouldn't hear such words.

Stryder's tent.

At least there she would either be alone or with others who knew the truth of the matter. There no one would be accusing the earl of murder. Instead, they would be trying to acquit him.

Rowena noted that a few of the knights' heads turned as she made her way through their tented area. Several of them glared openly at her, especially when they realized where she was headed.

No doubt they thought she had put Stryder up to the murders. She'd been accused of worse things. Not that she truly cared what they thought of her. Only Stryder's freedom mattered to her.

Reaching his tent, she stepped quietly inside. Kit was already there, sitting alone at Stryder's desk, his hands clenched tight in his lap. He looked so incredibly tired and sad. A tuft of his black hair stood out in front as if he had been tugging at it in frustration. His clothes were a bit rumpled, which for him was rare. He normally took great care to keep his tunic and surcoat scrupulously orderly.

"Kit?"

He jumped at her low tone and turned around in his chair to face her. "Rowena," he breathed. "I didn't hear you come in."

"Are you all right?"

He nodded, then shook his head. "I worry over my brother."

"As do I." She crossed the floor to stand near him. Placing her hand on his shoulder, she sought to give Kit some comfort. "I have to admit I'm rather surprised to find you here."

" 'Tis the only place I could find peace. I swear if I hear one more person malign my brother . . ."

She nodded in understanding. "I came for the same reason."

Kit stood up and offered her his chair. She smiled at the gesture as she took his vacated seat. He was ever a gentleman.

"Where are the others?" she asked.

"Looking for the murderer." He combed his fingers through his hair as if aware he had somehow mussed it.

"Have they any ideas?"

"Nay. I know they won't find the assassin. 'Tis an evil force at work here. I can feel it."

"You sound like Zenobia."

"Someone call my name?"

They both looked at the door to see Zenobia entering. Kit quickly made his excuses and left.

Zenobia frowned at his hasty exit. "Why is it he runs every time I draw near?"

Rowena shrugged. "Kit is rather shy with most people."

"Hmmm . . ." Zenobia frowned as she moved to sit in the chair across the desk from Rowena.

"So how goes the search?"

Zenobia sighed wearily. "Much like Nassir, 'tis ever frustrating. No one knows anything other than someone wearing a cloak like Stryder's was seen leaving the tent. Again."

Zenobia stood up and opened one of the drawers on Stryder's desk. "Where is the note you found in Cyril's tent?"

"The one in Arabic?"

Zenobia continued to open drawers. "Aye. Stryder had it last night while we were in here speaking of Cyril's death."

Both women searched the desk, but found nothing.

"Maybe one of the men took it?" Rowena asked hopefully.

Zenobia's frown deepened. "Perhaps. But I can't imagine why. I saw Stryder place it in the desk myself just before we took our leave."

"Nay," Christian concurred, as Val headed across the yard toward their group.

Val joined them. "We have a problem."

Swan rolled his eyes. "Just what we need. Anyone else have something they wish to add to our current predicaments?"

"What?" Nassir asked Val, ignoring Swan.

"Stryder is to undergo a trial by combat."

"How is that bad?" Swan asked Val. "There is no man in Christendom who can best him. He'll be freed in no time."

And yet by the look on Val's face, Rowena could tell the news wouldn't be good. In trial by combat, the king's champion represented the crown, but since Stryder was the only one of Henry's champions present, it begged one simple question. "Who is he to fight? Will they send for Sin MacAllister or Draven of Ravenswood?"

"That was Henry's first thought," Val said, his face deadly earnest. "Until Cyril's brother pointed out that Simon of Ravenswood is one of Stryder's dearest friends. Draven would no more kill Stryder than he would Simon."

"And Sin is one of Henry's dearest friends," Christian said. "Henry would never take a chance on losing him to Stryder."

Now it was Rowena's turn to frown. "Then who's left to fight him?"

"Oh, take a moment and think," Val said to the group. "Who is the one man present in this crowd that Stryder would sooner throw himself to the lions than kill?"

"One of us?" Swan asked.

Val shook his head.

"Kit?" Swan tried again.

"Damien St. Cyr," Christian said, his tone low and lethal.

Rowena sucked her breath in sharply at the name. Damien St. Cyr was the younger brother of the Queen of France and a man of extreme wealth, power and renown. She knew he was here, but since he kept to himself, she, like most of the court, had yet to see him.

"Who is that?" Nassir asked. "He isn't one of us."

Christian raked an irate hand through his blond hair. "Nay, but he should have been."

"How so?"

A bad feeling went through Rowena as she remembered Stryder's torn tunic. "Do you think the murderer might have taken it?"

Zenobia's eyes mirrored the horror Rowena felt.

"Who is this person?" Rowena asked. "That they would dare come and go from Stryder's tent?"

"I know not, but we had best find him soon. Otherwise someone else will pay a price most foul for our inadequacy."

Aquarius paused as he reread the note he'd stolen from Stryder's tent.

"I am such a fool," he breathed as he studied the script. It was flowing and elegant.

A woman's hand.

And all this time, he had assumed the Jackal or the Scorpion, like him, would be a man. He should have known better. Just as he should have recognized her face earlier.

Though to be fair, their captors hadn't brought them together often. Only at certain banquets and feasts where they were made to perform for the benefit of others. . . .

His stomach tightened as rage gripped him anew. Somehow he would repay his captors for their cruelty.

Silently, he made his way across the yard and into the castle with only one destination in mind. He only hoped that the other assassin would be alone so that he could confront her.

As he reached the door to her chambers, she spilled out of the room with three of her friends. Aquarius stepped back into the shadows quickly before they saw him.

Damn. He dare not approach her right now. Not while her friends could overhear them.

Kill or be killed . . .

Sooner or later, she was bound to be alone. Then the two of them would have a nice, long conversation.

Sick of heart and completely demoralized, Rowena and Zenobia made their way into the hall that was crowded with nobles who could still find no other topic than when Stryder would be made to pay for the lives he had taken.

Why couldn't they find the one responsible?

But then they were searching for a needle in a haystack. There were close to two thousand people in Hexham for the tournament.

Two thousand.

Anyone could be the murderer. A blacksmith, a knight, a marshal, a . . .

Rowena froze midstep as a whole new thought came to her. "Zenobia, you said to me on your arrival that your people trained women for battle. Is this not true?"

"Aye."

Her mind reeled with a whole new speculation. "Is it possible our murderer could be a woman and not a man?"

A sick look came over Zenobia's face. Without another word, she spun around and started back out of the castle.

Rowena rushed after her. "Zenobia?"

Zenobia didn't pause. Instead, she kept an angry, quick stride. "We are such fools!" she snapped. "Why didn't one of us think of that before?"

"Then I'm right?"

"Aye, Rowena, most likely you are right. In fact, it makes perfect sense. Who better to get inside a knight's tent and cut his throat? A woman could easily fool a man. 'Tis the last person he would suspect was out to kill him."

Part of Rowena wanted to shout out in triumph, but another part of her was ill. They had been wasting precious time looking for the wrong person.

Not to mention she shivered at the thought of one of the women courtiers taking part in such a horrible activity.

Zenobia didn't stop until they found the men in the list. Nassir, dressed as one of Stryder's men, stood with Christian and Swan. Nassir and Swan looked as if they had been practicing with swords before Christian had joined them.

"'Tis a woman we seek," Zenobia said, interrupting their conversation.

Christian frowned.

"What?" Swan asked, his face aghast.

Nassir said something that sounded like a curse in Arabic.

"Rowena made the connection," Zenobia said.

Swan recovered his gaping expression to scoff at the idea. "A woman is our killer?"

"Who better to kill us in our sleep," Christian asked quietly.

"The note," Nassir added. "Remember what it said. 'We didn't all go home.' Cyril was was one of the men who went down the *special* wing of the prison. Do you remember what he said that night?"

"None of them survived," Christian said, his voice leaden. "The men said they were either dead or missing."

"What special wing?" Rowena asked.

It was Swan who answered and his words horrified her. "The one where the Saracens kept their whores."

"They weren't whores," Christian snapped, his face suddenly flush with rage. "They were the women who had been captured, and a few young boys."

Feeling sick with the news, Rowena covered her mouth with her hand. Tears welled in her eyes. "They weren't freed?"

The men looked even sicker than she felt.

"I wish I'd killed Cyril myself," Christian snarled.

Nassir curled his lip. "Why didn't one of us go and double-check what they had told us?"

"Because we were all afraid of being caught that night," Zenobia reminded them. "The eldest of you was only a score of years. You were mere boys yourselves."

"Still," Christian said, his voice ridden with guilt and pain "One of us should have checked when they returned alone."

"We believed them," Swan said quietly. "Why would the have lied about freeing them? Besides, every second counted ar we were all terrified."

"Whatever we do," Nassir interjected, "we must never Stryder know."

Rowena frowned. "Why?"

They looked at her and she remembered the promise Stry had made to the youth in the cell next to his.

"Oh mercy, the youth was one of them on that wing?" asked, her throat tight.

They nodded.

Nassir took a deep breath and expelled it. "He will neve give himself."

Christian leaned back against the stone gate as if he needed to feel something solid at his back. "One night a few years ago, not long after we had escaped, Stryder and I were in Hamburg at a tournament when Damien showed up with a group of his men. I've never seen Stryder so pale. Two nights later, when Stryder was deep in his cups, I found out why. Stryder and Damien were once close friends. Foster brothers, in fact. Damien was with Stryder, Simon, and Raven when they were captured in Outremer."

"Then why wasn't he in the camp with us?" Swan asked.

"Because he wouldn't listen to Stryder. Instead of doing as Stryder said, and hiding his identity, Damien told the Saracens who he was. They took him away and Stryder never saw him again. Not until that night in Hamburg."

"Hide what identity?" Nassir asked.

"He's the great-grandson of William the Conqueror," Rowena answered. "His sister, Alix, is the Queen of France, and his nephew Henri is count of Blois, Champagne, and Troyes. Not to mention the small fact that Henri is also married to the daughter of Eleanor of Aquitaine and King Louis of France."

Zenobia frowned. "I think I'm rather confused. This is beginning to sound like he is his own brother's son."

Nassir shook his head at Zenobia's comment. "Is there any royal house this man isn't related to?"

"Mine," Christian said.

"Are you certain?" Zenobia asked. "You know Eleanor and Louis did go on Crusade and your father was French."

Christian cocked his head as if thinking that over. "Then again . . ."

Nassir held his hands up to interrupt the two of them. "Let us travel back to the point, lady and priest. Why would Stryder not fight this man?"

It was Christian who answered. "Because Damien bears two Saracen marks on his face. One across each cheekbone."

Zenobia turned pale.

Nassir cursed.

"What marks?" Rowena asked. "No one has ever seen Damien's face. He's always robed when in public."

"I've seen them," Swan said. "Only once when he lost his

helm in the midst of a training match. They're Arabic writing of some sort, but I couldn't read it."

"They're the marks of a slave," Zenobia said quietly.

"Aye," Christian concurred. "Damien hates Stryder with a burning passion. He blames him for the fact that they were captured."

"Stryder got them captured," Val said, his voice thick. "It's why he would never fight Damien. He blames himself for what happened to the man."

"Nay, it wasn't Stryder's fault," Christian contradicted. "Talk to Raven or Simon, who were there. It was Damien who caused their capture. Stryder took the blame and has carried it ever since. According to Simon, Damien's problem was and has ever been the fact that as a spare prince, he has ached for his own slice of power. Once they were in the Holy Land, he resented Stryder's authority and one day in order to prove himself, he led them against the Saracen band that captured them. Stryder led the others in to save Damien and ended up with all of them taken or killed."

Silence fell between them while each of them considered the ramification of Stryder facing a man he would feel sorry for and guilty over.

"When are they to fight?" Nassir asked Val.

"On the morrow, at first light."

The gravity of that statement hung heavy between them.

Rowena stood quietly as she considered what they should do. Like his men, she held no doubt that Stryder would refuse to harm Damien.

While they stood in the midst of the list in silent reflection, Kit joined their group, his face grim. "I take it from the looks of you that you've heard about the trial?"

Nassir and Christian nodded.

"Any thoughts on what we should do?" Swan asked.

"Kill Damien," Nassir said.

Christian scoffed. "We can't do that."

"Sure you can," Swan said. "You're not related to him, and no one from France or England has ever been able to defeat your country."

Christian was aghast. "I could never kill a man in cold blood."

"Nassir?" Swan asked. "You're our sand demon. Why don't you go after him?"

Nassir rolled his eyes.

"I'll kill him," Val offered. "I can challenge him tonight while we sup."

Swan shook his head. "Nay, you cannot. I've seen the man train. You're good, Val, but he's better."

"Then kill him in the hall."

They all turned arched looks toward Kit who spoke in a deadly tone. "You could go up behind him, pretend to stumble and then slide a grism into his back, straight into his heart. By the time anyone realizes he's been mortally wounded, you can be out of the hall and back in your tent."

Nassir and Zenobia exchanged a bewildered look. "How do you know about that?"

"I'm a minstrel. 'Tis a common known way to deal with enemies."

"I didn't know that," Rowena said.

Kit shrugged. "You don't travel with minstrels who write of war." Kit's eyes took on a strange glint. "Imagine what it's like when you stab someone who's not expecting it. The look of horror and respect in their eyes as they stare at you, knowing you're not so weak and helpless after all. The feel of that last gasp of their breath on your cheek before they fall dead at your feet."

A bad feeling went through Rowena. "Kit?"

He gave her an innocent look. "Aye?"

"Is there something you wish to tell us?"

He blinked innocently. "Nay, why would there be? I only repeat what I've heard others say."

Still there was an uncomfortable awkwardness between them all as each of them sized Kit up anew.

Could Kit . . . ?

Nay, Rowena decided. It wasn't in him to take a life.

She was sure of it. And even if he had, he would never allow Stryder to pay for the crime of it. He loved his brother too deeply for that.

It was a foolish thought. Her mind was seizing at any straw now. Besides, she fully believed the assassin was a woman. It made much more sense than Kit. The knights held even less regard for Kit than they did for Rowena. None of them would have welcomed Kit into their tents, and Kit would never have framed his brother.

Swan sighed. "Well, if we can't murder Damien—"

"Let me talk to him," Rowena said, interrupting Swan.

"How well do you know him?" Christian asked.

"Not very well, but we have been introduced a few times in the past."

"Why would he listen to you?" Zenobia asked.

Frustrated, Rowena looked at each of them in turn. "I'm ready to hear any other option the lot of you has that doesn't involve his murder. Can anyone think of something better?"

"I throw my lot in with Kit's suggestion," Val said, his tone surly.

Swan shoved at the much larger knight. "Very well then, Rowena, you're our only hope. If you fail to dissuade Damien from taking part in tomorrow's trial, then Stryder will die."

The full weight of that statement settled hard upon her shoulders.

Everything was now up to her.

Nodding, she took her leave of the group and headed toward the castle, but as she walked, she realized something.

This was the weight of responsibility that Stryder had lived with since his youth. He had been the leader of the Brotherhood. Their lives had all been in his hands, and to a degree those lives still were.

It was a horrifying burden that he carried with grace.

And in that moment, she realized something even more terrifying.

She loved Stryder of Blackmoor.

Knight. Knave.

Hero.

And she would do whatever she must to see him free of his prison.

Chapter 11

Getting in to see Damien St. Cyr proved to be even more difficult than getting in to see the king.

His chambers were just off those of the king and queen themselves. In fact, he had traveled here to Hexham in their royal company and had kept to himself almost exclusively since their arrival.

Unlike the other nobles, he never ate in the hall, nor did he venture out to train with the other knights. His time in the list was reserved at dawn or dusk with only the most renowned of tutors, and during those times no other knight was allowed to be near the area.

It made her wonder how Swan had ever glimpsed the man's cheeks, especially since the prince wore a gilded mask over the top part of his face. He was never seen without a full cloak, even in the dead of summer, with a cowl pulled up to conceal the mask.

Not that she knew what said mask looked like. She'd only heard other courtiers gossip about it. Many claimed that he had been burned as a young man and sought to cover those scars. Others said he was deformed from birth and that no one had ever glimpsed his real face or hair.

But if Swan was correct about the writing . . .

"He will see you, milady."

Rowena let out a relieved breath as his servant stood back and opened the door to let her inside the prince's private chambers.

Nervous and unsure, she entered his chambers slowly. They were lush with burgundy wall hangings and ornate, mahogany chairs covered by plush, dark blue cushions. There was a closed door to her right that no doubt led from this sitting area into the bedchamber.

Damien stood with his back to her, looking out a corner window. He was a tall man. One of intimidating size.

"Rowena de Vitry." He said her name in a voice that was silken and smooth. Deep and cultured. "What brings the renowned Lady of Love into the humble presence of a man such as myself?"

She swallowed and wished she knew more about the noble lord before her. But in truth, few rumors were ever spoken about him, and that in and of itself told much about his family's vast influence.

And Damien's power.

"I've come to ask a favor of you, milord."

He turned toward her then. Rowena could see nothing of his face or form. His thick cloak held him completely concealed from her. Even his hands were covered by dark gray gloves.

There was something so commanding about his presence that it sent a shiver over her.

"And what is this favor you would ask of me, milady?"

"You are to fight Stryder of Blackmoor on the—"

He let out a hiss so hate-filled that it made her jump and succeeded in cutting off her words immediately.

"Forgive me, Rowena. May I call you Rowena?"

Her heart hammering, she nodded.

He moved to stand just before her so that he towered over her slight frame. She had a feeling he did it just to intimidate her and it worked much better than she would have liked.

Damien lifted his gloved hand up to her chin and then tilted her head so that she was looking up into the merest of outlines hidden beneath the folds of his cowl.

"You are beautiful," he breathed. "I can see why he took you."

"I beg your pardon?"

"Never beg, Rowena. 'Tis degrading."

She tried to pull away, but he grabbed her arm and held her near him.

He laughed darkly at her efforts to free herself. "It won't do you any good to fight me, Rowena. I know all about you and that bastard. What the two of you did this morning while you thought yourselves safe in his cell. Who do you think had Henry separate you two even while Eleanor argued against it?"

She froze at his words. "I don't know what you mean."

His grip tightened. "Of course you do. No doubt you dream of feeling him inside you again even while you look at me."

She struggled to free herself of his oppressive grip. How dare he handle her so!

And yet he was one step away from two powerful thrones. No one would ever question anything this man did.

"Sh," he said quietly. His touch turned from forceful to soothing. "Forgive me for my manners. I don't normally attack women, I promise you. 'Tis just that my anger at your earl knows no bounds. The mere mention of his name . . ."

He released her so suddenly that she actually stumbled away from him.

Sadness engulfed the man. He seemed to deflate right before her eyes. "Ask me for no mercy or quarter where that man is concerned, Rowena. I have spent far too many hours of my life wishing him dead."

"Why? What has he ever done to you?"

He didn't answer. Instead, he spoke with a deadly calm that sent a chill over her. "Your secret is safe with me, milady. I will tell no one what I know of the two of you. But I would ask one small price for my silence."

She braced herself for more cruelty. "And that is?"

He waited several minutes before he spoke and when he did his tone was so low that she barely heard it.

"If you still believe in God, then say a prayer for me. He turned a deaf ear to my pleas long ago."

Rowena couldn't have been more stunned.

"Guards," Damien called out loud.

The door outside opened instantly.

"Take the lady and see her safely to her uncle."

"But milord—"

"Nay, Rowena," he said coldly. "Tomorrow God himself will decide the fate of the man. I only hope that I am the instrument that finally rids this earth of his pestilence."

* * *

Rowena hardly slept at all. The entire night was spent with her turning about in bed as Damien and his hatred roiled through her.

Did Stryder know whom he was to fight? Had someone maliciously told him?

What would he do? But then she knew. He would never kill a man he blamed himself for hurting.

Rowena woke up just before the sun did, along with her ladies-in-waiting. They, too, had spent a restless night, and like the rest of the court, they wanted to bear witness to Lord Stryder's trial.

Rowena rushed to get to the list, but while her women took a place in the stands that had been set up for the tournament, she snuck around the back to Stryder's tent, where the earl had been taken to suit himself up in his armor.

There were more than a dozen guards set around the tent and as she approached, the captain stopped her.

"He's to have no visitors."

"Please," she implored him beseechingly. "I only wish one word with him."

"Have a heart, Boswell," another guard said. "The man could very well die this morning."

The captain debated.

"Let her in for a moment," another one prompted. "He's only got a few minutes more before they start. Let him leave this world with the memory of a fair maid's face."

The captain's features turned stern as he looked at her. "Only a moment, so you'd best be quick about it."

Rowena gave him a chaste kiss on his grizzled cheek before she dashed into the tent.

She pulled up sharply.

Stryder stood with his back to her while Kit tightened the laces on his mail cuirass. She'd never seen two men look more dour.

"I still say you should have taken Christian up on his offer to run."

"I will not run, Kit, you know that. I can take any French champion."

Kit glanced past Stryder to see her. He paused, then released his brother.

Stryder turned, and at the moment their gazes locked, she felt a cold shock go through her.

Kit stepped between them. *"He doesn't know it's Damien."* The words were mouthed to her.

Rowena crossed herself and hoped that Damien's armor would shield him so that Stryder never learned who it was he faced.

"I'll wait outside," Kit said, leaving them alone.

Rowena was overwhelmed to see Stryder looking remarkably fit and awake so early. Before she could stop herself, she threw herself into his arms and held him close.

Stryder closed his eyes and inhaled the sweet scent of Rowena's hair. For the first time in his life, he hated the mail armor that kept him from feeling her soft curves that were pressed up against him.

All night long, all he had done was dream of her. Dream of tasting her lips, feeling her hands on his flesh.

Now he wasted no time in dipping his head down to capture that mouth that had haunted his sleep. He growled at the taste of her, at the feel of her hand clutching his hair.

He ran his hands down her back, letting his palms cup and press her closer to him. He wanted inside her so badly that it was all he could do not to rip the armor from his body and take her.

But there wasn't enough time for that.

"Sweetest Rowena," he murmured against her lips. "Thank you for coming."

Rowena felt tears prick her eyes at his words. "Did you think I wouldn't?"

"I didn't think they would allow it."

She scoffed at him. "Since when do I follow the dictates of others?"

He laughed at that and squeezed her so tight that she yelped. "Forgive me?"

She nodded, then pulled one of the ribbons from her hair.

"What are you doing?" he asked as she moved to wrap it around his biceps.

"A token for you, milord. One to bring you good luck."

He was humbled by her offering. "You who have no regard for war would offer me such?"

She looked up, her gaze searing and sincere. "Aye, Stryder. I would see justice done this morning, and you free so that you can give me my choice of husband."

He grunted at that. "And here I thought you had a more nobler reason for your actions."

She reached up and placed her hand to his cheek. "I am but teasing you. I want nothing to happen to you this day. If you should happen to die, I fear I would be most put out."

"Not nearly as much as I would be," he teased back. "Besides, I keep telling everyone that I hold no fear. I have no equal on the field."

Someone cleared their throat.

Rowena glanced over her shoulder to see the captain standing in the entrance. " 'Tis time."

Stryder inclined his head. He started away, but before he could take a step, Rowena pulled him back toward her.

She kissed him quickly on the lips. "I wish you the strength of Hercules."

He lifted her hand to his lips and placed a tender kiss on her palm. "I will see you anon."

Rowena nodded as the captain came forward to lead him toward the list.

She followed behind the men, then took her own place among her ladies in the stands.

"There you are," Elizabeth said as she took a seat beside her. "We had begun to fear something had happened to you."

Stryder entered the list, which was surrounded by archers in the event that he decided to run. Not that he would, but 'twas customary under the circumstances.

Two swords were being held by heralds in the center of the list. All he waited on was the appearance of the French champion to challenge him.

He almost laughed at the thought.

But then his humor died the instant he saw his opponent take the field. In fact, his entire body went cold at the sight of the royal French coat of arms over the gold mail armor. Even though the man's face was covered by his great helm, he knew him in an instant.

It was Damien St. Cyr.

Stryder cursed.

"That sentiment is entirely mutual," Damien growled as he stopped before him.

Stryder longed to curse fate again. How could Henry have done this to him?

"Don't do this, Damien. We were friends once, you and I."

"And now we are enemies. It's strange how fate turns, isn't it?" Damien reached for his sword.

"I don't consider you my enemy."

Damien tossed Stryder the other sword. "Then you're a fool and quite deserving of your death."

At the same instant Stryder caught his sword, Damien lunged at him. Stryder barely had time to parry the thrust and spin away from him.

"Don't make me hurt you, Damien. I've no desire to see any more pain placed upon your shoulders."

Damien roared as he attacked with the fury and power of ten men.

Stryder had to actually work to keep the knight from hurting him—a true rarity. Damien hadn't studied much during the years since they had been friends. Back in those days, the boy had been free-spirited and fun-loving.

His parents' youngest child, Damien had been doted on by both of them as well as his older sister, Alix.

Even though barely a year separated their ages, Stryder had always thought of Damien as a young brother in need of protection.

But the man before him was nothing like the boy he'd known. This Damien was angry and bitter. His rage glittered like ice in the greenish-gold depths of the eyes that glared out at Stryder from the slits in Damien's helm.

Stryder had no idea what the Saracens had done to Damien, but it was obvious they hadn't just held him kindly for ransom as Damien had said they would.

Damien kicked at Stryder's leg, then slashed at his head.

Stryder barely dodged the killing blow.

Damien dropped his sword, grabbed him by his surcoat and slung him into the low railing that segregated their area from the spectators.

Stryder let go of his own sword as they fought hand to hand. This wasn't the combat Henry had intended. To Damien it was personal.

And it made Stryder's heart ache. He'd tried many times to speak to his old friend over the past few years only to have Damien's men refuse.

"I never meant for you to be hurt," Stryder said.

Damien growled low and deep like an animal in pain before he slammed his fist down on his shoulder.

Stryder took the blow without flinching.

"Don't you dare be sanctimonious with me, you bastard. I promise you I'm not leaving this field until I bathe in your blood."

"Is that what you want?" Stryder asked as he dodged another blow. "Is that what it'll take to set the past right again?" He pulled his helm from his head and stared at his friend. "I still consider you my brother, Damien."

Damien backhanded him across the face.

Stryder staggered back as he tasted the blood on his lips. Licking the metallic taste, he righted himself.

"Fight me, damn you."

Stryder shook his head. "I don't wish to fight you."

Damien cocked his head at that, then turned to retrieve his sword. When he again faced Stryder, the coldness of his gaze chilled him.

"Very well then," Damien said. "But before I kill you and you go down in the scribe's rolls as a convicted murderer, allow me to tell you one thing."

"And that is?"

"I know the boy you broke your promise to in Outremer. Aquarius."

Stryder went cold at the news. "How do you know that name?" A sick feeling went through him. "You?"

Damien laughed at his question. "I should have been so lucky. Nay, I was never he, but I knew much about him. I could hear his screams on the nights when they tortured him after you and your Brotherhood left him behind. I heard his curses and his prayers for death."

Stryder couldn't breathe as pain consumed him. "He was dead when I left."

"Nay," Damien said with an evil note of glee in his voice, "he was not. He lived. In fact, he lives still and he hates you and all your Brotherhood who left him behind to suffer. He hates you even more than I do. Every time they beat him, he cursed you and swore he would see you dead."

"You're lying to me."

Damien shook his head and Stryder held the distinct feeling that his former friend took a great deal of pleasure from the pain he gave him. "If you doubt me, ask your brother for the truth."

Stryder frowned. "Kit? What has he to do with this?"

"Kit *is* Aquarius, you fool."

So stunned by the news, Stryder barely saw the stab wound coming. He moved to the side, but not fast enough to keep the blade from gashing his ribs.

Bellowing in rage, he rolled away from Damien and seized his sword.

Rowena rose to her feet as she saw Stryder wounded. The crowd around her all held a collective breath.

No one had ever wounded the earl before. No one.

Unlike the others, she knew why Stryder didn't fight with all his strength, but when he seized his sword and turned on Damien, she realized something had changed.

There was no longer any sympathy on Stryder's face. Only a rage so potent that even from her distance, it scared her.

Stryder attacked Damien like a man possessed.

Damien fought back, but it was useless. With one sweeping attack, Stryder unbalanced his opponent and had Damien flat on his back in the dirt.

Rowena drew in a sharp breath as Stryder made to kill the prince.

Then, just as she was certain the blade would pierce his heart, Stryder deflected it and buried it in the earth.

He kept his foot soundly on Damien's chest, pinning him to the ground.

"Sire?" Stryder's voice rang out in the early morning mist. "I have defeated your champion. I have no desire to kill a man to prove my innocence. I have never taken a life coldly and I've no wish to begin doing so now."

Henry nodded his head in approval. "Indeed, Lord Stryder. You have proven yourself merciful. Let no one else question your guilt in the murders. Release Our cousin and let Us see him tended."

There was no need. The instant Stryder removed his foot, Damien came to his feet and charged the earl.

Henry ordered his men to break them apart.

"This isn't finished!" Damien snarled as Henry's men pulled him away.

Stryder took a ragged breath as Rowena rushed toward him. Her heart racing, she wanted to throw herself into his arms and kiss him all over his face until they both fell on the ground. Only the knowledge that the entire crowd of nobles watched them prevented it. "Your needs be tended, milord."

His own men and Kit quickly joined them.

"Thank God you came to your senses," Christian said as he embraced Stryder briefly and pounded him on the back. "I was afraid you were about to let him kill you."

Stryder held a strange look on his face as he turned toward Kit. He searched Kit's gaze as if he were meeting a stranger.

"Is anything amiss?" Kit asked.

"I . . ." Stryder shook his head as if to clear it. "I needs be taken back to my tent."

They all surrounded Stryder, shielding him from the stunned crowd, and led him back to his quarters. But though they were all relieved and happy, Stryder appeared less than pleased by his victory.

Rowena and Zenobia exchanged concerned looks while the men congratulated Stryder and shoved each other like playful children who had won a victory.

She and Zenobia waited outside the tent while Christian and the other men helped strip the armor from Stryder.

As soon as Stryder was free of his armor, he grabbed a clean linen and held it to his side to help staunch the flow of blood while Christian poured him a goblet of ale. His friends were asking him questions, but to be honest, he heard none of it.

All he could hear was Damien's accusation.

Hear the sound of Aquarius's voice through the walls as the boy cried for someone to help him.

Then he saw Damien's face the day they had fought.

"Who do you think you are to lead us? I'm the son of kings and I am born to it."

After the death of their overlord and his knight, there had been six of them left behind to find their way from Outremer to France. Raven, as the youngest, had been ten-and-three, but luckily he was tall enough to pass for an older boy. The rest of them had been two and three years older than Raven.

To this day, Stryder wished he'd given the reins of leadership over to Damien when Damien had demanded them. But too young and vain himself, he had refused.

So Damien had left with two of their company to seek his own way. Like a fool, Stryder had gone after him with Raven and Simon in tow to bring them back.

And they had all ended up taken.

Because he was a fool.

Now he saw that day clearly. The sun had been blistering over the dunes as they were fought down and taken. Bloodied and beaten, they had been forced to their knees in the hot sand. The Saracens had tied their arms behind them.

Damien's eyes had been filled with hatred as he glared at Stryder.

"Tell no one who you are," Stryder had said between clenched teeth. "If they learn your pedigree, they will make you suffer for it."

"You're jealous," Damien had hissed. "I am worth more than ten of you." And so Damien had announced his titles to all present.

The Saracen leader had laughed aloud as he spoke to his men in a language none of them had known at that time. Damien had been taken and thrown across the back of a horse. He and the leader had ridden off while the rest of them had been marched across the desert to the camp where they had banded together with other captives.

God and Damien alone knew what the Saracens had done to make him pay for that arrogance. In Europe, Damien's position guaranteed him only the best of accommodations and care. At the hands of a nomadic race sworn to the eradication of a foreign army in their lands, such knowledge usually guaranteed death by impalement.

The look in Damien's eyes as they fought today had told Stryder that Damien would much rather have met that fate than whatever one he'd been given.

"Are you addled?" Christian asked as Stryder took the cup from his hands and downed the contents in one gulp.

"Can you hear me?"

Stryder shook his head to clear it of the past as he realized his friends had been asking him a multitude of questions.

"I am . . ." He didn't finish the thought. He couldn't. Not while he doubted everything about himself and his family.

Kit never spoke of the past. Never. Since the night Stryder had found him in Canterbury, his brother had refused to speak of the years they had spent apart.

But then Kit never spoke much of anything personal. Considering the pain of his own past, Stryder had never pressed the issue with him.

"Damien was lying."

"About what?"

Stryder hadn't realized he'd spoken aloud until Nassir had asked his question.

"Nothing," he said, making his way to his cot.

As he lay down upon it, Rowena and Zenobia rejoined them.

Rowena rushed to his side and brushed his hand away from the cloth so that she could inspect his wound.

Stryder closed his eyes and took comfort in the sensation of her hands on his cool flesh. He took comfort in the care he saw in her green eyes.

She was beautiful in her concern for him.

Unconsciously, he reached out and ran his hand through her long blond hair, letting it wrap around his fingers. It instantly soothed the fears inside him. The horror that he might have left his own beloved brother in the hands of his enemies.

"I need a bowl of wine and thread," she said to Nassir. "This wound needs be stitched."

Then she looked at Stryder and something inside him shattered. No woman had ever held such a look on her face when she stared at him. He hardened instantly. His entire body burned for a taste of her lips even while it ached from his injuries.

"I think he's been addled by that strike to his head," Swan said from behind them. "Look at him there."

"Aye," Val agreed. "His mind is not as it should be. Mayhap we should beat some sense back into him."

Stryder didn't care what his men thought. His mind wasn't addled. It was clear. Perfectly clear.

For the first time in his life, he understood some of what his father had felt for his mother. Understood the desire to just sit and watch a woman do the simplest of things while he ached for her.

But it changed nothing.

Damien. Aquarius. Kit. His men. They were what he lived for. They reminded him daily of the fact that he could never tie himself to his lands. So long as a child suffered, he had to do whatever he could to see that child home.

He could never rest. Never.

No matter how much his heart might wish otherwise.

He tore his gaze from Rowena to find Kit standing to the back of his men. A stern frown lined his brother's brow.

In all the time they had been in prison, Aquarius had refused to speak of his family. He had said nothing personal. Not even how he'd come to be taken.

All the child had wanted was to go home.

Could that boy have really been Kit?

Kit had been homeless when Stryder had found him. Their half-brother, Michael, had said nothing other than Kit had returned and then Michael had thrown Kit out. At the time Stryder had been too angry to ask where Kit had returned from.

Now he wished he had.

There were no marks on his brother's hands. Not like the ones that had been branded into the hands of the Brotherhood.

Nay. Kit couldn't be Aquarius. His brother loved him. Of that he held no doubt. Damien had promised him that Aquarius hated him and the boy would have every right to.

But there was no hatred on his brother's face as Kit watched him. Only concern showed in his blue eyes.

Damien had planted that seed there to hurt him. To weaken him. Even as a child, Damien had always known how to wound well with his tongue.

Saying something didn't make it true.

"Stryder?"

He turned his gaze to Rowena, who was watching him closely. "Are you all right?"

"Aye," he said, offering her a small smile as he let his hand fall away from her hair. "I wasn't expecting to face Damien in this contest."

Val shoved at Swan. "I told you we should have warned him."

"Nay, you did not!" Swan snapped back.

"I appreciate your looking out for my best interest," Stryder said to his men. "But in the future, I would appreciate a little warning on such matters."

They all looked about guiltily.

"But no harm was done. Let us think no more about it."

Swan and Val nodded and left the tent while Rowena set about stitching his side.

Grimacing at the pain, Stryder watched her delicate stitches. She took great care not to hurt him any more than was necessary.

"You're very good at that for a lady who hates war."

"Men are wounded for other reasons," she said quietly. " 'Tis a talent my mother said all women should possess."

Zenobia clapped, then rubbed her hands together. "I think Rowena is able to care for Stryder. What say the rest of us go and seek out our killer?"

Kit and Nassir nodded. Christian balked. "I think it an ill notion to leave them alone."

Nassir snorted at that, then grabbed Christian's arm and hauled him for the entrance. "Stryder is a man full grown, Abbot. The last thing he needs is to be hounded by us."

"But—"

"Come," Nassir said, pulling him from the tent.

Zenobia gave them a knowing glance. "Rest easy, Stryder. I shall make sure that the two of you are not disturbed."

Zenobia closed and secured the front of the tent.

"Not disturbed from what?" Rowena asked as she moved away from stitching him.

"From this," Stryder said, pulling her close so that he could finally taste the honey of her lips.

Chapter 12

Rowena moaned at the strength of Stryder's kiss. And to think she had actually feared for him this day. But there was far too much power in that kiss for him to be seriously injured.

Nay, her knight was fine.

He pulled her onto his cot, over his chest to cradle her gently in his arms.

She broke their kiss off instantly. "Careful, milord, you'll hurt yourself."

"I care not," he breathed, pulling her lips back to his so that he could ravage her senses.

Her heart leapt at his words and at the feel of his tongue sweeping against hers. The warm, manly scent of him filled her head as she swept her hands over the steely biceps that flexed and beckoned her with power.

What was it about this man that made her feel like this? It made her shivery, hot, and needful. Ever longing to be close to him when she knew deep in her heart that he posed the biggest danger to everything she wanted out of life.

She ran her hand over the muscles of his chest, feeling the way his flesh rippled and flexed under her palm.

Stryder took her hand into his and led it down the length of his body until she touched his rigid shaft.

"I dreamt of you all last night, Rowena," he breathed raggedly in her ear. "Of you touching me again."

She moaned at the sound of his voice and the feel of him in her hand. She ran her fingers to the tip of him where he was already wet. A shiver went through him that she felt with the whole of her body.

She found it hard to believe that this man who could kill could be so tender with her. That he could hold her like this and make her entire body burn for him.

Yet he did. He made her breathless and weak. And at the same time, he made her feel as if she could fly.

"I'm so glad you weren't killed."

"Are you?"

She nodded while she stared into those captivatingly blue eyes. "I never knew I could pray so hard for one knight to pummel another."

He opened his mouth to speak.

"Or for any man," she said before he could say a word.

He nibbled her lips with his teeth as he slid his hands down her back, to her hips. Rowena didn't protest him sliding her skirts up until he bared her bottom to his questing hands. She groaned deep in her throat as his hand found the part of her that throbbed for him.

Stryder clenched his teeth at the sweet moisture of her that coated his fingers. He shouldn't even be thinking of taking her. Especially not now, when his mission was so clear.

But he couldn't resist her. He needed to be inside her right now in a way he didn't understand. He had to have her and he would kill anyone who tried to interrupt them.

Ignoring the pain of his wound, he pulled her gently into his lap and slid himself deep inside her waiting warmth. He closed his eyes and just savored the feeling of her.

He could stay inside this woman forever. There was some foreign, inner calm he felt whenever she was near him. It was as if he could find no fault with the world.

No fault with himself.

It was a tranquility he'd never imagined could exist.

Rowena gasped at the fullness of Stryder inside her body. What she felt for him terrified her. What they were doing was madness when both of them wanted to be free.

And yet she was helpless against her body's ravenous need

for him. Her heart's desire to be near him. To soothe this man whose eyes were always tormented, like a stormy sea forever bereft of sunshine.

He guided her with his hands, showing her how to make love to him from above. Her rich blue dress pooled around them, trailing to the ground.

She watched his face closely and wondered if her own features mirrored the pleasure he gave her. His breathing was rapid as he bit his lip and growled while his hands urged her to move faster.

"That's it, love," he whispered as she found a rhythm that pleased them both.

Stryder cupped her face in his hands while he let her thrust for both of them. It was all he could do not to tear her gown from her until her body was bared to him so that he could touch her all over. Sate the longing he had to stare at her lush curves until he was drunk from it. However, the last thing he wanted was for her to be embarrassed anymore than was necessary should someone interrupt them. He trusted Zenobia could give them privacy.

But just in case . . .

Rowena turned her face in his hands and kissed the inside of his wrist. His heart quickened at the gesture.

She was marvelous. Truly, an unexpected pleasure.

He felt her body tighten against his shaft as she quickened her strokes. A smile played at the edges of his mouth as she came for him.

It was the most beautiful sight he'd ever beheld. Her cries of pleasure filled his ears and warmed him through and through.

Pulling her down to his lips, he swallowed those cries before anyone else heard them and lifted his hips, driving himself even deeper into her body.

He could feel her heart pounding against his chest as he held her and thrust faster until he found his own release while she kissed him deeply and fully.

Hissing in pleasure, he savored the sensation of her wet heat until his body was completely drained and sated. There was nothing on this earth like his nymph.

No one could ever compare to her. Nor could any give him a more blissful moment.

Rowena rested herself on her elbows so that she could stare down at Stryder. She kissed her way along the edge of his whiskered jaw and simply inhaled the warm, masculine scent of him.

"Did I hurt you?" she asked, worried about his wound and the bruises that were forming along his body.

"Nay, lady. It would take much more than your mere weight to harm me."

Rowena lay herself down upon his chest, her cheek to his heart, which pounded and soothed her while he toyed with her hair. He lifted his other hand to trace the line of her nose.

"You are so soft."

She placed a kiss over his heart, then moved so that she could look up at him. "You are not."

He smiled down at her, his eyes hot and searing. "Tell me why I can't resist you, Rowena. You write of love and desire. Why do I desire you when all my reason tells me I shouldn't?"

"If I knew the answer to that, then I would understand why I'm here with you when I shouldn't be." Biting her lip, she pulled back from him. "What are we doing, Stryder?"

"I think we're falling in love."

Silence hung between the two of them as those words echoed in the quiet stillness.

Rowena knew the truth of it. She felt it with every part of her and it made her want to run away in terror.

His jaw flexed as his fingers brushed against her cheek. "And I can't afford to love you, milady. I can't."

"I know. And I don't want to love a man I can never keep. One who will never be content to lay aside his sword in the name of peace and live tranquilly by my side."

He sighed at her words. "Nay. I can never lay aside my sword. Not so long as children like Damien are out there being hurt. And it's not just the Saracens who harm them. We free just as many of their children who are held by our people as we do our children being held by them. I can see no end to this war and until I do, I have no choice except to do everything I can to help those who are suffering."

"You can't save the world, Stryder."

"If I save one person, then I have saved *their* world. Homes are not built of one single slab, but rather they are made of hundreds of stones. If one stone is crushed, then the entire house is compromised, if not ruined. I might not save them all, but I have to save as many as I can."

And that was what she loved most about him. "I want you to win this war you fight."

Stryder kissed her lips, then withdrew from inside her. He moved to the side so that she lay beside him on the narrow cot. He cuddled her tenderly as he covered them with the blanket.

"I wish you could win yours, Rowena. I wish asking for peace was as simple as you singing one of your songs."

Rowena glanced down to where his wound was red and swollen. She ached for him. Just as she ached for herself. "So what are we to do?"

"We shall have to avoid each other as much as possible."

Tears welled in her eyes as she noted the deadness of his own. The last thing she wanted was to not see him. "What of the tournament? If you win, you will have to marry me. How can you win the song competition if we don't see each other?"

"I can have Kit teach me something so that I will win your contest. You will have your freedom of choice, my lady. I swear it."

And what if I want you? She swallowed against the sudden lump in her throat. If she had a choice, 'twould be the one thing she would want.

The only husband she would want.

But that was a whimsical dream and well she knew it. Stryder of Blackmoor was beyond the reach of any lady. So long as his quest beckoned him, he would never settle down.

"Very well then." Rowena forced herself to get up and adjust her dress. If they could no longer see each other, there was no need in her torturing either one of them further.

It was best to leave now while she could almost bear the thought.

Although, to be honest, the pain in her chest wasn't really bearable. It hurt and it cut. She didn't want to leave him, but just as he had said, she understood why it was necessary.

She only hoped the agony inside her ebbed eventually. Perhaps she might even one day find another to love. . . .

Nay, there would never be another who could mean as much

to her as Stryder did. But some things weren't meant to be, and their relationship was one of them.

Stryder braced himself for the sudden coldness of his body as she withdrew from him. It was for the best, and yet his soul cried out for him to hold her close.

Then he did the hardest thing he'd ever done in his life. He watched as she made her way out of his tent.

Stryder pressed his hand to his eyes and cursed beneath his breath. How had this happened? How had he allowed a mere slip of a termagant to slide into his well-guarded heart?

And yet she wasn't a shrew. If she were, she would never have conquered him so skillfully. She was merely a woman of great convictions. Bold, intelligent, and determined. All traits he admired.

Now she was gone.

Pain the likes of which he'd never known consumed his heart.

"You have to be the greatest fool in all of Christendom," Zenobia said as she entered his tent. "Nay, you are the greatest fool in all the world."

Without uncovering his eyes, he growled at her. "Leave me be, Zen. I've no patience for you at present."

"Good, for I have none for you, either. Never have I suffered fools gladly."

To his complete astonishment, she came over and slapped him across his good ribs.

Stryder grimaced at the unexpected pain and moved his arm so that he could glare up at her. "What are you doing?"

"Be grateful you're injured. That alone keeps me from taking my sword and giving you the thrashing you deserve."

He snorted at her threat. " 'Twould take more than you to do me harm."

"Mayhap, but not with the anger I hold at present. How could you allow Rowena to leave you?"

His gut tightened at the thought, even though his head understood the reason. "It's for the best."

She slapped his side again.

"Have you gone mad?" he asked, rubbing his ribs.

"Nay, but methinks you have. You love that woman. So why are you pushing her away?"

"What do you know of it?"

She stood with her hands on her hips and her face showed every bit of her ire at him. "I know all of it, as does Val, Swan, Nassir, and Christian. There's no great secret given the light that comes into your eyes at the mere mention of Rowena's name. Never mind the way you watch her like a hungry wolf whenever she draws near you."

"Bah! What foolishness you speak."

She rolled her eyes at him, then said something in her language he didn't quite understand.

"Did you call me a pig?"

"I called you a pigheaded boar."

"Isn't that redundant?"

She moved to slap him again, but this time he grabbed her hand before she made contact. Instead, she kicked her foot up under his cot.

"Ow!" he snapped as she kicked his buttocks.

"I love you like a brother, Stryder, but I swear there are times when I could strangle the very life out of you."

" 'Tis a good thing you care for me then. Given my treatment, I shudder at what you would do to me should you decide you hate me."

Her face turned stern. "Pray you never find that out."

Zenobia turned away and headed for the entrance. She paused and looked back at him. "Tell me something, Stryder. When you are too old and aged to tourney, too old to carry your sword and battle for the weak, who will sit in the hall beside you to keep you company?"

He looked away at that. In truth, he chose to not think about such things. If he were lucky, he wouldn't have to deal with such a fate.

However, Zenobia was in no mood to give him any sort of quarter from those thoughts. "You can't stop time from moving forward, nor can you defeat every demon who walks this earth. All your life you have been running away from the ghost of your parents and the fear of becoming your father. But tell me honestly, Widowmaker, what would have happened had your mother loved your father the way he had loved her? Imagine that for one moment. A marriage where two people live and die for each other. Both of them hopelessly in love for all their lives."

"Do you think it possible?"

"Simon lives in happiness. You told me so yourself."

Aye. Simon and Kenna were indeed happy in their vows. But as he had pointed out to Rowena earlier, they were still newly married. What they had might last forever or it could end on the morrow.

Not to mention the fact that his marriage had also curtailed Simon's loyalty to their Brotherhood. "Simon stays in Scotland now, forever removed from our service."

"Is he?" Zenobia asked with an arched brow. "What of the youths we send to him? Without Kenna and Simon to understand their problems and to help them readjust to life outside of captivity, those children would be lost to us and their families. Unrecoverable. It seems to me he serves our cause better where he is than he did trailing along after you."

Stryder grew quiet as he considered that. But it wasn't just that one matter that had to be weighed. "You make it sound so simple. If I were to take Rowena as my bride, I would have the responsibility of not just my lands, but hers as well. Henry would never allow me freedom to travel. I must struggle even now to get him to allow me to leave England. As overlord of both domains, I would ever be forced to his side."

"Nothing is ever simple," Zenobia said quietly. "Nor is anything worth having unless you have to strive for it. But don't strive too long, Stryder, or you may very well find yourself the loser in this. Have you given thought of how you will feel when you see the woman you love given over to another man to possess?"

Stryder blinked as Zenobia left him alone with an image in his mind so disturbing that he could barely draw breath.

Nay, he hadn't thought of that. "Rowena won't marry another!" he called out after Zenobia. His side protested his raised voice by throbbing instantly.

Zenobia stuck her head back in the tent. "Keep telling yourself that, and on the day of her wedding, I shall be there to comfort you."

In that moment, he almost hated his friend for what she was

doing. Throwing his pillow at her, he then turned his back to her and did his best to push her words out of his mind.

Rowena would never betray either one of them by choosing another husband. Her freedom was too precious to her.

What if Henry forces her to choose?

What if she loves another?

Those words hovered in his mind like a demon plague. It was possible. Some other man could woo her. A man of poetry and song. One who would stay by her side and give her his children.

The thought tore through him.

Ultimately the decision of whether or not she had her freedom to choose a husband depended solely on him. He would win the tournament without question.

But the song competition . . .

She will hate you forever if you lose it.

Would she?

Dare he chance it?

Stryder lay in silent debate as his mind and heart warred. 'Twas possible he might not win it. There were many others at court far better at song than he was. Would it be his fault if someone else was superior?

Would Rowena really blame him?

Set her free.

Stryder cursed. Aye, he would set her free. Look now how distracted he was and they barely knew one another. The last thing he could afford was to claim a woman whose very thought overshadowed everything else.

Such as the fact that they had a killer to locate before the assassin struck again.

Aquarius slipped into the room quickly. Silently. No one was there except his target, who sat alone at her dressing table. She brushed her long, blond locks and hummed a fair tune while she watched herself in the looking glass.

She was beautiful, he would give her that. With lush, graceful curves that were displayed perfectly by her deep crimson gown.

Relying on his training, he skirted up behind her and grabbed her arm so fast that she opened her mouth to scream.

"Say nothing," he hissed, pulling back the sleeve of her gown to show him a list in Arabic that was tattooed onto her pale skin. 'Twas similar to the one he carried on his own arm. Only the names were different. "I knew it was you."

She snatched her arm away from him. "What are you doing here?"

"I wanted to know why you framed Stryder of Blackmoor for murder."

She set her brush back on her table and gave him a cool, calculating stare as she lowered her sleeve and relaced it so that the names were no longer visible. "Where are your manners, milord? 'Tis been years since we last saw one another. Have you no kindness for a woman you once took with great passion?"

He winced at her words as he recalled the times they had been forced together for the enjoyment of others. The banquets where they . . .

"I try my best never to remember those days."

"Then I'm happy for you. I find they haunt me constantly no matter how much I try to forget them."

He felt for her, but that didn't change anything. What she had done was wrong. "You haven't answered my question."

She gave him a droll, aggravated stare. "Why do you think? You helped me and I wanted to return the favor."

"Return what favor?"

"You killed Cyril for me. I didn't remember who you were until the night I saw you leave his tent. I went inside to fulfill my bargain only to find him already dead. At first, I was terrified. I thought you had been sent to finish my list and me, but once I calmed down, I realized he must have recognized you earlier that night."

Aquarius looked away in shame. Aye, it was true. Cyril had known him. The fool had even goaded him when he had awakened to find Aquarius standing over Cyril's cot. Those taunts had ended the moment Aquarius had shoved his dagger straight into the man's heart.

"You dropped the note?" he asked her.

"Aye. I went back to retrieve it later, but could find no sign of it."

He pulled it out of his purse and handed it over to her. "You'd best destroy this before anyone else learns of it and realizes as I did who wrote it."

She nodded, then tucked it down the front of her crimson gown, between her breasts.

Aquarius stared at her, his gaze burning. "Do me no further favors where the earl is concerned."

"Nay?" she asked, arching a brow. "Are you aware *Kalb al 'Akrab* is here?"

Aquarius went cold at her words. *The Heart of the Scorpion* was the name of the assassin who had been charged with keeping all of them in line. He was the one they sent in to kill them should they ever betray who and what they were. Damn. The Scorpion and *Kalb al 'Akrab* were no doubt the same person. He should have known that.

But no one knew his name or his likeness. All of their kind who knew him were now dead by his hand.

"Aye," he breathed. "I found one of his couriers."

"I recognized him as the Scorpion the moment I saw him," she said. "Unlike you, he wasn't kept hidden so much, but rather our captors took great pleasure in trotting him out to abuse."

"How do you know for certain that he's *Kalb al 'Akrab*?"

"I know not for certain exactly. But I wasn't wrong about you being Aquarius, and I know your time for killing Stryder has passed. Remember? I was there the day they let you go and I heard the Saracen guards laughing that soon the Widowmaker would be dead. It was why I tried to frame him. I was hoping that if he were dead, at least you would be free of them and prove to me that they really will let us go once we complete our list." She looked away as terror filled her eyes. "My worst fear is that they'll come for us once we fulfill our bargain. I know of no one who has lived through completing their list. Do you?"

"Until you, I had no knowledge of any others assigned my duties. Only *Kalb al 'Akrab* was ever mentioned to me, and I was hoping he was nothing more than a fabrication they made up to keep me in line."

Her gaze sharpened. "Why haven't you killed the Widowmaker?"

"The time isn't right."

She moved to stand before him, her body rigid with anger. "Have you turned craven? My master said that you were the coldest, most efficient killer of all of us who were sent out. What are you waiting for?"

"What master?"

She stiffened but didn't answer. "You were lucky. They sent you out alone. The rest of us have those we know watch us. I take my orders often from their messengers."

A sick feeling went through Aquarius. "Why have they kept themselves from me?"

"They assumed you would complete your mission. Why haven't you?" she insisted again.

"Why do you care? I thought you and your friends wanted Stryder to live and marry Rowena."

She scoffed at that. "Think you I want her married? 'Tis bad enough I returned home to the loving bosom of my family." She spat those words with a hate-filled venom that chilled him. "As soon as my father learned I was no longer virgin and wouldn't command a high marriage price since I had been used, he quickly ushered me off to her house so that he wouldn't have to look at me and feel shamed for what had happened because he was careless. Unlike you, I traded one prison for another. The last thing I want is to see Rowena married to a man who will never stay put in this country. He'll be off on adventure while we are forever locked in Sussex so that she can train her milksops and their idiotic poetry."

"Elizabeth—"

"Nay," she said, pulling away from him. "Don't touch me and don't use my name. I never want to hear it from your lips."

He let his hand drop. "Why didn't you just kill Stryder yourself?"

"I tried, but he would never be alone with me, then I thought that if I became the countess of Blackmoor he might protect me."

"So you killed another Brotherhood member to frame him?" he asked, trying to understand her motivation.

"Aye. Roger was the one who raped Mary."

Aquarius winced as he recalled the night the Brotherhood members had fled the prison. A small group of them had been sent to set them free. Instead, they had taken their pleasure of them and then left them locked in their cells while they returned to the others with false tales of how the whores were all dead.

For years he had hated all the Brotherhood members. Who wouldn't? After their escape those of them left behind had been ravaged by their enemies.

Mary had died during one of her punishments after the Brotherhood had fled. She had been a timid woman. Small and delicate. The Saracens had crushed her like a frail flower.

To this day, Aquarius lived only to have enough strength to return to their prison and kill the ones responsible. Unfortunately, he doubted he would ever have the chance.

"I took great pleasure in killing Roger," Elizabeth snarled. "And I would have taken greater pleasure in seeing Stryder die too."

"He suffers enough."

She curled her lips at him. "What do you know of it? There will never be enough suffering where he is concerned. We are the ones who suffered most back then and still do. Tell me truthfully, is there a night that goes by where your nightmares don't haunt you?"

"Aye," he lied. "I gave enough of my life to those demons. I refuse to give them anymore." At least he tried his best to live by that. During the light of day it was easy.

It was only at night when he slept that he couldn't banish the nightmares.

"I'm happy for you," she said snidely. "I can never forget what was done to me. Know you that I can't even have children now? They brutalized me so savagely after the one time I was pregnant at their hands that in all this time, I have never conceived again. Never." Her eyes sparkled with unshed tears.

Aquarius wanted to comfort her, but he knew she was past that. Nor would she welcome his touch and the unwanted emotions it would no doubt evoke. As one of the few males in her ward, he had listened to the women as they suffered through their pregnancies and had even helped to deliver some of their babies.

Elizabeth in particular had had a difficult time birthing her son.

"Is your son still in Outremer?"

She nodded. "They hold him as guarantee that I will complete my mission. I shudder every time I think of him in their care. There's no telling what lies they are filling his head with. Or what they do to him."

Rage filled him. Her son would only be around seven or eight years old now.

"I'll get him for you."

She laughed aloud at that. "As if you could. If you return, they'll see you dead. Indeed, I know I am right, and that *Kalb al 'Akrab* is here to kill you."

"It'll take more than him to kill me."

She snorted at that. "Boastful men. Braggarts. It's all any of your kind are, and I've had enough of it. If you won't kill Stryder, I will, lest they tire of waiting and come to reclaim us. His life is not worth whatever freedom I do have."

Aquarius gave her a hard, meaningful stare. "I won't let you kill him."

"Nay?" she asked in disbelief. "And if I tell him who you are?"

"I will see you dead first."

"Rowena?"

Rowena paused at the deep-timbered voice that sent a shiver down her spine. It was one she hadn't expected to hear addressing her ever again.

Turning about slowly, she faced Damien St. Cyr. "Milord," she said, curtsying before him.

"There's no need to be so formal, milady. Or cold. I didn't kill your knight, after all."

There was something different about Damien this afternoon. Something more relaxed and calm.

Like Stryder, he'd changed out of his armor. Now he wore a gray tunic with a crimson and gold surcoat and black hose beneath his voluminous black cloak.

"It seems God has indeed judged him innocent."

She thought she detected a note of bitterness in Damien's voice. "I hope you weren't hurt much, milord."

"Only my pride, which has been wounded so often that I am sure it will heal from this, too." He bowed to her. "I'll take my leave of you, milady. I only wanted to apologize once more for my curt, unchivalrous behavior toward you yesterday when you came to see me."

"Think nothing of it, milord."

"Damien," he said, his voice seductive. "Please, call me Damien."

Rowena curtsied and inclined her head to him.

Damien *tsked* at her. "You are suspicious of me?"

"Do you blame me?" she asked.

He laughed at that. A deep, hypnotic sound. "And you don't even try to deny it."

"Should I?"

"Most do. I have to say I find your honesty refreshing." She had a distinct feeling he was smiling at her and it truly bothered her that she could see no hint of his face.

"Good day, milady. May it lay treasures at your feet."

She frowned as he walked off and left her standing in the middle of the hall.

She didn't move until she heard another voice just behind her.

"Whatever did he want with you?" Zenobia asked as she moved forward to stand by Rowena's side.

The two of them watched as Damien vanished through the door, headed somewhere outside the castle.

"He apologized," Rowena said. She was still unable to believe he had done such. It seemed completely out of character for him.

"For?"

"Being rude to me yesterday when I asked him not to fight Stryder."

Zenobia looked as surprised as she felt. "How unlike him to apologize for anything."

Rowena frowned at her. "Do you know him?"

Zenobia looked away guiltily.

"What?" she asked as a wave of trepidation came over her. There was something sinister in the way Zenobia looked about.

"I know many things about those my father held in his prison, and it shames me to no end," she whispered. "Not so much the stories the Brotherhood tells, which are bad enough, but the ones I heard from my father's men, who oft bragged over their cruelty to the ones they 'guarded.'"

Rowena touched her arm in sympathy. "Is that why you helped them escape?"

Zenobia nodded. "My father forgot that my mother's people were different from his. We are not ornaments to sit quietly at a man's side, especially when we see injustice. The Ayasheen are descended from the Amazons. It is our birthright and duty to fight, and I can still hear my mother's voice in my ear that no one should be deprived of their dignity. Her people believed that enemies should either be respected or executed. If you execute them, then they worry you no more. If you allow them to withdraw with dignity, then they will do so. But when an enemy is held down and made to suffer continuously, sooner or later he will strike out, and woe to you when he does. For there is no more fearsome a power than that of long-festered vengeance."

Rowena nodded. "Your mother was very wise."

"Aye, she was indeed. You remind me a lot of her."

She was surprised by Zenobia's comparison. "Me?"

"Mmm. My mother used to call me *Karima*. It means 'little monkey' in her language. She would say that I run about and shriek, throwing things and aggravating others until I get my way. She was quiet and steady, like an unmovable wall, firm in her resolve and confident with herself."

Rowena smiled at her. "That sounds much better than 'stubborn as an ass,' which is what my uncle calls me."

Zenobia laughed at that. "Stubborn is only wrong when it causes you to act against your best interest."

"How so?"

"Remember I told you of the man I love?"

"Aye."

"'Tis his stubbornness that keeps him from me. Rather than accept what I offer him, he travels the world forever seeking a peace that will never come to him. Sometimes what we want and what we need aren't compatible."

"What are you saying?"

"If Stryder wins this troubadour contest and you are given your choice of husband, who will you choose?"

That was easy enough to answer. "I will choose my freedom, of course—at least for as long as Henry will allow it."

"Because you need it or because you want it?"

Rowena looked away as truth struck her. "Neither. I will choose it because the man I want is much like yours. He won't stay with me and should I force him to it, he will resent me for it. Better I should grow old alone than married to a man who will only learn to hate me for binding him to me against his will."

To her surprise, Zenobia laughed again. "You are my mother, *patrulla*." She took her arm and led her toward the stairs. "Come with me, Lady Rowena. I lost the man I love, but you . . . you have me, and together let us see what we can do with yours."

"Do you think we can win him over?"

Zenobia let out a long, measured breath. "All we can do is try."

Chapter 13

S tryder walked through the tournament field of knights feeling much like a leper at banquet. The morning's battle might have acquitted him in the eyes of the law, but in the eyes of everyone else, he was a murderer.

Whispers of gossipmongers, both male and female, followed him everywhere he went. There were no ladies mobbing him. For once he could probably strip himself bare and no woman would dare come near.

Perhaps murder did have some advantages. . . .

Sighing, he saw his brother sitting underneath a tree, alone, plucking at his lute while he made notes on a piece of vellum.

Stryder made his way over to him.

Dressed in his orange and red clothes, Kit looked up as Stryder's shadow fell across him. " 'Tis a dismal feeling, isn't it?" Kit asked as Stryder paused by his side.

"What is?"

"Not belonging. Having other people judge you for what they believe you are and not for what you really are." Kit gave him a wry smile. "Too bad you have no older brother to go and thrash them for you. I would offer my services, but they only laugh at me whenever I try to defend myself or someone else."

Damien's words came back to him as Stryder squatted by Kit's notes. "Has it always been that way with you?"

Kit looked away from him.

"Kit?" Stryder asked, drawing his brother's attention back to him. "Where were you when I went to Michael to find you? He said he had thrown you to your own means when you returned. Where had you been?"

"Nowhere."

"Kit . . ."

His brother looked aggravated by the inquisition. "Take not that tone with me, Stryder. I'm not one of your men to quake in terror of it. I happen to know you would never hurt me."

Nay, he would not. Ever. But he wanted answers to this. If Kit were in fact Aquarius . . .

"Why won't you trust me?" Stryder tried again, this time more calmly. "After these last few years together, I still know very little about you."

"You know enough." Kit's gaze locked with his. "You are the only brother I have ever known. The only family, for that matter. And until the night you saved me in Canterbury, I never knew what it was like to belong anywhere. For that I thank you, and I would never betray you or any you hold dear."

Those words were so odd. . . .

Stryder offered him a brotherly smile of affection. "I regret the years I wasn't there for you, runt. I wish you'd never known a day of sadness."

"I know." Kit looked back at his paper.

Stryder paused to watch three men walk by, men who glared maliciously at him and Kit.

He rose to his feet and the men immediately quickened their steps.

"I envy you that power," Kit said quietly as Stryder looked back at him. "What I wouldn't give to make people tremble in fear of my displeasure."

"Then why don't you train as a knight? I would teach you everything I know."

Kit scoffed at that. "I'm frail. Too thin. More woman than man."

Stryder beat back the anger those words evoked. "Raven is thinner than you are and younger than you to match, and yet he wins more fights than he loses. And you most definitely are not more woman than man."

Kit locked gazes with him. His brother's eyes were piercing.

Searching. That intense stare made something inside Stryder almost cringe. "And if I told you I was attracted to other men, what would you say?"

"Nothing," Stryder answered honestly and with conviction. "I know that for the lie it is. Not that it would matter to me even if you were. We are brothers, you and I. Nothing changes that. Ever. Wherever I am, you are always welcome and I will kill any who says otherwise."

Kit's eyes teared as he looked away.

Stryder knelt beside him again. "Kit?"

Kit glanced back at him as a single tear fled down his cheek. "Why is it only you and Rowena who have ever seen that truth in me? No woman will look at me unless she's trying to use me to get to you. Why is that?"

"I know not. Any more than I can understand why they misjudge me now. But you know something? I care not what these fools think. Do you?"

He saw the indecision on his brother's face.

"Kit . . ."

"I'm considering it."

Shaking his head, Stryder rose to his feet and held his hand out to his brother. Kit took his hand with a strong grip. Stryder hauled him to his feet.

He inclined his head toward the list. "Come, little brother. There is something I would show you."

Kit followed after him without question.

"You know, Kit, the best way to make a maid crave you is skill with a sword."

Kit arched an amused brow at him.

Stryder shook his head as he understood that look. "There was no double entendre intended," Stryder said with a dark laugh.

He left Kit standing at one end of the list and went to pull two throwing daggers out of a straw dummy. Returning to his brother's side, he handed one over.

"It takes a light touch, but . . ." Stryder let fly the dagger, which landed just below where a man's heart would be. "'Tis rather easy once you practice a bit. You think you can do that?"

Kit raised the dagger and barely looked at the dummy. He

threw it fast and hit the straw-filled knight straight between the eyes.

Dumbstruck, Stryder stared at the knife. As did every knight on the field.

"Beginner's luck," Kit said nonchalantly.

Again Damien's accusation ran in Stryder's head.

Was it possible?

Stryder looked at the knife, then at his brother. "Are you sure there's nothing you wish to tell me?"

"Nay."

Still suspicious, Stryder watched as Kit turned and went to retrieve his lute and paper. His brother might dismiss what had just happened, but Stryder knew better. It took a lot of practice and skill to throw a dagger like that.

A lot.

When and where would Kit have learned such? And what other skills had his brother acquired that he knew nothing about?

Late that afternoon, Rowena sat in the great hall with her lute in her lap as she sang to a very small group of troubadours, mostly women, and a few men who sought to curry her uncle's favor. Other ladies, mostly those who had young sons they didn't wish to see die in battle, had come to hear her. They alone seemed to agree with her viewpoints against war.

At least no one was mocking her.

Oddly enough, there were two of her own ladies-in-waiting missing—Elizabeth and Bridget. She assumed they were both off with some man who had caught their fancy.

It was very typical of both of them, and it was something she would never hold against either one. She loved her friends too dearly for that.

Everyone was being respectful and attentive until the door behind her that led to a back hallway opened. There was a collective gasp and frown from the group before several heads went together and whispers instantly began.

Rowena turned to see what had so captured their attention. Behind her, she found Damien and three of his men entering the hall. It was something unheard of.

Damien pulled up short as he realized he was the center of

everyone's attention. "Forgive me," he said quietly to Rowena. "I was hoping not to interrupt you."

"Think nothing of it, milord. I can—"

"Please, Rowena, play. It is, after all, why I came here this day. I wish to hear your songs."

To her utter astonishment, he and his men took seats off to the side, in the back of the small crowd.

Suddenly unsure of herself and completely self-conscious of the fact that Damien was staring at her with eyes she couldn't see, she began her song anew and tried her best to ignore a man whose very presence set her ill at ease. Indeed, she could feel the weight of his steely gaze on her as if it were a touch. It unnerved her greatly.

There was something extremely disconcerting about Damien, and it wasn't just the fact that she had no idea what the man looked like. It was as if darkness itself was cloaked around him.

Rowena sang three more songs to finish her recital. Her audience, including Damien, applauded graciously. She curtsied to them and as she righted herself, a sudden movement on the gallery high above the hall caught her attention.

Looking up, she was startled as she met the deep blue stare of Stryder, who stood watching her.

He offered her a warm smile before he stepped back, out of her line of sight.

Her heart leapt at the thought of him being here to hear her when she knew how much he hated such things.

Without thinking twice, she set her lute aside and made for the spiral stairs. Several people tried to stop her, but she quickly excused herself and rushed upstairs.

She ran down the long hallway where he must have escaped. Where could he be? The only way to leave the hall was down the stairs she had flown up.

Yet there was no sight of him anywhere. Had her eyes deceived her?

"Stryder?"

She started past a door when she heard his quiet response. "I'm here, Rowena."

She stopped and turned to see him stepping out of the shadows. It was so good to see him upright and dressed.

Before she could stop herself, she threw herself into his arms and kissed him soundly.

Stryder growled at the taste of her. At the heated demands of her tongue dancing with his. She tasted of warmth and softness. Of hope.

Most of all, she tasted of Rowena and her unique femininity.

He cupped her face and drank his fill of her lips, letting the hands that skimmed his back take him away from the doubts and fears in his mind.

She pulled back slowly. "Why did you come after you said we should keep our distance?"

"I didn't think you would see me."

"But you saw me?"

"Aye." He cupped her cheek with his warm hand. "You're a very talented lady."

"You hate talented women."

"I don't hate you."

She covered his hand with hers and kissed his palm. "You're not helping me to put distance between us."

"I know. You're like a siren luring me."

"Perhaps we should have your men lash you to a mast?"

He laughed at her reference to Odysseus, who had sailed his ship safely through the sirens' lair only because his crewman had tied him down. "Best get Swan to do it. He'd make sure the ropes held. I'm not so sure about the others."

She smiled at that. "And where is your motley band of friends?"

"Scattered to the ends of the county looking for clues."

"Rowena!"

They both turned to see Joanne at the top of the stairs. Her face was pale, her eyes filled with tears as she rushed toward them.

"What's wrong?" Rowena asked, terrified of what had her friend so distraught.

Tears fell down her cheeks. " 'Tis Elizabeth. She's dead."

Chapter 14

Rowena was grateful for Stryder's support. Without it, she was most certain she would have crumpled as a wave of grief so profound hit her straight in her heart. It was the most crippling pain she had ever known.

Tears stung her eyes and fell completely unchecked down her face. "What do you mean Elizabeth is dead?"

Joanne wiped at her own eyes. "One of the king's guards fished her body from the lake. They think she must have slipped and fallen into the stream, and her skirts were too heavy for her to swim."

"Nay," Rowena breathed through her tears. "'Tis not possible. Why would she be at the lake alone?"

"You know how she was," Joanne said. "She told me this morning that she was going to meet someone there."

Joanne took her into her arms and they held on to each other as they sobbed from the loss of their beloved friend.

How could Elizabeth be gone from them? Since the day Elizabeth had joined their household, she had been a necessary part of their lives.

Rowena felt Stryder's strong hand on her back, rubbing her gently. She turned away from Joanne and pulled him close, needing to feel his strength. His comfort.

"I'm so sorry, Rowena," he whispered against her hair as he cradled her to his chest.

"She can't be dead," Rowena wailed. "She can't."

While she cried, she could hear a commotion from below. Voices echoing through the hallway as nobles were told of Elizabeth's fate.

"I wish we had never come to this tournament," Joanne spat. " 'Tis been evil from the onset. And now this . . ."

"Sh," Rowena said, taking her friend's hand. " 'Twas an accident, a stupid one. But an accident nonetheless."

And there were preparations that needed to be done. Someone would have to see to Elizabeth's body.

With a strength of will Rowena had never known she possessed, she pulled herself together. "Someone will have to notify Elizabeth's family," she said quietly.

"I can send one of my men," Stryder offered.

She gave him a tremulous smile. "I think it best that your men stay here to defend you if needs be. My uncle has men he can send. But I appreciate the thought."

Stryder inclined his head to her.

"Rowena?"

She looked past Stryder to see her uncle coming toward them from the stairs. His face was saddened and pinched.

"You've been told?" he asked gently.

She nodded and fought against another wave of tears.

"Is there anything I can do?" Stryder asked.

"Don't leave me alone," Rowena whispered. "I don't think I can cope with all this by myself."

Joanne let out a baleful wail as her legs buckled. Stryder barely caught her before she hit the floor.

Rowena's stomach tightened even more as she remembered Elizabeth telling her the tale of how Stryder had carried Joanne when they had first arrived. Her friend's face had been all awash with light happiness as she asked Rowena if Stryder would make her Queen of All Hearts.

"Oh, Elizabeth," she breathed, her heart breaking from the loss. All the dreams that Elizabeth had held for her future . . .

All their hopes . . .

But she couldn't think of it right now. If she did, she would join Joanne and no one needed the additional burden. There was too much to do.

"Take her to her chambers," she said, leading the way for Stryder. Her uncle followed a step behind them.

"I have already dispatched someone for Cornwall," her uncle said quietly. "Though to be honest, I doubt if her family will respond."

Rowena sighed at that as she held open the door for Stryder to carry Joanne into the room at the end of the hall. She rushed around him to turn down Joanne's fur-covered bed, and stepped back for Stryder to place her upon it.

"Why won't her family respond?" Stryder asked as he stepped away from the bed.

"We know not," Rowena said. "Elizabeth was a distant cousin who was sent to live with us a few years back. She had spent almost five years with me when we were girls, and then her father summoned her home at ten-and-six to wed."

"Elizabeth was married?" Stryder asked as he watched Rowena cover Joanne up.

"Nay," her uncle answered. "Her betrothed eloped with another and she didn't return to us for several years."

"She was so sad in the beginning," Rowena said. "She would sit for hours, staring out the window, saying nothing to anyone. It was as if her spirit had been broken. Then one day, she decided to rejoin this world."

Stryder stared at her with a fierce scowl. "Any idea what happened?"

"Nay, she would never speak of it. Nor of her family. It was as if she had no past at all."

"Like my brother . . ."

"Kit?" Rowena asked.

"Aye, he was much like that when I first took him in."

Rowena remembered that herself. When she had first met him on the troubadour circuit, Kit had been withdrawn and crestfallen.

"Strange coincidence, isn't it?"

Stryder didn't answer. His thoughts were whirling. Indeed, their behavior reminded him of some others he knew. Himself included. "Tell me. Did Elizabeth ever venture to Outremer?"

Rowena and her uncle exchanged a puzzled look.

"Not that I know of," Rowena said. "Uncle?"

"I know not. Her father never spoke anything of her leaving his home until he sent her to live with us."

Rowena tilted her head to look up at Stryder, who considered that. "What are you thinking?"

"I don't know. Foolishness most likely." Stryder inclined his head toward Joanne. "Will she be all right?"

"Aye, she just needs to rest." Rowena closed the burgundy curtains around the bed, then led them from the room.

By the time they reached the hallway again, everyone was rushing about, murmuring.

Most of all, they were whispering about where Stryder might have been when Elizabeth fell into the lake.

"After all," one elder woman said to a friend as they headed toward the stairs, "I heard the girl bragging many a time that she would wed the earl of Blackmoor. Mayhap she annoyed him one time too many."

"Well, you know his father killed his mother . . ."

"And curiosity killed the cat," Rowena said from behind them.

They turned to see her, Stryder, and her uncle, then hastened off in embarrassment.

"I never!" Rowena snapped as the older women vanished.

"Leave them," Stryder said. "Those rumors have been with me all my life. I no longer even hear them."

"Aye, but you do." Rowena touched his arm comfortingly. "You're just too well armored for your own good."

Stryder caught her uncle watching their exchange. Clearing his throat, he disengaged himself from Rowena's grasp.

"Is there something the two of you wish to tell me?" her uncle asked.

"Nay," they both said in unison.

Lionel looked back and forth between them suspiciously. "Are you certain?"

"Completely," Rowena said.

They rejoined the thronging crowd of onlookers downstairs who were gathered in the great hall as the door opened.

Stryder grabbed Rowena against him as soon as he saw the blanket-covered body being brought into the room.

"Stryder, what—"

"Sh," he said quickly, making sure she couldn't see her friend or the ones who carried her. "There are some memories no one needs to have."

Her uncle gave him a nod of approval as Stryder guided her toward the rear of the hall and to the exit that led toward the kitchens. Lionel stayed behind to tend the body.

"It was Elizabeth, wasn't it?" she asked, her voice thick with pain.

"Aye, love."

She closed her eyes. "Thank you."

He kissed her hand gently. "Ever at your service."

Rowena paused to give Stryder a hug for his thoughtfulness and she savored the warmth of his body. The feel of his strength and comfort.

"Is this ever going to end?" she asked. "I'm beginning to share Joanne's thoughts. I am more than ready to go home and put this tournament behind me. How can we continue to have festivities after so many have died?"

"The same way we managed to laugh while we were in prison. You have to, otherwise you will go mad from the grief. Sometimes it helps to shout. Let the angels hear your rage."

"Is that what you did?"

He nodded. "Other times I would goad my captors just so that I could get a taste of them before they beat me back."

"What if I'm not as strong as you are?"

"I would never take you on in battle, Rowena. Methinks you could easily best me in that regard."

She smiled at that.

"Stryder!"

Neither of them had time to look or respond before someone threw them to ground.

Stryder struggled against the unknown assailant until he heard the whizzing sound of arrows being fired.

"Rowena?"

"I'm here," she said, her voice quaking from fear.

The weight removed itself to show him Kit, who then pulled the dagger from Stryder's waist and took off running.

Stryder rolled over to see a shadow dodging along the wall. It was obvious that was what Kit was after.

"Rowena," he said, urging her back toward the kitchens, "run inside. Now!"

She didn't hesitate to obey him.

Stryder ran after his brother. It didn't take long to catch up to him. Side by side, they chased after the shadow until Kit stopped suddenly and tossed the dagger straight for their target. It hit the shadow and caused him to flip head over heels off the wall.

Stryder watched in stunned appreciation as Kit skillfully scaled the battlement wall, even better than most knights, to reach the place where the man had vanished. It took him a few minutes longer to get to the top where Kit waited. They both looked down to see the body that had fallen over to the other side.

Kit cursed at the broken, unmoving body that lay far below on the jagged rocks that were piled up against the backside of the castle. Rocks that had been chosen for their lethal edges should anyone try to lay siege to the castle. A scaling ladder pushed off the wall would guarantee serious, if not mortal, injuries to any knight who fell from said ladder and struck those rocks.

"He's dead," Kit spat. "There'll be no questioning him now. I knew I should have struck before he made it to the battlements. Damn. He was supposed to fall on this side, not that one. I should have realized he would pitch himself over rather than be caught."

Stryder gaped at Kit. "You and I need to talk. We *definitely* need to talk."

Kit met his gaze for only an instant before he looked away. He started off the wall.

"Wait!" Stryder snapped.

Kit stiffened. "I'm not your dog, Stryder, to come and go at your command."

"Nay," he said, placing his hand on Kit's shoulder. "You are my brother. And I want a few answers, starting with how you knew that man was after me."

Kit raked his hand through his black hair. "I saw him attack Christian and I followed him quietly, trying to take care of him on my own. Unfortunately, he escaped.

"In the last hour, since you left the training list, all of your men have been attacked. So my next guess was that they would be coming for you. As I made my way here to warn you, I saw him again and chased him. You and Rowena just happened to get in our way."

Stryder didn't know what part of that shocked him most, his brother giving chase to an assassin or the assassin making so bold a move on all of his men during the light of day. "What do you mean, my men were attacked?"

"They are all fine. I don't believe the attacks were meant to do anything other than toy with them. They were just caught off guard, and for that I apologize. I didn't think the assassins would attack in the middle of the day, and I had no idea they would be going after anyone else." Kit directed his gaze to the wall where he had killed the assassin. "At least there's one less of them to worry over now."

Stryder wasn't amused by Kit's tone of voice, or the gleam in his brother's eye. "Has anyone been hurt?"

"Christian's arm was slashed." A haunted look descended over Kit's face.

"What are you not telling me?"

Kit climbed down the wall without answering.

Stryder jumped down after him.

His brother didn't pause as he headed back the way they had come.

"Kit!" he snapped, rushing to catch up. He grabbed Kit by the arm and pulled him to a stop. "What is going on here? And don't tell me again that you don't know. I know you better than that."

Kit refused to meet his gaze as his face mottled with color. It was obvious whatever it was, it upset Kit greatly.

"You can tell me anything," Stryder said, gentling his tone. "You know that."

A tic started in Kit's jaw. "I don't want you hurt and I don't want you dead." Kit finally met his gaze levelly. Sincerity burned deep in the eyes that were an exact match for Stryder's. "Whatever else you might think or hear, you must believe those two things about me."

Agony seized him as Damien's words returned to goad his anger. "You are Aquarius, aren't you?"

Tears welled in Kit's eyes before he looked away and Stryder had his answer. His brother's entire body shook and he hung his head shamefully.

Stryder couldn't breathe as he remembered how many times he had spoken to Kit through the walls of their prison. How many times he had promised his brother that he would save him while never knowing that it was Kit he was talking to. Kit whose cries had haunted him all these years.

In the end, he had left him there to be abused.

Stryder wanted to die with the knowledge of what had happened.

He pulled his brother into his arms and held him tight. "Oh God, Kit, I never knew it was you. I swear I didn't knowingly leave you there. Had I had even an inkling that you were still alive, I would have torn down the walls to get you out."

He felt Kit's tears against his neck. "I know that now, Stryder."

Stryder pulled back and braced one arm against Kit's thin shoulder. He lowered his head until their gazes were level. "Do you honestly?"

"If I didn't know it for truth, you'd be dead now." Kit's gaze was eerie and haunting. "By my hand."

Stryder was uncertain of this new side of Kit. He was used to his brother being humble and shy, not rigid and deadly. "How many men have you killed?"

Kit withdrew from him and unlaced the dark green leather bracer he wore on his left wrist. He rolled his white sleeve back to show Stryder what appeared to be a list written in Arabic on his arm.

"There are twelve names here," he said quietly. "All of them are dead save you."

Stryder touched the names he couldn't read that the Saracens had tattooed on Kit's arm. "When?"

"I killed them before I met you. Originally, I had intended just to return home and kill no one except you. I went to Michael's hoping he would shelter me from *Kalb al 'Akrab*, but when he threw me out, I knew I had no choice other than to fulfill my bargain. Without a haven, I dared not do anything other than what they had instructed me to do. There were times when I traveled that I was certain one of them watched me. Indeed, I would find notes of warning along the way, but I never knew who left them or when."

"But what of Cyril?"

Once more Kit refused to meet his gaze.

"Is he on your list?"

Kit shook his head. "Nay. I killed him because he recognized me as Aquarius."

That didn't make any sense. Cyril was in the same cell as Stryder. He would no more recognize Aquarius than Stryder had. "How would he know you?"

Kit flinched as if he'd been struck. Before Stryder could blink, Kit started away from him.

"Kit?"

"Leave me alone!" he roared. "I have no desire to remember that night any more than you do."

A sick feeling came over Stryder as he remembered how many times he and the rest of the Quinfortis had pulled Cyril away from some of the younger boys in their prison.

"Tell me he didn't—"

Kit turned on him with a hiss. "Don't you dare say it! And don't look at me." Kit's breathing was ragged as he raged. "I was there for five years after all of you escaped. Five years! Don't you or anyone else judge me for what I had to do to get free. You and your precious Brotherhood never returned for the rest of us. Never. You were too busy freeing others, and don't think for one moment that our captors didn't take great pleasure in informing us of every raid your Brotherhood performed that freed more. But never us. We waited and waited and waited, and none of you ever returned for us."

"Us?"

"*Us,*" Kit repeated angrily. "I wasn't alone."

Stryder closed his eyes as pain seized him. "Why didn't you kill me too, then? Why did you spare me when you didn't the others?"

"I was going to," Kit said, his voice hollow and deep. "That night in Canterbury when you rescued me and paid for me to have the room next to yours. I crept into your room while you slept, fully intending to cut your throat."

"What stopped you?"

"You did," he said simply. "Remember? You were in the throes of a nightmare and you came awake calling out to me, or Aquarius, rather."

Stryder nodded as he recalled that night. It was a nightmare he'd had since the night they became free. It was one where he heard Aquarius calling to him and he was trying to break down a door to get to the youth.

On the night Kit spoke of, Stryder had awakened to find Kit standing by the foot of his bed. "You said you heard me and that you were concerned."

Kit nodded. "I was hiding the dagger behind my back so that you couldn't see it. You were so trusting of me as my soul begged me to go ahead and kill you."

"Yet you refrained."

"Aye. Because when I asked you what you were dreaming of you told me how much you regretted not saving me and I knew it for the truth. Your pain was too genuine to be feigned. I realized my masters had been playing with my mind, lying to me. I hadn't seen you in years. As Christopher you owed me nothing at all, and yet you reached out to me when no one ever had. God knows there are far too few men like you in this world. I couldn't bring myself to kill you, even if it meant my dying in your place."

Stryder frowned at his words. "What do you mean?"

Kit let out a deep, tired breath. "I was given two years to fulfill my bargain, and my time has since passed. I was told to either kill all of you or they would kill me."

"No one has tried to kill you?"

"Not until today. It seems my masters have grown tired of dealing with us all and have sent in a new group to dispatch us."

"How so?"

"Elizabeth was one of us," he said wearily. "It appears she must have found *Kalb al 'Akrab* after all and confronted him. I know she didn't finish all the names on her list and she still had time to complete her mission. There was no other reason for her to die and I know she didn't drown. It's just too coincidental. Nay. They killed her. I know it."

Kit gave Stryder a sheepish stare. "She was the one who framed you for Roger's murder."

"And Cyril's? Why did you frame me for that one?"

"That was an unfortunate accident. The witness must have glimpsed me and in the dark thought that I was you. After all, how could Christopher de Montgomerie fell a knight of Cyril's skill?"

Stryder took a deep breath to quell his conflicting emotions. He was angry at Kit and fate for what had happened, and he felt guilty for leaving his brother behind. Most of all, he felt sick that he had failed so many people so needlessly.

"Elizabeth thought she was doing me a favor by convicting you," Kit said morbidly before he started away from Stryder. "I shall pack my things and leave your company."

"What do you mean, leave?"

Kit paused to look back at him. "What else is there for me? You don't want a whore in your company."

Stryder's temper broke. "Never say that word to me! What happened to you was never your fault. I was there, remember? I know the truth of what happened to you and I will not allow anyone, especially you, to use that word."

Something akin to relief flashed in Kit's eyes. There was still a wall between them, but he could feel Kit's resistence to him faltering.

He was reaching him.

Stryder patted Kit on the back, then urged him toward the kitchen where Rowena had escaped to. "Come, we needs gather everyone together and find a solution to this."

Kit stopped midstride. "Will you tell them who I am?"

"Nay. Your secret is safe with me, little brother."

Kit nodded gratefully as he followed along.

They found Rowena in the kitchen with a rolling pin held in her hands as if ready to do battle.

Stryder smiled at the sight of her there. She was truly lovely, but never more so than whenever she was holding her ground against anyone who threatened her.

She lowered her weapon. "Is the danger over?"

"Yea. Kit saved both our lives."

Kit shook his head in denial. "All I did was warn you."

Rowena smiled at his brother, then laid a quick, chaste kiss on his cheek. "Thank you, Kit."

Kit looked terribly embarrassed as he put Stryder between them.

From the kitchens, they made their way to Swan's tent. The same blue and gold as Will's, the inside was similar except it lacked a desk and had a smaller bed. Stryder's men were already gathered there: Zenobia, Swan, Val, Nassir, and Christian, whose arm was bandaged.

"Are you all right?" Stryder asked.

Christian nodded. "It was just a glancing blow. Enough to make me angry, but not enough to do much damage."

"Kit said all of you were attacked."

"Aye," Swan said. "Someone threw an ax at my head while I practiced, but no one saw who threw it."

"I had someone come up behind me and try to stab me," Val said. "I caught his arm and knocked him back. He turned and ran so fast that I didn't even get a good look at him. All I know is he was almost a head shorter than I am."

"I had a dagger tossed at my head," Nassir said. "Zenobia saw it coming and tripped me in time to save me."

Zenobia looked at him sweetly. "Ever my pleasure to embarrass you in public." She turned to Stryder. "But I didn't see who threw it at him either. Only the sunlight catching the blade made me realize what it was."

Like Nassir, he was grateful for her quick reflexes. "Did anything happen to you?" Stryder asked her.

"My wine was poisoned."

Stryder felt his jaw go slack.

"Have no fear," she said, "It was *dharindus*. I'm not sure what you call it in your language, but it is a fairly common poison in Syria. I knew the instant I smelled the wine that it was tainted."

"Why are they attacking us now?" Swan asked, rising to his feet. "And why *all* of us?" He looked around. "Which one of you angered our enemies?"

"I think I did when I didn't die," Stryder said.

Nassir stroked his chin thoughtfully. "Who is controlling them?"

Stryder forced himself not to look at Kit lest he give his brother away. "I believe it's someone called *Kalb al 'Akrab*."

"Heart of the Scorpion?" Val asked gruffly. "What has that to do with all this?"

"The Watcher of the West," Zenobia breathed as a light came into her eyes. "My people believe the star *Kalb al 'Akrab* is responsible for causing discord and conspiracy. Many of my people take an oath by it to exact revenge on our enemies. It would be the perfect name to give to a spy sent here to eliminate all of you." She looked at Stryder. "Where did you hear that term?"

Stryder didn't answer.

"I gave it to him," Kit said, surprising them all.

Stryder heard Rowena gasp, but she said nothing as Kit continued.

" 'Tis the name of an assassin executioner."

Stryder stepped forward. "Kit . . ."

" 'Tis fine, Stryder. I don't need you to protect me anymore. I'm tired of hiding."

Stryder's chest was tight as Kit unlaced his sleeve and showed his men what he had shown him earlier while Kit relayed everything else to them.

Rowena moved to Stryder's side and in truth, he welcomed her nearness, especially the hand that she placed inside his own. It soothed him profoundly while he hurt for his brother, who was bearing the most shameful of secrets to his men.

Nassir took Kit's arm and read the names on it. "Aubrey, James, and Vincent aren't on here, and yet they were killed by assassins."

"I'm not the only one they sent." Kit met each of their gazes in turn. "All of you have been looking for someone like Zenobia or Nassir, but it's not the Saracens who are going to kill you. It's people like me. We blend seamlessly because we are one of you. We dare not tell anyone where we've been or what has happened to us. We have no Brotherhood to help us. We're nameless shadows born of shame and horror. We have no conscience left and all we want is to be free."

"You killed Charles?" Swan snarled as he took Kit's arm and read the names. "You bastard!"

Stryder caught him before he could strike Kit. "Don't you dare!"

He forced Swan back.

Swan glared at both of them in rage. "He didn't do anything

to deserve death. Charles was my foster brother, you worthless dog."

"I know," Kit said, his voice breaking with pain. "They allowed me to pick three names that I wanted as a reward. The rest, such as Charles, were assigned to me."

"What three did you pick?" Christian asked.

"The only three I knew. Hugh of Wales, Geoffrey of Navarre, and . . ." His gaze went to Stryder.

"You would nurse a viper at your breast?" Swan asked Stryder, his lips curled in disgust.

"My brother is not a viper," Stryder said between clenched teeth. "And before you judge him, I caution all of you to remember he was there for five years after we escaped. *Five* years alone. He didn't have a Brotherhood to protect him. No friends to help him make it through the endless days. Tell me who among you wouldn't have done whatever you had to to get out of there?"

Stryder looked at Val. "Would you still take the moral high ground had we left you behind?"

Val looked away.

"Or you, Swan? How long would you have lasted without Simon and me, and the others?"

Anger and tension snapped in the air as everyone held their ground that they were right and the others wrong.

"Your point is well taken," Christian said at last, breaking some of the malignant atmosphere. "There's no need to condemn Kit for surviving. We all did things back then that none of us wishes to remember."

He passed a meaningful look to each one of them. "Kit risked much by confiding in us when he could have just as easily killed all of us in our sleep. He has put his entire life into our hands and he knows it. We could easily turn him over to Henry for justice's sake. But I, for one, will not punish him any further."

"How do we know he's not the one who came after us today?" Val asked.

"Because you're still living," Kit said with an arrogance Stryder had never heard before. "Trust me, I don't make those kinds of errors."

To Stryder's surprise, Christian stepped forward and held his arm out to Kit. "I, for one, welcome you to our ranks." A wry smile twisted his lips. "After all, it's better to have an assassin with you than against you."

"Aye," Zenobia agreed, holding her hand out as well.

Nassir and Val followed suit.

They all looked to Swan.

"Very well," he said, joining them. "But if you ever make a move on me, boy, I will be your first failure."

Kit shook his arm.

"So now then, what do we do?" Christian asked. "How do we find this *Kalb al 'Akrab*?"

"You can't," Kit said quietly. "No more than you can find the rest of us. We have been trained to hide beneath your very noses. You'll be looking for someone above reproach. Someone you would never think to blame."

"Someone from the Holy Land who hates us," Stryder said.

Rowena's face went pale. "I can think of one person who fits that description."

"Aye," Stryder agreed, "but we can't make that accusation. Not without inarguable proof. If we daresay anything against him, our lives are forfeit. Not to mention he could be innocent of this. Look at me. How many of you doubted my innocence in killing Roger?"

"We never doubted you," Val said, his tone offended.

"Nay?" Stryder asked, arching a brow. "Not even for a second? Or what about my killing Cyril?"

They looked about uneasily.

"Exactly," Kit said. "Stryder almost died because of a mistake. For that matter, I'm not even sure the Scorpion is a man. We're making an assumption with no facts to support it. Besides, looking for the Scorpion is a waste of time. He or she's not interested in any of you. *Kalb al 'Akrab* is only sent after us when we grow a conscience or try to escape without fulfilling our bargain."

Val folded his arms over his chest and gave him a look of disbelief. "If we're safe, then why is Christian wounded and why were the rest of us attacked?"

"As a warning to me," Kit said. "No doubt Elizabeth was a similar sacrifice because she tried to cover for me or maybe, like I said, she confronted him or her. She told me she had a suspicion, but she refused to elaborate." Kit sighed. "Nay, I think the Scorpion is playing with us."

"How can you be sure?"

"Again, because you're all living. If you were meant to die, you would have been attacked while you slept or when your guards were down. Not in the middle of the day when you could see the attacks coming." He looked at Zenobia. "And not with poisons the Scorpion would know you could identify."

Zenobia nodded. "He has a point."

Swan moved forward. "It seems to me I know one way to draw the Scorpion out."

"And that is?" Stryder asked.

Swan glanced speculatively at Kit. "We have something he wants."

"You're not endangering my brother."

"Stryder, he's right," Kit said calmly. "I am the one thing he will expose himself for."

"Then I say we get you out of here, to someplace safe."

Kit shook his head. "There is no such place. The Scorpion will find me no matter where I go."

"Perhaps. But this time you won't be there alone," Stryder assured him. "You'll have us with you." Stryder stepped back and addressed the group. "After nightfall, I want Nassir, Zenobia, and Christian to take you to the Scot in northern England."

"And if the Scorpion follows him?" Rowena asked.

"If it's who I think it is," Stryder said, "he won't. Besides if a noble goes missing, we will know instantly who the Scorpion is and I can send Swan after them to warn them."

"I think not," Swan said. "I don't want to be the next dead man found."

Stryder passed an evil glare at him.

"Have no fear," Val said. "I shall go with you and keep those evil beasts from slaughtering you."

Swan scoffed at that.

"It's the only plan we have," Stryder said sternly. "Tell the Scot that he is to keep Kit safe no matter what."

"Don't worry," Christian said. "The Scot burns for nothing more than someone to breech his walls looking for one of us. I think he would relish the idea of laying hands to an assassin."

"All right then," Stryder said. "Until it's time to leave, everyone act normal and let no one know what we've learned."

"And what have we learned?" Swan asked. "That someone is trying to kill us. We knew that before this."

Val elbowed him in the stomach. "I say if we need a sacrifice, we use Swan. He makes far too much noise for my tastes."

Stryder ignored them.

"Nassir, Zenobia, will you stay with Kit until tonight? I don't want him to be alone."

Nassir nodded.

Assured they would keep him safe, Stryder took Rowena's hand and started for the door.

"And now look at this," Swan said, indicating their clasped hands.

Val slugged him so hard, Swan crumpled into an unconscious heap on the floor.

Stryder arched a brow at his large friend.

"I warned him I wanted silence. You two go and don't worry about us."

Feeling a little less sure about leaving his men to their own ends, Stryder led Rowena from the tent.

Rowena let out a tired sigh as they walked back toward the castle. "What an awful event-filled day this has been."

"Aye, it has."

She pulled him to a stop and ran her fingers over the scar on his hand that the Saracens had burned into his flesh. "Why won't they just let all of you go?"

"Because we're still fighting them."

"And if you stopped?"

"Believe me, Rowena, I would give anything to lay aside my sword. But how can I when I know there are more men down there like Kit? More women like Elizabeth? Would you have me abandon them? To just turn my back on them and say, who cares?"

"Nay, I would not."

"Then what would you have me do?"

"I would have you find this Scorpion and expose him. He alone knows the identities of the assassins. Find him and we stop this."

"And just how do you propose we do that?"

"I'm not sure, but I think I may know of a way."

Chapter 15

Rowena was numb for the whole of the next week as Elizabeth was buried and the crowd tried to put aside the tragedies that had plagued the event thus far. It was as if a pall hung over everything and everyone, and what was normally a festive occasion more times than not was only half-hearted. The days of the tournament progressed slowly as knights and squires practiced for the oncoming events.

But all the while, Rowena missed her friend.

Stryder and his men were more concerned than ever for her safety, so much so that Stryder even forwent his plans to stay away from her while they looked into the truth of what had happened to Elizabeth. Her only solace came in meeting with Stryder to teach him a song while he continually fought against learning one.

It had become quite a habitual routine. After supper, Rowena would travel with him to his tent, where he would grimace and complain for a full half an hour or more before he would sit and let her teach him the notes and words.

Neither of which he ever tried to duplicate well.

Then he would finish the lesson off with a kiss, and Swan would find some way to interrupt them so that Stryder would be forced to take her back to the castle.

It was enough to make her want to take her lute to Swan's bottom. But he meant well, and for that she almost tolerated his interference.

During the daytime, while Stryder practiced his swordplay and jousting, Rowena tailed Damien everywhere he went, trying to catch him in the midst of some dubious behavior that would show him for who and what he was.

Elizabeth's killer. He was the Scorpion. She was sure of it.

In fact, she had spied him only a few moments ago heading toward the king's counsel room where Henry had been holding court all morning.

Why would Damien be interested in venturing there while the king was gone unless he was looking for information about the king that he could hand over to Henry's enemies?

She was sure he was up to something evil. Insidious. Just like she had been when she had followed him into the woods two days ago.

Of course then, the dubious event had been him meeting with a farmer to buy fresh berries, but . . .

He was guilty of treason, and she would prove it.

Rowena held her breath as Damien slipped into the king's room like a silent specter.

More careful this time, as she was learning from her previous mistakes at being caught by him, she peered through the cracks in the door to see what he was doing.

There was no sign of him.

Rowena tapped her chin in indecision. Should she slip into the room as well or wait for him to reappear?

Stryder had warned her most earnestly against following after Damien. After all, if he was the killer as she suspected, he wouldn't hesitate to take her life as well.

But the prince seemed to like her well enough, and if she turned up dead, then Stryder would know for certain who had done it and no doubt he would avenge both her and Elizabeth.

There was still no sign of movement or sound from inside the room.

Now or never . . .

Taking a deep breath, she cracked the door ever so slightly and glanced around.

No one was in there that she could see. Where could he have gone? There was no other exit out of the room.

She stuck her head in a bit further.

"Looking for me?"

Squeaking, she jumped as Damien's deep voice startled her from behind.

She swung around to find him in the hallway, standing with his arms crossed over his chest. How she hated that cowl that kept him completely concealed from her. It was extremely disconcerting to speak to someone when you couldn't see their face or eyes.

"I . . . I . . ." she stuttered as she tried to think up another fabrication, "was looking for my uncle."

He cocked his head, or cowl rather, to the side. "And why would he be in there when Henry is not?"

She held her hands up and gestured as she tried her best to come up with a reasonable excuse he might actually believe this time. "Because he likes to sit on . . . nay, wait. He . . . he forgot something."

"He forgot something?" Damien asked in that calm, even tone of his that somehow reminded her of a still, bottomless lake. "Well, if you tell me what it is, I can ask Henry or his marshals if someone has found it."

Well, that wouldn't work. The instant he did, he would know she was lying to him . . . again. "Nay, uh, I think he found it already."

"Which is why you were here looking for him even though he's nowhere to be found?"

She glared at Damien, wishing she could see his face. Then again, she had a distinct feeling he was laughing at her. Perhaps 'twas best she didn't see his face after all.

"Well, since he has indeed found it," she said, inclining her head toward him, "I shall take my leave of you and head back to the great hall."

She hurried away, but with every step she took, she could feel his gaze on her like a tangible, almost lethal touch.

At the top of the stairs she turned to see that he hadn't moved even the slightest bit. "Are you waiting for someone, milord?" she asked him.

"I was just waiting to see if you would look back. You shouldn't be so predictable, Rowena. It could get you into trouble."

She swallowed at his words. "Is that a threat?"

"Nay, Rowena. I would never threaten such a rare lady as yourself. Only others who aren't as entertaining as you are."

A tremor of fear went through her. "So you admit to threatening others?"

"Hmmm," he said, as if considering that. "Aye, I have. For that matter, I've even been known to kill a few of them from time to time."

He turned at that and went back into the study.

Rowena blinked twice as his words rang in her ears.

He admits it! Rowena's heart skipped a beat as she realized what Damien had just done.

She rushed down the stairs and out of the castle with only one destination in mind. Stryder.

It took her several minutes to find him training in the list with Raven, who had returned just the day before from his trip to York. Unfortunately, as Zenobia had predicted, he and Will had arrived too late to help their friend. The two of them had been quiet and withdrawn since their return.

But at least Rowena had good news for all of them.

"I have proof!" she announced proudly as the men fought before her.

Stryder lowered his sword as soon as he saw her running toward him. Until he caught a flash of silver.

Whirling fast, he barely had enough time to dodge Raven's attack.

Raven pulled back immediately. "I'm sorry, Stryder," he said breathlessly. "I hadn't realized you were distracted."

His youngest knight looked at Rowena, blushed, then excused himself.

Stryder pulled his helm from his head as Rowena danced around him like a small child who had just been given a gift.

"He's guilty!" she proclaimed for the millionth time, and since it had been that many if not more, he didn't have to ask who she was referring to.

Stryder sighed. Poor Damien. 'Twas a wonder the man hadn't killed Rowena for her persistence.

He looked at her wryly. "What did he say now?"

She counted her two items off on her fingers. "He threatened me *and* he admitted he's killed people."

He arched a brow at that. "I'm guilty of both of those myself and yet you still live. Healthy and sound in spite of all the aggravation."

She gave him a menacing glare. "But, but—"

"Rowena, love," he said, interrupting her tirade against Damien, "you must stop dogging Damien's steps. Everyone has noticed that you all but follow him to the garderobe. The man is toying with you."

"He admitted it," she insisted.

Stryder strove for patience. "What exactly did he say?"

"Well, he said my nosiness might be bad for me and I asked if he were threatening me. He said nay, he would never threaten me, and so I asked if he had threatened others. He said aye, and that he'd even been known to kill a few of them. See! Proof!"

He shook his head at her. "Those are words, milady. Nothing more, nothing less. You can't convict one of the most powerful, well-connected men in Christendom of being an assassin without incontrovertible proof. Damien is far too smart to give that to you. Trust me, I know him."

She looked away as if frustrated with him. "I can't believe he's going to get away with what he has done," she said, her voice thick with heartfelt emotion. "Elizabeth is dead because of him and I want him to pay for it."

He removed his gauntlet and touched her creamy cheek lightly. Her soft skin went a long way in soothing his ire with her persistence. In truth, he admired and respected her temerity. "We have no proof that he killed her. All we know is she drowned. It could have been an accident."

She looked up at him with those passionate green eyes that were untainted by the tragedies that had marked his life. "Do you really believe that?"

"Honestly, nay," he admitted, "I do not. But no one is going to listen to us unless we catch him midstrike."

She let out an aggravated breath. He saw the tears darken her eyes before she blinked them back. "I owe Elizabeth."

"I know, sweeting," he said as he caressed her cheek. "I understand the need to put her spirit to rest, believe me. But getting yourself killed isn't going to bring her back. You must stop following him. If he is guilty, *we* will catch him."

"Very well." She lifted her skirts, gifting him with the precious sight of her ankles before she headed back toward the castle.

Stryder watched the sway of her hips as he hardened, aching for a taste of those ankles . . . those legs . . .

Mayhap tonight he could bribe Val to knock Swan unconscious again so that he and Rowena could have one night of undisturbed freedom.

Pulling his other gauntlet off, he tossed it into his helm with the other one, and made his way to his tent. When he arrived, he was stunned to find Damien in there, waiting for him.

His old friend stood in the center, looking straight at him as he came inside.

"She is spectacular, isn't she?" Damien asked, his voice rumbling like thunder through the quiet stillness.

Stryder didn't answer. Though he had no issue with Damien, he more than understood why the prince hated him. "Why are you here?"

Damien didn't answer his question either. "She's quite a trophy for the tournament. I'm told new lords have been arriving daily since Henry made his proclamation that the winner will be Rowena's husband. Most of them plan to lock her in a convent should they win. They may not appreciate the lady and her untoward tongue, but they are all in love with her lands."

Stryder forced aside the anger he felt at Damien's words. The man was only trying to raise his temper and he would never give him the satisfaction of knowing it worked. "Why are you telling me this?"

Damien shrugged. "I just thought you would be interested."

"Well, I'm not," he said in a deadly, calm voice. "There's not a man here who hasn't fallen in tournament to me. Most of them multiple times."

"Are you sure about that?" Damien asked.

"Aye."

"Very well then. Hold tight to your arrogance."

Damien headed for the exit, but paused to turn around. "By the way, I intend to enter the joust for her hand. I concede that you did best me with the sword. Hand to hand has never been my strong suit, but the lance is another matter. No one, not even you, Lord of Blackmoor, can challenge me there. But don't worry, Stryder. I shall take *good* care of your lady once we're wed."

That succeeded in breaking his calm. When Stryder spoke, it was from between clenched teeth with his voice carrying the full weight of his wrath. "Nay, you will not. Win, lose, or draw, I intend to see Rowena free to choose her own husband."

Damien laughed evilly at that. "Do you honestly believe Henry will allow her such a freedom? Rowena needs a powerful lord in charge of her lands. Someone with strong political ties. Win, lose, or draw, I will have her. Mark my words." With that spoken, Damien swept out of the tent, leaving his cloak to billow out ominously behind him.

Stryder followed him outside. "She will never marry you!" He ignored the knights who turned to stare at him while Damien paused, then turned back to face him.

The prince looked at him for several heartbeats before he spoke in a calm tone. "Women like her can easily be wooed with song and poetry. With letters of love from the one they desire. Tell me, have you ever written her a love letter? Oh wait, I forgot. You're nothing but an illiterate buffoon. All you're fit for is brute strength and knocking grown men to the ground. Do you really think that in the end, she will choose a barbarian like you over someone like me?"

Damien turned on his heel and headed down the line of tents.

It took every ounce of will Stryder possessed not to attack Damien over those words. As an old friend, Damien knew the history of Stryder's parents. The mere fact that Damien had hurled the difference of his being a knight and Rowena being cultured at Stryder made his blood boil.

But no more so than the truth of what the bastard had said.

In the back of his mind, he saw Rowena last night as she teased him about the fact that he didn't catch on to her songs quickly and that his fingers often fumbled the chords.

That he was ever a knight and never a troubadour.

Rowena loved troubadours and their songs.

And she had spent her life preaching against knighthood. . . .

He heard his mother's faint laughter ringing in his head as he remembered the times she had criticized his father for his oafishness.

"Want me to kill him in his sleep?"

Stryder looked over his shoulder to find Will standing there with a murderous gaze directed at the place where Damien had vanished.

"You heard?"

"Aye. Several dozen heard," Will looked around at the men who were still staring at Stryder.

Stryder sent them a glare that made them flee instantly.

"Too bad you're not Kit making those threats," Stryder said churlishly. "Then I might say yea."

Will laughed at that. "My sword is ever at your command. One word . . ."

"Nay. He's not worth your life." Stryder went back inside his tent while Will followed after him.

"Don't take his words to heart," Will said. "He's a bully and an arrogant braggart."

That was true, but then Damien was also an excellent challenger for the joust. Highly trained and accurate to a fault, Damien, like him, had never been defeated.

Stryder had never faced him in a joust and didn't really expect to lose to him.

But when it came to Rowena's heart, Stryder wasn't so sure. Could her love be taken from him as easily as his mother's had been taken from his father?

It was ever human nature to change, and women's nature to be fickle with their hearts. Not to mention, Damien was a prince. He was cultured and literate. He even shared Rowena's love of poetry and music.

Grinding his teeth, Stryder pushed the matter out of his thoughts. There was nothing he could do except talk to Rowena tonight when she came to him and see if there were any truth to what Damien said.

Rowena could sense something even darker than normal about Stryder the instant she entered his tent. He sat at his desk with a piece of paper before him. A deep frown marred his handsome brow and his attention was solely on the paper.

He had yet to even hear her approach and that more than his frown told her just how intent he was on his task.

Knowing he couldn't read, and curious about what had him so transfixed, she approached silently to peer over his shoulder.

Her breath faltered as she saw what he was doing.

He was trying to copy the one letter's contents onto another piece of paper.

"Stryder?"

He turned sharply, then wadded up the paper he'd been writing on. He snatched the paper up so fast that he overturned the inkwell, then cursed as he righted it. Of course, it was too late, as ink had spilled all over the desk.

Stryder grabbed a cloth to dab at it.

Rowena moved forward to help him.

"What were you doing?" she asked as they wiped up the spilled ink.

"I . . . I . . ." he let out a long, deep breath as if he were too tired to try and think up a lie. "I was trying to teach myself to write a letter to someone."

She felt a strange weepiness in her chest at his words. Imagine a man like him humbling himself to learn to write at his age. "Why?"

He replaced the quill pen to its wooden holder as he shrugged. "I had something I wanted to say and I grow tired of having to tell others what I wish to have written. I thought it was time that I learned to write for myself. After all, Simon once got me into a great deal of trouble by being my scribe."

She had no idea who this Simon was, but she wasn't interested in him. She only cared about Stryder. "What were you trying to write? Perhaps I could be of service."

He looked rather uncomfortable about that.

"Is it a letter of war?" she tried again. "Do you need someone to issue orders to some of your men or to the Brotherhood?"

"Nay, 'tis a personal letter."

No wonder he was nervous about it. Stryder could be very private at times with everyone. "Would you rather I sent for one of your men?"

He snorted. "I wouldn't trust them with this."

"Would you trust me?"

He met her gaze with something akin to embarrassment, though why he should feel such, she couldn't imagine.

He debated silently for several minutes before he stepped back and pulled his chair out for her.

Rowena took a seat at his desk. She pulled a fresh piece of vellum from the drawer and placed it on the desk. Taking the quill, she dipped it in ink and looked up at him. "Whenever you're ready, milord. To whom should I address it?"

"Leave the name blank. I have many things to say and if you will just write some of them down, then I can copy them later so that this person will know I wrote them in my own hand. It's important to me that this person knows that."

How strange. But unwilling to question him on something that obviously bothered him, she poised her hand over the paper. "All right then. Just tell me what to pen."

Stryder rubbed his eyes as he took up pacing between the desk and his bed. Silence hung in the air while Rowena waited patiently.

She'd never seen Stryder like this before. He was rather jumpy and skittish, more like an untried youth than the fierce knight she'd come to know so well.

After he paced for a bit, he finally spoke. "Fair greetings. I hope this letter finds you well."

Rowena wrote the words down for him.

"I have been counting every minute of every day we have been apart."

Her stomach shrank at his words. Who could he be writing such a letter to?

"And on every morning when I awake, the first thought I have is of you."

Rowena stopped to give him a glare, but he was too busy pacing to take notice of her displeasure.

"In all my life, I never thought that I would find anyone like you. Someone who makes me laugh even when I no longer have strength even to smile. All I have to do is think of you and my heart is instantly gladdened. Indeed, I keep every one of your smiles stored especially there in my heart and in my mind.

"You'll never know how truly sorry I am that fate would not

see us united. That things couldn't have been different between you and me. But then there is much in my life that I regret."

Tears stung her eyes as she realized what he was dictating and to whom he would one day send this letter.

Without glancing at her, he drew a deep breath. "I hope this note finds you well and that you will smile when you think of me and not be saddened as I am saddened. I would never wish to be the source of your unhappiness. Instead, I hope you have all you desire and that someday, should things be different, you might again welcome me into your arms.

"Ever yours, Stryder."

Stryder moved to stand by her side where he glanced down at the paper. "Did you get everything written?"

Rowena sniffed back her tears as she shook her head. "Nay, milord."

He let out an exasperated breath. "But how is she to know of my feelings if I don't write them to her?"

"She knows, Stryder." Rowena looked up at him and saw the same pain she felt mirrored in his blue eyes.

"But if I don't write it—"

"It makes no difference to her whether or not you write it," she said, taking his rough, callused hand into hers. "Only that you think it and feel it."

He knelt down beside her and stared longingly into her eyes. "I do feel it, Rowena. I feel it every time I look at you. Every time I think of you."

She bent down ever so slightly to capture his lips with hers. Oh, the taste of this man . . . it made her dizzy and weak. Made her soar high above this world.

He was her heart and her soul.

He was everything to her.

And she wanted to let him know just how much he did mean to her. But not with words. He had reached out to her with what she needed and now she would give him what he craved.

Stryder closed his eyes as Rowena left his lips and buried her mouth against his neck. Her tongue teased his flesh with delectable strokes that tore through him. She'd never been bold with him before, but he delighted in the way she took control of their desire.

He still felt like an ass for saying what he had. But he did want her to know how he felt about her. He owed her that much and more for all she had given to him.

"You know," she said, pulling back from his neck. "I've always been wrong about something."

"And that is?"

"I thought there was nothing in the world more seductive than a troubadour singing his observations about his lady love. But I was wrong."

She trailed her fingernail down his arm, raising chills in its wake. "The most incredible seduction is when a knight who is renowned for his strength speaks from his heart. Not as a knave out to woo a woman because he can, but as a man who wants only to give of himself." Her gaze seared him as she stared into his eyes and he saw her innermost sincerity. "I love you, Stryder. I always will."

Savoring those precious words, he kissed her deeply, tasting the full, sweet honey of her mouth. He balled his fists in her hair and let the cool, silken strands caress his war-scarred fingers, let her gentle softness caress his battle-hardened heart.

She loosened the laces of his breeches as he reached behind her back and undid her pale yellow gown. He growled deep in his throat as she sank her hand down into his breeches to cup him in her hand.

"I like it when you're bold with me, Rowena."

"Do you?" she asked, her voice thick.

"Aye."

She seemed to take courage with that. She tugged at his black surcoat, which was trapped under his knees. Stryder shifted his weight so that she could pull it off him. It was quickly followed by his black tunic.

"Mmm," she breathed as she ran her hand over his bared chest. "You are far too handsome for any man."

Before he could comment on that, she dipped her head down and gently suckled his nipple. Stryder swore he could see stars as unexpected pleasure tore through him. His breathing ragged, he looked down to watch her as she teased and tormented his flesh with her tongue and mouth.

How could he let this woman leave him? How could he give her freedom when all he wanted to do was hold on to her forever? And yet he had no choice in the matter. None whatsoever.

She nipped his flesh playfully before she pulled back. The wicked smile on her face made him even harder as she pushed him gently to the floor.

Stryder lay back on his rug and let her have her way with him. It was refreshing to see her like this . . . a tigress who was as hungry for him as he was for her.

She tugged the boots from his feet, then his hose. Still fully dressed, she removed his breeches, leaving him bare before her.

He'd never had a woman study his body so intently before.

Smiling, she stood up and returned to his desk.

"What are you doing, Rowena?" he asked, suspicious of her actions.

She returned with the quill. "I'm teaching you to write," she said impishly.

Stryder frowned as she sat down beside him and then wrote something across his stomach. Chills sprang up all over him.

"What are you writing?"

"*Amor vincit omnia,*" she said with a smile. "Love conquers all."

Lifting himself up on his elbows, he stared at the ink stains on his stomach while she wrote something else beneath it.

"And that?"

She bit her lip as she gave him a devilish stare. "I belong to Rowena."

He arched a brow at that. "I do, do I?"

She nodded playfully.

Stryder pulled her to him and pinned her to the ground. She lay beneath him, her eyes shining and bright.

He kissed her and kissed her again before he pulled back and quickly divested her of her clothes and shoes. "Now let's see what I can do."

He took the pen from her hand and, looking down at his stomach, he did his best to copy her words.

Rowena watched him, her heart pounding as he wrote his *b* and *g* backward when he spelled "belong." Still, it was the most beautiful sight she had ever beheld.

He looked at her expectantly. "How do I spell my name?"

She covered his large, masculine hand with hers and showed him how to write his own name. "S-t-r-y-d-e-r."

He sat back on his heels to inspect his work. "Did I do it correctly?"

Rowena's eyes misted as she saw his less than elegant script that said she belonged to him. Even though some of the letters were malformed and hard to read, it was still the most wondrous sight she'd ever beheld. "It's lovely, milord."

"Aye," he breathed, giving her a heated once over. "You are indeed."

Rowena hissed in pleasure as he dragged the feathered end of the quill over her bare breast. She shivered all over from it. She'd never felt the like!

Stryder's eyes smoldered as he gave her an evil grin. He explored every inch of her body with his lips and that feather. Who knew someone could have so much fun with a mere pen?

Rowena writhed in sweet, agonized bliss from the torture of his hot, blistering touch.

He was so warm and hard. So tender. She loved the feel of his muscles surrounding her. The sensation of his prickly, hard, masculine body sliding against hers.

She kissed him, one, twice, thrice, inhaling his scent, and letting the power of him intoxicate her. The candlelight played over his tawny flesh and danced in the rich highlights of his dark hair. She ran the backs of her fingers over his stubbled cheeks and jaw, letting the manly feel of his skin scrape her gently.

"You are magnificent, Stryder. No wonder women chase you."

He dipped his head down to kiss the valley between her breasts, then he nuzzled her ever so tenderly. "But I don't want them to chase me, Rowena. None of them have what I desire."

Stryder growled as he licked and teased the honey of her skin. She was so soft and delicate in a world where things seldom were either one. Softer than velvet, her caresses tore through him.

She wrapped her silken legs around his waist, tightened her grip, then rolled over until she had him pinned under her.

Stryder smiled as he looked up at her smiling face. Her pale hair fell forward, over them, down to his chest where it tickled his naked skin, his nipples.

She looked like some wild nymph that had crept into his tent. Her eyes flashing, she bit her bottom lip as she skimmed his flesh with her hungry gaze.

"May I have my way with you, milord?"

He hissed at her question and at the thought of her doing the most sweetly torturous things to him. "Ever at your service, milady."

She kissed him then. Stryder moaned at the unmitigated wildness of her kiss before she tore her lips away and moved slowly down his jaw to the underside of his chin where her breath scalded his throat. She licked and nibbled, driving him wild as she made her way to his chest, his stomach, his thighs.

He raised himself up on his elbows so that he could watch her as she explored the lengths of both his legs. And when she reached his feet, he jerked in bittersweet pleasure as she tickled him.

She laughed before she tickled him again.

Stryder smiled. How he loved watching her make love to him. No woman had ever made him feel so special, so desired, and it wasn't just physically.

All women wanted his body. With Rowena there was something different. She was interested in more than just his titles and groin.

With her, he could be himself and trust her with his dearest kept secrets.

Rowena reversed her direction, moving slowly back up his legs until she reached the center of his body. She paused to breathe one hot, tingly breath over the very tip of his manhood.

Stryder dug his heels into the rug as chills swept over him. His entire body involuntarily jerked.

Rowena hesitated as if losing her nerve, then she took him into her mouth.

Closing his eyes, Stryder savored the feel of her wet, sleek mouth taking him in. Her tongue swept against his flesh, making him harder, heavier.

He buried one hand in her hair as he watched her pleasure him. The sight of her blond hair fanned out over him almost succeeded in undoing him.

But he wasn't ready for that.

Not yet.

Rowena was startled as Stryder rose up quickly.

"Don't stop," he said breathlessly as he reached for her and pulled her body toward him.

She wasn't sure what he intended until he lay himself beside her so that she lay over his chest with her feet at his head.

"Stryder?"

His warm hands slid over her back as her breasts pressed against the hard ridges of his abdomen.

"Aye?" he asked, nipping the back of her thigh with his teeth.

"What are—" She broke her words off with a cry as he buried his lips against the center of her body and his intent became obvious.

Taking a moment to savor his caresses and licks, she then returned to taste him with equal enthusiasm.

Oh, he was ever splendid. Rowena trembled at their mutual giving and sharing. It was what she loved most about her warrior. He wasn't content to just take from others. He was ever so giving of himself. Considerate and kind.

Stryder was the very antithesis of everything she found desirable in a man, and at the same time, he was everything she had ever wanted and more.

There was nothing she wanted except to be with him. To keep him close to her and yet she knew he wouldn't stay. He would ever be a falcon out to throw his jesses and flee whatever cage she tried to force him into. A woman couldn't keep a man so proud and dedicated for her own.

And she ached with the truth of it.

But she wouldn't think of the month's end that would see them separated. Instead, she preferred to think only of the time they did have together. To focus on the fact that for a little while, she had tamed her falcon and taught him to feast from her hand.

Rowena moaned as her body exploded.

Stryder took no mercy on her as he felt her climax. Instead, he licked and teased until the very last tremor had gone through her and she was begging him for clemency.

Laughing, he rolled over, pinning her under him. He got up and turned about so that he could crawl up her body. Laying himself between her thighs, he stared down at her as he slid himself deep inside her hot, wet body.

She arched herself against him, drawing him even deeper. No longer in the mood for tender love play, Stryder thrust against her, seeking a temporary solace that would keep him from thinking of the inevitable.

He wanted to be with her like this so that he could drown out the sound of Damien's voice that threatened to take Rowena away from him.

He didn't want to let her go and he didn't know how to keep her.

Was it possible to have both?

Nay, he knew better. This was the real world where dreams very seldom ever came true.

And when he finally found his release, he roared with it.

Rowena cradled Stryder to her as she watched the pleasure on his face as she felt him shuddering. His warm seed poured into her, connecting them in a way nothing else could.

She cupped his head and lifted herself up to kiss him. He laid them both back as he nibbled her lips and stroked her face with his hand.

She felt his heart pounding against her breasts. He lay his head down on her shoulder and held her quietly as they both floated back down into their bodies.

"Stay with me tonight, Rowena," Stryder said quietly. "I want to lay with you in my arms while I sleep."

She started to tell him it was impossible, then bit back the words. She had covered for her ladies-in-waiting to go trysting with their lovers enough times that they owed her a favor just this once.

Not that her uncle would seek her out in her bedchamber this late. He never did.

His routine was flawless. After supper each night, he would retire to Henry's quarters where he and the king would play chess for a bit and then Lionel would seek his own bed.

He never disturbed her.

She could stay and no one would ever know except for them and her ladies.

"I shall need you to fetch Bridget in the morning and have her bring me a fresh gown so that no one will know I stayed here," she said quietly.

He pulled back and stared down at her incredulously. "You'll stay?"

"Aye."

His eyes dancing, he picked her up from the floor and carried her to his bed.

Rowena covered herself with his blanket as she watched him gather their clothes and bring them to the arming chest beside his overly large cot. Here in his bed, she was inundated with his intoxicating scent. It clung to the blanket, the pillows and most of all, it clung to her, marking her effectively as his.

He pulled closed the thick canvas material that separated his sleeping area from the rest of the tent and blew out the candles.

The sudden darkness was a bit frightening until she felt the bed dip beneath his weight.

Stryder gathered her into his arms and held her close to his naked body. Sighing in contentment, she folded herself into him and just inhaled his warm, masculine scent.

"Stryder?"

He tensed at the sound of Swan's voice on the other side of the divider. "I am sleeping, Swan. If you value your life, disturb me not."

"Are you alone?"

"Swan," he said, his voice sharp and deadly. "Turn about, head out of my tent, or so help me, I shall send you to attend duties in Outremer."

"Good night, milord," Swan said stiffly, then he added in an equally sharp tone. "And you'd best be alone."

Stryder let out a disgusted noise as they heard Swan leave. "I swear, I should hire him out as a wet nurse."

She muffled her laughter against his shoulder. "He would make a good one, wouldn't he?"

"Aye, provided the poor child assigned to him didn't murder him in his sleep."

She laughed again, then settled down to rest quietly in his arms.

Closing her eyes, it didn't take her long to drift off into sleep. But as she surrendered herself to Morpheus, one thought hovered in the back of her mind.

She had been with Stryder far more times than she should have and within the week she should have her flow.

What if she didn't?

Stryder awoke just before dawn to find Rowena snoring ever so softly beside him. He smiled at the sound and at the sight of her nestled against his shoulder with her hand tucked underneath her chin. Her long, blond hair fanned out behind her, falling over the edge of his cot.

She was beautiful in the faint light. Tempted for a quick tryst, he refrained. She looked tired and no doubt could use her sleep. She'd told him that she'd been having trouble sleeping ever since Elizabeth's death.

But she'd seemed to sleep peacefully in his arms. The thought warmed him.

Kissing her hand, he reluctantly withdrew from her, being careful not to pull her hair or wake her. He had much to do today, including the need to rally his men and have Swan send a messenger to the Scot to make sure everyone had arrived safely.

Stryder looked back at Rowena and smiled. What he wouldn't give to wake up every morning like this . . .

Sighing at the needless thought, he quickly washed, dressed, and went to break his fast.

Rowena wasn't sure what time it was when she came awake to someone talking outside of Stryder's tent.

When she first opened her eyes, it took her a few seconds to remember where she was. Heat burned her face as she realized she was naked still in the earl's bed. Someone, hopefully Stryder, had placed her blue gown on top of the arming chest. There was no sight of the yellow gown that she had worn the night before.

Someone had also placed a washing bowl, towels, and a large water pitcher for her.

Rowena threw back the covers to wash and dress, then laughed quietly at the sight of Stryder's writing on her stomach. Her body hot with the memory of his touch, she placed her hand over it and smiled tenderly.

That she would take care to keep a little while longer.

A bit fearful of being caught naked in his quarters, Rowena washed quickly and pulled her gown on. She was grateful Bridget had sent one that laced in the front and not the back. Leave it to her friend to think of that.

She rolled her fresh stockings on, then slid her feet into her shoes and started out of the tent.

No sooner had she started down the hill than she saw a group of knights gathered in a circle and heard an old woman's voice speaking Arabic, asking if anyone could understand her.

The knights were bullish and hostile toward the old woman as they insulted her in Norman French. If anyone understood her questions, they didn't speak up.

"I understand you," Rowena said, making her way through the crowd.

The men parted with an air of anger, but then she was used to that, and she paid them no heed as she sought to help the woman.

In the midst of the knights' circle, she found an old woman dressed as a Saracen servant. She was holding the thin, frail hand of a boy who was no older than eight. He also wore Arabic clothing, but his features and pale skin were clearly European. Strands of his golden blond hair had come loose of his hat and he had very large dark hazel eyes.

He was terrified as he looked at the large men surrounding them.

"Milady," the Saracen woman said as she bowed low before Rowena. "Please, can you help us?"

Rowena offered her a smile. "What can I do for you, good woman?"

She rose slowly and pulled the boy forward to stand in front of her. He stood there staring up at Rowena as if he were even more afraid of her than he was of the knights. Still, he was a handsome boy.

"I was told to bring Alexander"—it took Rowena a moment to recognize the name through the woman's heavily accented Arabic words—"to his father. I was told he would be here with the other knights of his kind."

That made sense. Most European knights who were renowned were here for the tournament. And the boy could belong to any of them. "And who is his father?"

The old woman nudged the boy forward. "Show the lady your sign, boy."

The boy shook his head and cringed away from Rowena.

"It will be as Allah intends, Alexander. Show her your father's symbol."

The boy's eyes were filled with tears as he looked ready to bolt for cover. He reluctantly tugged at a chain that was around his neck until he brought out a small heraldic emblem. It was the kind that many knights wore around their necks.

Rowena moved forward so that she could see whose coat of arms were painted on it.

Alexander's medallion was old and worn with most of the enamel missing. Even so, she knew instantly who it belonged to.

Her heart stopped. Aye, she knew his father.

Well.

"Who is your mother, Alexander?" Rowena asked, forcing her voice to stay gentle and even in tone.

The boy looked up at the old woman.

"Tell her," the old woman urged.

"Elizabeth of Cornwall," he said, his tone as fearful as his eyes. "But they told me she died."

Rowena couldn't breathe. Aye, he did look like her friend. She could see Elizabeth's features plainly now that he had spoken of her, but she saw nothing that marked him as the son of his father.

"What are they saying to you, lady?" one of the knights snapped as the crowd grew restless.

"No doubt they're lies. I say we should kill them."

Rowena frowned at the men around her. "Do you mind?" she said in Norman French, glaring at them all. "Can't you see they are terrified?"

"And well they should be."

"I say we string them up as a warning to others of their kind."

Rowena straightened herself up. "You'll have to go through me to do it."

"That won't be a problem."

As one of the men moved forward, he was pulled suddenly backward.

"Actually, 'tis a problem," Stryder said angrily. "To get to the lady, you must first defeat me."

One of the knights spat on the ground. "Leave it to you to defend a Saracen dog."

Stryder turned on the man with a glare so intense, Rowena felt a wave of fear from it. "Are you issuing a challenge?"

The knight, along with the others, quickly withdrew.

Rowena took a ragged breath, grateful once more for Stryder's interference.

He faced her, his features lightening instantly until he swept a puzzled look over the boy and old woman. "What are they doing here?" he asked.

"They are looking for the boy's father."

Stryder nodded, his gaze completely innocent. "Should I fetch him?"

"Nay, there is no need."

"How so?" he asked with a frown. "Is his father dead?"

"Nay, Stryder," she said as she indicated the boy's necklace. "His father is you."

Chapter 16

Stryder blinked, then blinked again as her words went through his mind and were rejected. "I beg your pardon?"

"See for yourself," Rowena said, shaking her hand that held a tiny medallion in it. "He wears your badge and they both claim the badge belongs to his father."

Stryder stared at the two of them, his mind reeling. How could this be? He'd never fathered any child, never mind one who had a Saracen nurse.

"Do they speak Norman French?" he asked Rowena.

"Nay."

"Good," he said, relieved by that one reprieve, "because I don't want to ask the child who his mother is. Did you by any chance ask?"

"Aye."

"And?"

"He says Elizabeth."

Once more he was almost struck dumb by her words and the boy's claims. "*Your* Elizabeth?"

"Aye," Rowena said, her eyes troubled.

Oh, this didn't bode well for him. The last thing he needed was for Rowena to think he had been with one of her ladies. "But I never touched her. Never. I swear it."

Rowena touched his arm, her gaze tender. "I know, Stryder. Believe me, I know."

Relieved that Rowena was being reasonable and not screaming at him for seducing her friend, Stryder knelt down before the child and took the small medallion from Rowena's hand to study it.

It was indeed his father's emblem. One he had carried with him into the Holy Land when he wasn't much older than the boy in front of him.

Stryder closed his eyes as he remembered the day he had been taken into captivity. He had forced this emblem into Damien's hand.

"Tell them you are my brother. They won't hurt you if they think you are no one of consequence."

Damien had curled his lip in disgust. *"But I am of consequence."*

Even so, Stryder had forced Damien to take it. Damien had grabbed it from him, and Stryder hadn't seen it since. In fact, it had been years since he even thought about it.

The boy licked his lips as he looked from his medallion to Stryder and then back again.

"Are you my father?" the boy asked him in Arabic.

Stryder was afraid to answer that question lest this be some sort of trick the assassins were using against him and his men. And if it was, he would kill whoever toyed with an innocent child in this manner.

"Where did you get this?" he asked the child.

"My uncle gave it to me."

Stryder cocked his head as he looked up at the child. "Your uncle?"

"Aye. He was from a place called France. We came through there to get to here, Nana said, but she didn't know where exactly my uncle lived when he was a boy. He used to tell me all the time about France and my father and how the two of them used to play pranks on other boys and on their cook. Do you have your own cook?"

Stryder shook his head at the boy as he tried to keep him on topic. "And what specifically did your uncle tell you about your father?"

"That my father was the bravest knight in all the world. He said that one day I would find him and that my father would take care of me just as he tried to take care of my uncle. But my uncle said he was a bad boy and didn't listen to him. He told me that the devil always comes for little boys who don't listen to their elders."

Stryder thought about that. The more the boy spoke, the more his uncle sounded like Damien, but that was absurd. As much as Damien hated him, he found it hard to believe the man could ever say anything kind about him.

Never mind tell an innocent child tales of their boyhood together.

"And your mother?" Stryder asked. "Why didn't you live with her?"

He looked up at the old woman.

"She was taken from him, milord, as soon as he was weaned," the old woman answered. "He doesn't remember her."

"And his uncle?"

She shrugged her thin shoulders. "He was taken away three years ago under protest. We know not what happened to him."

Stryder's stomach lurched as he thought of Damien with the child. They must have been kept together for quite some time for a child so young to remember so much of what Damien had said.

"And what of the boy?" Stryder asked the woman. "Where has he been kept?"

"In a guarded orphanage with other boys his age. So long as his mother obeyed her masters, they promised her he wouldn't be harmed. Word was sent that she had died and I was told to bring him home to his father."

That made even less sense. "Told by whom?"

"Servants don't ask questions, milord. We only do as we are told."

Stryder apologized, then looked back at his "son."

"What is your name, child?"

"Alexander."

He smiled gently and held his hand out to the boy. "I am Stryder of Blackmoor, little Alexander. Your father."

The boy looked as stunned as Stryder had felt when he had heard the same.

Alexander's eyes teared brightly. "Are you truly my father, the great English knight?"

"Aye, lad. Forever and always."

The boy launched himself into his arms with a happy yelp.

Rowena felt her own eyes start to tear as she watched Stryder and the boy embrace. There for a moment, she had almost feared that Stryder would deny him, but she should have known better.

He would never be so cold to a child.

The old woman started away from them.

"Wait," Stryder said, rising with the boy cradled in his arms. Even though Stryder was large, the boy was still too big to be held. His long skinny arms and legs were wrapped tight around Stryder as he laid his little head on Stryder's shoulder and kept his eyes closed tight.

"What is your name?" Stryder asked the woman.

"Fatima."

He inclined his head to her. "Thank you, Fatima, for bringing my son to me."

She nodded, then started to leave again.

"Fatima?" Stryder called after her. "Will you not stay with us and help Alexander adjust to his new home?"

"I must return. My master will be very upset if I don't."

Stryder set the boy back on his feet. "Do you have family to return to?"

"Nay. My son died as a child and my husband not long after. I have worked for my master at the orphanage ever since."

"Then stay," he insisted, "and help Alexander. I will send money to your master to pay for your freedom."

The old woman wept at those words. "You would free me, a useless old woman?"

Stryder gave her a chiding glance. "You're not useless, Fatima. You traveled a long way to bring my son to me. I think Alexander would like to have a familiar face around, is that not right, Alexander?"

Alexander nodded fanatically. "I love Nana," he said. "She tickles me when I'm good and tells me lots of stories."

Stryder held his hand out to the old woman. "Stay with us, please."

Fatima didn't touch him, but she did bow.

"Nay," Stryder said, helping her up. "No more bowing except when you pray. You're a freewoman now."

Fatima's lips trembled as she took Alexander's hand into hers. "Your uncle was right, little one. Your father is a good man."

Rowena stepped back out of their way as Stryder led them toward his tent. She followed along behind them as Alexander skipped along, asking questions.

"Do you live here all the time, Father? Or do the English travel like the nomads? Will I be a knight like you when I grow up? Nana said I was a freeman, but I don't know what that means. She said my father, or you that is, would tell me one day. Will I finally get to ride a horse? We rode on a boat to come here. It was expensive and we couldn't eat anything but flat bread and water. If we were good at home and did our chores, they would let us have milk. Will you let me have milk when I'm good too?"

Stryder laughed at the child and his incessant questions. "I should let you have milk even when you're bad."

"Really?" Alexander looked triumphantly at Fatima. "Did you hear that, Nana? I can have it when I'm bad too."

"I hear, scamp. We shall see."

Stryder showed them his tent. Alexander ran around and inspected every bit of it.

"A sword!" he shouted as he found Stryder's arming chest.

Stryder rushed to take it from him. "Careful, child. 'Tis very sharp."

Alexander bounded around then, pretending he held a sword of his own as he battled imaginary knights, dragons, and monster scorpions.

Rowena watched Alexander "battle" with laughter in her heart. "You must have had your hands full with him," she said to Fatima.

"Aye, he even fell overboard the day we started our journey."

Alexander paused in his play. "The sailors were very angry that they had to save me," Alexander said seriously. "They said they would feed me to the sharks if I fell again, so I was very careful not to slip and fall."

Swan came into the tent, then froze as he caught sight of Stryder scooping Alexander up and tossing him over his shoulder.

"What is *that* doing here?" he said, indicating Alexander.

"*That* happens to be my son, Alexander," Stryder said hotly. "And I pray you show him proper respect."

Swan looked horrified. "Nay, nay, nay, this cannot be. First 'tis bad enough that Rowena shows herself here every time I glance away, but now this? Tell him Simon is his father and send him to Scotland."

Stryder was aghast at his knight and when he spoke, he was careful to use Norman French so that Fatima and Alexander wouldn't understand him. "Simon has children aplenty already. The boy believes me to be his father, Swan. His mother is dead and I won't denounce him."

When Stryder's gaze met Rowena's she understood why. She remembered the look he'd had on his face when he had told her about his own father denouncing him. The bitter pain that had been evident even after all these years.

He would never hurt a child the way his father had hurt him.

Swan threw his hands up. "Fine. But have you given thought as to what we're going to do with a child in our travels? How are we to ferret out the Scorpion while the boy trails along after us babbling and doing all those annoying things children do? And what of the people out to kill you, Stryder? Now they have another target."

Rowena watched as the color faded from Stryder's cheeks. He reached out and placed his hand on Alexander's shoulder as the full weight of that settled on him.

Neither of them had given thought of that.

"I can take him to live with me in Sussex," Rowena offered. "I owe that much to Elizabeth."

"And if you marry?" Stryder asked her. "What will your husband say?"

She scoffed. "I will not marry, I've told you that."

"If Henry decrees otherwise?"

Rowena opened her mouth, but was cut off by Swan. "Don't even propose that the two of you wed. Think for a moment, Stryder. Again I say to you, if you leave a son and wife in England while we are abroad, they are living pawns. Anyone who wants control over you merely has to capture them."

"I have guards," Rowena said.

Swan gave her a droll stare. "As did Henry, and yet Sin MacAllister was able to crawl unseen into Henry's tent when Sin was only a boy and lay a knife to the king's throat. We are not dealing with incompetent fools here. Our enemies are highly trained and cannot be seen until 'tis too late."

"Is something wrong, Father?" Alexander asked as he looked back and forth between Stryder and Swan.

"Nay, child." Stryder looked back at Swan. "Take the boy and his nurse. See them fed fully while I think this over."

"Yea, Stryder. You think about this carefully. We are not men as others. How many times have you warned all of us that we aren't able to have families because of the burden we carry?"

Swan gentled his face as he looked at the boy. "Alexander?" he said in Arabic.

The boy looked at him suspiciously.

Swan held his hand out to him. "I am one of Lord Stryder's men, and you may call me Swan. Come and I will see that you and your nurse have food to eat."

The joy leaped back into Alexander's face. Taking Swan's hand, he let the knight lead him from the tent with Fatima following after them.

As soon as they were gone, Stryder raked his hands through his hair. His face tired, he looked at Rowena and offered her a half-hearted smile. "Good morning, milady. I never even got the chance to say that to you."

She walked into his arms and laid a gentle kiss to his cheek. "Good morning."

Stryder wrapped Rowena in his arms and let her presence soothe him for a few seconds while he thought over what he should do.

"Why does life have to be so difficult?" he asked. "I look at other men such as your uncle and they seem to be able to live their lives at ease without such conflicts."

"All is not as it appears, Stryder. You don't see the inside of my uncle's heart to know how hard his life has been. Unlike you, he is the youngest son of my mother's family. 'Tis why he was chosen to be my guardian. He will never inherit his own land nor mine, even though he has been a good lord to my people and vassal to Henry. 'Tis why he has never married. Instead, he has had to stand aside and watch the woman he loves marry a lord because that man was landed while he could offer her nothing. I am sure he must resent me at times for having been born an heiress, yet he never shows it."

"How could anyone resent you?"

She squeezed him at the kind question.

He sighed and released her. "What should I do, Rowena?"

It amazed her that he even asked her opinion. How unlike any man to care what a woman thought about anything. It was why she loved him so much.

Marry me, the voice in her head whispered.

But that was something she wouldn't say out loud, especially since she had been the one who refused his suit.

"I know not, Stryder. However, I am quite certain that you will do whatever is right for everyone involved."

"You say that with much more conviction than I feel. I have been wrong so many times. . . ."

"But you have been right more times than not."

He shook his head. "I wish I shared your faith in me."

She placed her hand on his shoulder and kissed his biceps. "Have no fear, Stryder. Things will turn out as God intends them."

Rowena released him and stepped back. "I shall leave you alone to think. Should you need me, I shall be in the kitchens making sure Swan is feeding Alexander—and I don't mean to a wild boar."

Stryder gave a half laugh at her jest. Of course, with Swan one was never certain if he would actually do the outrageous or not.

He watched Rowena leave his tent while his mind whirled.

"What should I do?" he breathed.

Stryder's quest for an answer to that question led him straight to Damien's door. He strode toward it with raw determination.

"Halt!" one of the two guards flanking it said as he drew near.

Stryder ignored them.

They started to grab him only to find themselves flat on their backs as he moved them aside and swung open the portal.

Damien looked up in startled surprise.

But it was Stryder who was shocked most as he came face to face with Damien, who wasn't masked or robed. His old friend sat on a padded chair, flanked by two robed Arab physicians as one of them took a cup from Damien's hands.

Damien's hair was still the same golden blond shade, but unlike the days of their boyhood when he had kept it cut short, Damien wore it long and braided down his back. His amber and green hazel-colored eyes glowed with unmitigated rage.

Stryder couldn't breathe as he saw the black tattoos that had been placed upon Damien's cheeks. One below each eye, they ran parallel to the man's cheekbones. Stryder had no idea what they said, but it was obvious they were words and not symbols.

If not for those marks, Damien's face would have been flawless in its beauty.

"How dare you!" Damien snarled, coming to his feet. He rushed to a table on the other side of the room where he seized a golden mask and held it up to shield his face from Stryder. The mask was an exact duplication of what Damien's face would have looked like had it not been damaged by his captors.

The physicians started toward Damien, but he pushed them away. "Leave me!" Damien snapped.

The guards came forward to take Stryder, who quickly shrugged off their hands.

"I want to talk to you," Stryder snarled, "and I won't leave here until I do."

Damien stood, glaring at him as he tied the mask to his face. With a furious jerk of his head, he indicated to his guards and physicians to leave them alone.

They did so reluctantly.

Stryder continued to watch Damien as he waited for them to close the door and leave them in peace.

Dressed in a scarlet surcoat and hose, Damien still wore gloves even though he was indoors. For once the prince didn't bother to reach for his cape as he closed some of the distance between them.

"Whatever you have to say, you'd best make it quick," Damien said in a low, gravelly tone.

Stryder went straight to the heart of the matter. "Why did you send Alexander to me?"

Damien pulled up short at the name, then his features went blank. "I have no idea what you're talking about. Who is Alexander?"

"You know who he is, Damien," he said between clenched teeth. "Don't play your games with me or with that child. So help me, if you do, I will see you in the ground regardless of the consequences to myself."

He had a strange feeling that his words somehow pleased Damien.

Damien moved to stand behind a chair, with his hand on the high, ornate back of it. When he spoke, his tone was low, almost as if he was afraid someone would overhear them. "So you will protect him?"

If he didn't know better, Stryder would almost swear he heard hope in Damien's voice.

"Are you planning on using him against me?"

Damien laughed coldly. Ironically. "Nay. I will not."

"Do you swear it?"

Damien smiled. "Even if I did, would you believe me?"

Nay, he wouldn't. How could he when Damien had already confessed to the fact he hated him?

"Why did you tell him I was his father?"

Damien looked away and took his time answering that question. "I didn't know what to tell him when he asked me. So I tried to think of someone he should admire and strive to be." Damien locked gazes with him and the hatred there was searing. "The only person I could think of who was honorable was you."

Stryder truly didn't understand the man's reasoning or his unwarranted hatred. "And you hate me because of that?"

"I hate you for many reasons."

"Yet you send me a child to raise?"

Damien tightened his grip on the chair. "I will see you duly compensated for all his expenses."

"I don't want your money, Damien. Nor do I need it. I only want you to leave the boy alone and not toy with his emotions or his mind."

"Have no fear there. I will stay completely out of his life. Tell him his uncle died. It's all he needs know."

Stryder nodded. "I just have one last question."

"And that is?"

"How much do I send to Fatima's master to buy her freedom?"

Damien cocked his head.

"It's how I knew it was you, Damien. Besides the medallion

the boy carried, there was also the matter of his appearance here from Outremer. It would take someone very important to get the two of them to England without harm. You should be more careful."

Damien didn't acknowledge his warning in the least. "Why are you keeping Fatima?"

"Because Alexander loves her and he needs someone around him he knows. You of all men must understand what it feels like to be a stranger in a foreign land where no one understands you when you speak and you have nothing but strangers around you."

A muscle worked in Damien's jaw as he looked away. "I will take care of her master."

Stryder nodded, then turned to leave.

"Wait."

Stryder watched as Damien left him and went to his bedchamber. A few moments later, he came back with a carved wooden knight the size of a man's palm and handed it to Stryder.

"Tell Alexander that Edward has missed him."

Stryder frowned at the toy and Damien's vague message.

This time when he turned to leave, Damien grabbed his arm fiercely and held him in place. "Don't raise him to be the fool I was, Stryder. You make him grow up to be a decent man."

Damien released him and strode back to his bedroom without another glance in his direction.

The double doors echoed ominously before Stryder heard them lock.

Now that was an interesting encounter. . . .

Stryder still didn't know why Damien had sent Alexander to him nor why it was so important to him that Stryder keep the child and raise him.

Sighing over the oddness of it all, he left the room and made his way to the kitchens.

Rowena stood off to the side while Swan played with Alexander. For a man who said he wanted nothing to do with children, it hadn't taken him long to become friendly with the boy.

"All right, Alexander," he said as Alexander held up two celery stalks. "Here comes the fireball from the trebuchet." Swan held an extra large raddish in his hand, spinning it as it fell toward the celery stalks and Swan made noises simulating fire and flying arrow sounds. Not to mention the sound of men crying out for help from the falling radish, or rather "fireball."

Alexander laughed as Swan knocked the celery stalks over.

"Oh my head," Swan said, picking one celery stalk up and trotting it over the tabletop like a man limping. "It's on fire! Ow, ow, ow!"

Alexander laughed harder.

Rowena exchanged a horrified look with Fatima, who sat beside Alexander, finishing off her bowl of leek-pea porridge.

Stryder came in and Swan immediately put down the celery stalk and sat up straight.

"Don't play with your food," he said sternly to Alexander who looked baffled by Swan's sudden change in manner.

Clearing his throat, Swan gave Stryder a fierce glare. "I'll go now."

Stryder met Rowena's gaze and laughed. "Was he playing the flaming celery stalk game again?"

"Does he do that a lot?" she asked.

"Aye, but it frightens me less when he does it for the amusement of children and not himself."

Rowena laughed at that.

He moved to kneel down beside Alexander. The boy tugged at his ear until Stryder handed him a small wooden toy.

"Edward!" Alexander shouted, grabbing the toy. "Wherever did you find him?"

She saw pain cross Stryder's brow as the boy kissed his doll. "Your uncle sent him to you. He said to tell you that Edward had missed you."

Rowena watched Stryder's face. There was something he was hiding.

"Oh, Edward," Alexander cried again, holding the knight close. "I thought I had lost you. But that's all right. We're together now and we can fight more dragons and . . ." he glanced to the table where Swan had dropped their vegetables, "celery now."

While Alexander played with his knight, Rowena pulled Stryder aside. "Where did you get that doll?"

Stryder shrugged as he continued to stare at Alexander play-ing with his toy. It wasn't until then that he realized something.

Just how much Alexander favored Damien . . . right down to his eyes, which were brownish green, but they were close enough in form and color to proclaim Damien as the boy's father.

He let out a long, drawn-out breath as that realization settled over him.

Now everything made sense. Why Damien had kept Edward. Why he had laughed when Stryder asked if he would threaten the child.

And yet none of it made sense. If Damien hated him so much, why send his son to him to raise?

Unless Damien was afraid of the Saracens learning that Alexander belonged to him.

Even so, why couldn't Damien take the boy to his home in Paris? There he had the entire French court to guard the child. And yet it couldn't be that simple. If it were, Damien would have taken him home long ago.

There must be a lot more to Damien than he had guessed. If they were right and Damien was the Scorpion, then the child could become a pawn of either government to be used against Damien as an Englishman and as a Frenchman.

Poor Damien, but he had to give the man credit. Who would ever think to look to Damien's most hated enemy to find his son?

It was a brilliant move.

And it warned him just how careful he needed to be of Damien.

"Stryder," Rowena insisted. "Please tell me what is going on here."

He took her hand into his and kissed it lightly. "I can't, Rowena. I'm not sure myself and I don't want to endanger the child by saying anything more." He glanced around to the staff, who were for all intents and purposes ignoring them, but usually that was only a ruse. Servants gossiped. Often.

Rowena must have caught his meaning, for she nodded and went back to play with Alexander.

Stryder watched the two of them. They were precious together. But as he watched them, Swan's words came back to haunt him. His knight was correct. He couldn't just marry her and leave. To do so would leave her open to any attack from anyone out to cripple him.

But now that he had Alexander . . .

"Father?"

He looked to the boy. "Aye?"

"I need a chamber pot."

Fatima stood up. "Where may I show him?"

"I'll take him," Rowena said, holding her hand out to the child. "No one will think anything of us being together."

Hand in hand, they quickly left.

Fatima returned to her food while Stryder set Edward back on his feet next to Alexander's trencher.

"My lord?" Fatima asked. "May I humbly ask you why you look so saddened by Alexander's presence? He is a good boy and of very little trouble compared to others of his age."

"I know, Fatima," Stryder said as he toyed with the soldier's arms. "I am only concerned since I can't see a way to save the world and raise my son at the same time."

"What do you mean?"

"There's so much evil out there to protect him and others from. How can I fight for that and keep him safe simultaneously?"

She looked twice as puzzled by his words. "I still do not understand, milord. You are but one man with one sword to fight all the world. This is indeed a good thing. But when you are gone so too is your sword. So it seems to me that while it is important to fight the bad man, it is just as equally important to raise a good one. Raising *more* than one would be even better. That way when you are gone, you will leave a whole generation behind who will fight for what is right."

Stryder was awed by her wisdom. "Thank you, Fatima. I had never looked at it that way before."

She nodded and finished eating her food.

Stryder stood silently cogitating her words. That was what Zenobia had meant when she had been speaking of Simon. Though to be fair to Fatima, Zenobia hadn't phrased it nearly so eloquently.

Aye, he had something to fight for all right.

And for once, it wasn't the Brotherhood.

Chapter 17

The day flew by as Stryder introduced Alexander and Fatima to his men and showed them around the castle. He also commissioned new clothes for both of them from a visiting tailor—something that wouldn't make the two of them stand out so vividly from the rest of the people there.

At sunset, Fatima went off to pray while Alexander napped in Rowena's room under her careful supervision.

While his son slept in a bed he longed to be in, Stryder had gathered his men together in his tent.

"Something's wrong, isn't it?" Will asked, his tone gruff and surly as he took up a cocky stance by the desk. "I can feel it in my bones."

"Nay," Stryder contradicted. "Not exactly."

Swan let out a sound of disgust as he stood by the entrance with his arms folded over his chest. " 'Tis that woman again. She has ruined his mind."

Stryder growled at him. "It's not Rowena."

"The boy, then," Will said, looking to Raven. "We can send him—"

"It's not Alexander," Stryder said, cutting Will off as well.

"Then why are we here?" Swan asked.

"Because I wish to have a word with all of you. I've been thinking for a while now about our futures."

Swan cursed. "It *is* Rowena. You want to marry her. I knew it."

"It's not just Rowena," Stryder said. "There are many matters at stake."

"Like whether or not we continue," Raven said as he took a seat at Stryder's desk. "You know, Swan, we don't need Stryder to lead us every step of the way."

Swan's nostrils flared. "Bite your tongue, rat. You know not what you speak."

"Nay, let the lad have his say," Val said. "It's not fair for us to ask Stryder to give any more of his life to our cause. Any more than it would have been to stop Simon from marrying Kenna."

"But we *need* a leader," Swan insisted.

"I'm not dying," Stryder said. "I will still be here. I'll just be spending more time in England."

"Guarding your family?" Swan asked, his voice laden with venom. "I thought *we* were your family."

Val grabbed him by his tunic. "Don't you dare try and place guilt on his shoulders like that. We *are* family. All of us. And part of being a family is giving support to our brother when he finds something he needs."

Swan broke his hold. "We need Stryder."

"Stryder needs Rowena," Raven said quietly from the desk. "You've seen the way he watches her. And he has a son to raise. Personally, I would like to see Alexander safely ensconced in a home."

Raven looked at Stryder. "All of you know I never knew my parents. My mother died at my birth, my father before I was sent to foster." His gaze went to Swan. "You may not care for your blood relatives, but you know who they are and you can go visit them any time you wish it. You've no idea what it's like to wonder what a father's love would be like or a mother's touch. I swore my service to the Brotherhood so that children such as I would have those things I lacked."

Raven stood up and held his arm out to Stryder. "Either here or abroad, I will serve you wherever we go. But for Alexander's sake, I hope you choose to stay here and be his father."

Val nodded. "We can tourney on our own and still pose as a relay between Outremer and England."

Will curled his lip and made a noise of disagreement, but finally he joined them. "Love, bah. I never thought you'd buy into such foolishness, but I hope that damned fool emotion serves you better than it has ever served me."

They all looked to Swan, who hadn't budged. "I stand by my words. I will not throw my lot in with the likes of you to see our cause fail."

"I don't need your permission," Stryder said. "I only wanted all of you to know this from my lips."

"And so we know it," Swan snapped.

He left the tent.

"He'll come around," Will said. "Or I shall thrash him until he does."

Stryder snorted at that.

Rowena opened the flap. His three men were instantly awkward as they quickly took their leave.

"Did I interrupt something?" she asked as she brought her lute into his tent.

"Nay, we were finished." He frowned as he glanced back at the opening, expecting to see Alexander trotting along behind her.

"Alexander is being watched by Bridget and Fatima in my rooms."

Stryder nodded. "Good. I wanted a few minutes alone with you. I've been thinking—"

"What is this?" she asked, breaking him off as she moved to his desk.

He frowned as he saw her pick up the list of matches for the tournament that Will had been reading to him earlier that evening. " 'Tis nothing. Just our opponent listings."

Her face went flush as she flipped through the stack of papers. "My word . . . how many men are on here?"

"One hundred and fifty."

"One hundred and fifty?" she repeated in disbelief. "This says there will be three straight days of jousting."

"Aye, there were so many entrants this year that Henry decided to lengthen the time accorded for the jousting."

She looked at him incredulously. "Why are they all here?"

"Because of Henry's decree naming you as the prize."

She stiffened as she reviewed the names. "Half of these men openly despise me. And the rest I know not at all. Wherever did they come from?"

"All over, Rowena. As you have said yourself, you own one of the best pieces of property in the known world. There are many here who would sell their souls to have it. Marry you and a man goes from landless knight to powerful baron. You've never been without, so you can't imagine just what a temptation you are."

She slammed the papers down and looked horrified. "So I am the prized goose and nothing more?"

"Rowena, you knew this all along."

"Aye," she said angrily, "but I didn't know men would be crawling out of all corners of Europe just to pummel each other for a piece of property that just happens to be attached to my hand."

He was baffled by her logic and her indignation.

"And this!" she gestured to one of the names he couldn't read. "Damien St. Cyr has entered the joust? Damien?"

"Aye, has no one told you?"

"Obviously not. Why would he enter?"

"You amused him this past week as you sought to expose him."

"Amused him?" she shrieked. "The man killed my best friend and is a cold-blooded murderer. I could never marry one such as he. I would sooner die."

Stryder tried to soothe her. "Worry not, milady. You shan't have to marry him or any of the others. I will win the tourney for you."

She cocked her head supiciously. "Are you certain?"

He stiffened, offended by the question. "There's not a man on that list that I haven't thrown to the ground multiple times in joust."

"Including Damien?"

Stryder hesitated.

"So you haven't bested him?"

"Nay, not in the joust. But I hold no fear of his winning, and neither should you."

She pressed her hands to her head as if she had an ache in her temples. "Oh Stryder, you cannot imagine how I feel right now knowing all these men are here to fight each other to bloodshed over me." She looked at him. "Will you still marry me? Now? Tonight? Take me far away from this madness."

How he wished he could. But it wasn't that easy. "Nay."

"Nay?"

"Nay, Rowena, we can't. If you wanted to marry me, you should have said aye three weeks ago when I asked you."

"What do you mean we can't marry now? Why not?"

He gestured toward the papers on his desk. "You saw the list yourself, Rowena. Those men came here because Henry promised the victor you. If I were to marry you less than one week before it begins, they would attack Henry and dethrone him."

"You can't be serious."

"Believe me, I would never jest over something like this. We have to see this through."

Her eyes flashing, she faced him with her cheeks darkened by her wrath. Dear heaven, but she was beautiful when she was angry. "I see. I have to sit by like a good goose and cheer on my butcher."

However, her anger was starting to ignite his own. "I'm not a butcher and you're not a goose. And why are we arguing over this when you wish to marry me?"

"Because I hate to see men fighting each other over such foolishness, and it sickens me that I am the reason grown men are going to try and kill each other."

"I thought that was the whole idea of courtly love. Sacrificing your life for your unattainable lady, even though you may never have anything more than a passing glance from her?"

She gave a most undignified snort at that. "And that is not the love I write of. I find nothing romantic in unnecessary bloodshed."

Stryder pulled her close enough so that he could kiss her temple. He inhaled the sweet, floral scent of her hair. "After Friday next, you shall never again have to fear unnecessary bloodshed. I will win you in tournament so that you won't have to fear them."

She nodded as she calmed a degree. "And I shall come dressed in white feathers, like all good geese do."

He sighed at her stubbornness. "Would you rather I lose?"

"Nay! Most especially not to someone like Damien St. Cyr."

"Then why are we fighting?"

"Because!" She turned on her heel and stormed out of his tent.

Stryder stood there in complete stupefaction, trying to understand what had just happened.

"Women," he growled. No man would ever understand them. Raking his hand through his hair, he headed for the comfort of men. At least they said what they meant and they made sense when they spoke.

Stryder spent the next few days readying himself for the tournament without any more lessons from Rowena. In fact, she barely spoke to him other than to honk like a goose and flap her arms whenever he tried to talk to her.

And God have mercy on him, but Alexander had taken up the habit as well.

"Aren't I funny, Father? Rowena said it would make you laugh."

Groan, more like. But Stryder refused to hurt the boy's feelings. So he patted him on the head and sent him off with Fatima while he cursed Rowena for being childish.

Stryder spent the night before the tournament in the chapel as was his habit, saying a prayer for strength and for all the souls he'd known who had died away from the reach of their families.

'Twas late in the evening when he made his way back to his tent to find Rowena waiting there. Dressed in a long cloak, she was sitting by Alexander's small cot, watching the boy sleep.

"What are you doing here?" he asked, half expecting her to honk at him again.

She didn't.

Instead, she rose slowly to her feet and moved to stand before him. "I gave Fatima the evening off. I didn't know you would be gone so long. I was hoping you would return before Joanne and Bridget vanished, but alas there is no one who can watch Alexander now."

He laced his fingers through her hair. "I wouldn't have been late had I known you were here, waiting and not honking at me."

She smiled at him and pressed her lips chastely to his. "I'm sorry for my behavior and even more so that I employed Alexander's help to annoy you. It was wrong of me."

Stryder cleared his throat. It was hard to feel rankled at her while she stood there apologizing and looking so inviting to him.

"I forgive you."

"Good." She pulled away and honked.

Stryder rolled his eyes.

She laughed. "I am but teasing." She glanced over her shoulder to where Alexander lay sleeping as if to assure herself the boy hadn't moved.

Then, she opened her cloak.

His breath caught in his throat as he saw her sheer chemise that accentuated more of her body than it covered. Her pink nipples were swollen and puckered, just begging him for a taste.

But more than that, her chemise showed his clumsy script where he had written the words "I belong to Stryder."

She laid her hand against his cheek. "I haven't forgotten."

She let her cloak fall closed and then tried to peek under his tunic. "Have you?"

"Nay, but unlike you, I was forced to wash mine off after Val and Raven saw it. They mocked me for days."

"Did they?"

"Aye, 'tis why Raven is off polishing my armor tonight."

"And Val?"

"He limps still."

She laughed at that. Stryder parted her cloak once more so that he could pull her barely concealed body against his and caress her skin through the sheer fabric. "Mmm," he breathed against her ear. "I wish I were inside you right now, tasting you. . . ."

Her cheeks pinkened at his words. "Milord, your son sleeps only a few feet away."

"I know, which is why you're not on the floor at this moment with me kissing you."

He cupped her face with one hand, kissed her deeply, then released her.

Rowena stepped back and smiled up at him. "You need your rest. On the morrow you have three men to defeat."

"Aye, I do."

She took both of his hands into hers and stared at the scars on them as if they made her ache. "I'm sorry I didn't say yea when you asked me to marry you, and I pray that no one is hurt in this travesty, least of all you."

He nodded. "You are aware that when I win this, I fully intend to keep you."

"I know. Alexander needs a mother." There was a pain in her eyes that made his heart lurch.

"Rowena—"

"Sh," she said, laying a finger over his lips. "I know I can't keep you at home, Stryder. I've no desire to try. As you said in your cell, 'tis for the best that we marry. It solves all our problems and it gives Alexander a home."

He'd never loved her more than he did at this minute. She asked nothing for herself. Nothing.

Kissing her hand, he bid her good night and watched her leave.

The morning came too slowly for Stryder, who tossed and turned with images of Rowena as a goose on his table.

Too bad she hadn't been wearing the sheer gown, but rather she'd been baked.

The nightmares had been terrible.

Fatima came to tend Alexander while Druce and Raven suited him up for the matches.

His first joust was at ten and as he took the field to wait his turn, his gaze searched the stands until he found what he was seeking.

Rowena sat in the stands with her ladies-in-waiting, wearing a white gown trimmed in down, and a crown on her head made of white goose feathers.

He laughed in spite of himself, especially as he saw her uncle's face beside her.

Leave it to his lady to vex any man near her.

Rowena hated the fact that her uncle and king commanded her presence at this debacle.

Every time two men charged each other, she cringed and closed her eyes. She'd always hated the sound of the horses' hooves, of wood striking flesh and metal, and the inevitable sound of a body slamming into the ground.

How could men be so barbaric to one another?

The hair on the back of her neck rose. Rowena turned her head, expecting to find Stryder staring at her.

He wasn't. Damien sat below on the back of his large, white

destrier. Both of them were covered in golden mail armor. She couldn't see Damien's eyes or his face, but she could feel his cold gaze on her body.

She quickly averted her eyes.

It seemed she waited for an eternity before Stryder finally rode.

He unhorsed his first challenger with no effort at all. A cheer went up through the crowd.

Reaching the end of this list, he turned his black horse about. It reared, pawing at the air while Stryder dropped the broken lance.

He righted his horse and inclined his head to her.

Rowena bit her lip, thrilled even though she shouldn't be. Before she could stop herself, she blew a kiss at her champion.

"What is it you do?" her uncle asked.

"Nothing," she said, looking down and plucking at her sleeve.

"Did you . . ." he looked at Stryder, then back at her. "Did you just blow a kiss at the earl of Blackmoor?"

"You're seeing things, uncle."

"Aye, she did," Bridget said from beside her. "She loves the earl, milord."

Rowena scowled at her friend.

"Is this true?" he asked her.

There was no need in denying it. "Aye, uncle, 'twould seem so."

His face turned deadly earnest. "Then I pray for your sake, Rowena, that he doesn't lose."

"He won't," she said with conviction. He had to win this. More than just her future depended on his success.

Once the matches were finished and the nobles had gone to sup, Stryder had expected Rowena to come to his tent that night. He'd made all the preparations, including sending Alexander to sleep with Raven.

But she never showed, and when he went to the hall to ask after her, he was met by her friend Joanne, who told him Rowena was ill that night and unable to attend the festivities.

When he tried to go to her room to check on her, her uncle kept him away.

"We can't have anyone think we are favoring one knight over any other, now can we?"

Angry at the truth, Stryder made his way back to his tent, where he spent a lonely night dreaming of a woman dressed as a goose making love to him.

By the time he took the field in the morning, he was exhausted.

As before, Rowena was in the stands, dressed in another goose gown. But she looked rather pale this day.

Concerned, he again tried to see her and was denied access to her by her uncle and the king.

So he sent Alexander to her instead. His son rushed through the crowd, dodging bodies until he made his way through the stands to Rowena's side.

His heart pounded with pride as she took the boy and sat him in her lap so that he could watch the matches. She still looked wan, but there was a little more color in her cheeks now that she was chatting with Alexander and pointing things out to him.

A few minutes later, when it was Stryder's turn to joust, Raven grabbed his reins and held him in place when he would have ridden out to meet his opponent.

"What are you doing?"

Raven indicated the stands with his head where Stryder looked to see Alexander running toward him.

Alexander stumbled as he reached them, making Stryder's horse a bit jumpy.

As Stryder soothed the beast, Raven quickly scooped Alexander up out of harm's way.

"Careful, bit," he warned. "Your father's horse might think you a small mouse to be trampled."

Alexander was breathing hard as Raven held him up to Stryder. "The Lady Rowena sends you this, Father."

Alexander handed him a scrap of paper that had something written on it. "She says to tell you that she cannot see you until the last match is won, but to hold that close and then she will read it to you and you will be overjoyed."

Stryder hugged Alexander and thanked him.

Raven set him down and the boy ran back to Rowena while Stryder tucked the note into his gauntlet.

"A letter," Raven scoffed. "You brave life and limb and instead of a kiss, all you get is a worthless piece of paper." He shook his head. "God spare me the arrow, and if Cupid must shoot my heart, then let it kill me."

Stryder ignored him as he took his lance from Raven's hand and faced his opponent.

He raced his stallion down the field and unhorsed the other rider on the first pass.

Stryder tossed his lance to the ground, then looked back for Rowena.

Her seat was vacant and there was no sign of Alexander anywhere.

Disappointed, he let out a tired breath. No doubt the sight of him bearing a man to the ground was upsetting to her.

Wishing he could spend some time with her, he dismounted and went to wait for his next match.

That night after the jousting had ended, there was no sight of either Alexander or Rowena in the great hall or his tent. All he received was a visit from Fatima telling him that the lady had wanted company tonight and so she had kept Alexander in her bedchamber.

So much for sending in his spy.

Damn.

His heart heavy, Stryder pulled his note out and stared at it. Yet again in his life, he wished he could read. Instead, he traced the beautiful script with his finger, wishing Rowena was with him.

Earlier, he had almost asked one of his men to read it for him, but had stopped himself. It might contain something personal. She had said she would read it to him and so he would guard it close until she did.

Aching for her, Stryder lifted the paper to his nose where he caught the faintest whiff of her scent. His body stirred instantly as an image of her in her sheer gown hovered in his mind.

"You are a witch," he breathed. "Ever tormenting me."

But she was a witch he loved, and on the morrow, she would be his.

At least that was what he thought.

* * *

The morning dawned bright. For once, Stryder slept well, and when he took the field, Rowena sat in the stands with Alexander. The two of them waved at him.

His heart light, he bore down his next two opponents and at the end of the day, the event turned out just as he had thought it would.

Everything came down to him against Damien.

They listened as the heralds called out the results. It was almost over.

Rowena would soon be his and no one would be able to separate them.

Damien reined his horse in beside him and gave him a smug look that not even Damien's helmet could mask. "Look your last on your lady, Stryder. In a few minutes, she will belong to me."

"Nay," Stryder said, knowing the truth in his heart. "She will never belong to you."

And in that moment his mother's face came to him and he had an epiphany.

Rowena did belong to him, just as he belonged to her, and it wasn't in a way he had thought.

She had touched his heart, his soul, and now, as he was about to face his childhood friend turned enemy, he finally understood why Rowena was a goose.

Just as he understood that the only reason Damien wanted her was because Stryder did. She meant nothing to Damien.

But she meant everything to Stryder.

Rowena was right. Some battles could never be fought by sword or by lance. Not by arrow or siege.

There was only one way to win his lady.

Rowena held Alexander close as he chattered away about how his father was going to beat the other knight. How no one could ever defeat a knight as great as his father. "My uncle said so," Alexander said with conviction. "And my uncle never lied to me. Never once."

She squeezed the little chatterbox as she waited for the match to begin.

As with all the other knights before them, Damien and Stryder faced off. Damien's armor glinted of golden wealth. Stryder, who could just as easily have had expensive armor, wore a plain silver mail suit over his leather aketon. His was a practical suit of war.

The horses stamped until the herald raised the flag. The two knights kicked their horses forward.

Rowena held her breath, waiting for the sounds she hated.

But for once they didn't come.

Just as Stryder would have made contact with Damien, he veered his horse away from the lance and the list.

Her jaw, along with every one in the stands, fell slack.

Stryder tossed his lance to Raven who stared at him as if he had lost his senses.

Indeed, he must have. Why had he not jousted against Damien?

The herald ran to Stryder and said something she couldn't hear even though the crowd was so silent that she could hear her own heartbeat as everyone waited to learn what was going on.

Was the earl injured?

Had his horse been damaged?

Stryder looked over at her, shook his head at the herald, and then kicked his horse from the field.

The herald ran to the stands where Henry and Eleanor sat. Taking a deep breath, he shouted out, "The earl of Blackmoor has forfeited the match, Majesties. The victor and winner of the tournament is Damien St. Cyr, duc de Navarre, comte de Bijoux and Averlay and he names the Lady Rowena as the Queen of All Hearts."

Rowena sat in stunned silence, unable to believe what she had just witnessed.

"I'll be damned and burned in Lucifer's deepest pit," someone said from behind her. "I can't believe this spectacle. Remember last year when the earl almost killed his best friend rather than see himself lose a match?"

"Aye," another man said. "The bitch of Sussex must truly be her namesake for the earl to forfeit after all this. I never thought I would live to see Stryder lose a match."

"And to throw it, no less. She must be the worst sort of womankind."

Pain seized her heart at their harsh words as her uncle snapped to his feet to confront the men behind them.

"How dare you!" he snarled.

He said something more, but she couldn't hear it for the ringing in her ears.

"My father lost?" Alexander wailed. "How can he lose?"

Rowena picked the child up and gave him to Joanne. She needed to get away from the crowd. From everything as her mind reeled from what had just happened.

Her knight had refused to fight for her.

She stumbled from the stands and headed blindly toward the castle.

Stryder had ridden off?

He had forfeited?

"Oh God," she breathed. "Please let me be dreaming. Please, don't let this be real."

Yet it was.

Stryder was gone and he didn't want her. He who would kill over any little thing had left her there alone to suffer the worst sort of humiliation.

He who lived to fight had refused to fight for *her*.

Unmitigated agony washed through her until tears streamed down her face.

What kind of fool was she?

Wanting to die, she made her way to her room so that she could just lie down and pretend that this day had never happened.

"Rowena!" Bridget snapped, pulling at her as she lay on her bed in a numbed cocoon of pain. "The song competition is beginning. You must get up."

She refused. Rowena never wanted to leave this bed again.

"Up!" Joanne said, tugging at her. "King Henry himself said that he will send his guards up here to fetch you if you refuse."

"Why bother?" Rowena wailed. "Stryder wouldn't joust for me, think you he will sing? I have no desire to go back down there where they can whisper and talk about me."

Her friends exchanged shamed glances.

Joanne tried again. "You are under royal command, Rowena. Please."

Hating her birthright more than ever, Rowena forced herself to rise.

Her friends seized her instantly and started straightening her clothes and smoothing her hair.

"Nay!" she said, pushing them away. "I'm the bitch of Sussex. 'Tis not my appearance that makes men desire me. 'Tis only my lands."

Bridget gave her a peeved glare. "At least wash your face."

Shaking her head, Rowena left the bed, swung open the door and headed with angry strides down the stairs. Why should she make herself presentable?

At least this way, they had something more tangible to mock.

But as she reached the great hall, her courage faltered a bit. There was quite a crowd in there. A large crowd that turned to stare en masse at her as she entered.

Heads came together, but she cared not.

Holding her head as high as any queen, Rowena strode through them, daring them to laugh. Some did. But she didn't care.

She couldn't feel their condemnation. All she could feel was the breaking of her heart.

She went to the chair to the right of Eleanor's that had been reserved for her.

"Child," the queen said gruffly as soon as Rowena sat down, "have you had an accident?"

"Aye, Majesty," she breathed under her breath. "I have been trampled and crushed. I fear I shall never be the same."

The queen patted her hand. "You have already missed the first three troubadours."

"Were they any good?"

"Nay. Count your blessings."

But not even Eleanor's humor could cheer her. "How many are entered?"

"Only a dozen."

Rowena took a deep breath and waited as the next male began his song. And as she listened, she began to agree with Stryder. Love songs did in fact reek like rubbish. They weren't speaking of real love, only of odes to women's throats and dried-up thighs.

She no longer wished a pox on knights. She wished one on all these horrible men who sang to her of made-up emotions of unrequited love.

And as every one sang, she had to bite her tongue to keep from shouting, "What do you know of it? If your heart were really broken you couldn't breathe, let alone sing."

Yet they droned on and on while every set of eyes in the hall was trained on her.

"Take heart, child," Eleanor said. "There is only one more to be heard and then you can return to your chambers."

Or could she? After this, she would have to meet with Damien to discuss the planning of her wedding, not to mention the banquet tonight where she would be crowned Queen of the tournament.

Mayhap this last milksop wouldn't be so horrendous after all compared to the horror that was waiting for her.

Staring at the floor, she didn't even look up as the final contestant entered.

Not until she heard a deep, rich baritone that filled the hall with the most beautiful sound she had ever heard.

Her heart pounding, she looked up to see Stryder holding his mother's lute.

Only it wasn't a love song he sang.

More like a limerick, it was a song about a woman who fancied herself a goose.

And a man who gobbled her up.

Laughter and applause rang out as soon as he strummed the last note.

Breathe, breathe.

It was the only thing Rowena could think. And even that couldn't get her to take a breath as Stryder approached her.

He smoothed her hair and straightened her feathered crown. "Methinks my goose has molted."

Rowena laughed as more tears streaked down her face.

"Well," Henry said. "We never thought We would see such a day as this. Our head champion reduced to a mere troubadour."

Rowena laughed giddily. "Aye, but he is incomparable as both."

Henry snorted at that. "Eleanor?"

"I judge Lord Stryder the best. What say the rest of you?"

A cheer went up among the women, and a few boos and hisses from the men.

But neither Stryder nor Rowena heard them as they stared at each other.

"So, Lady Rowena," Henry said, "you have your freedom to choose your husband. Who will he be?"

Damien stood up.

Until that moment, Rowena hadn't even realized he was present in the hall.

He didn't speak or move.

"Have you someone in mind?" the queen asked.

"Aye," Rowena breathed. "I want someone who can sing to me whenever I wish it. Someone who is fierce and strong, and who has all the qualities a noble knight should have. In this land of knavery, I want a champion who isn't afraid to stand up for himself or for others."

She met Stryder's eyes. "For the Lady of Love, there can be only one husband."

"And that is?"

"The one true prince among all the knaves. Lord Stryder, earl of Blackmoor."

She expected Damien to protest, but to her surprise, he didn't. He merely motioned to his men and quietly left the hall.

"What say you, Lord Stryder?" Henry asked. "You threw your perfect record so as not to have to wed her. How stand you on her wishes?"

Stryder's gaze never left hers. "I stand at the lady's side, my liege, where I intend to be ever at her service." He reached out and wiped the tears from her eyes.

"Well done then," Henry said. "We shall see you two wedded in the morning."

The king and queen rose to their feet and as they passed by, Rowena heard Eleanor mumbling, "I told you so, Henry. You should listen more to me than to your advisors."

Ignoring the crowd in the hall and her uncle, Stryder picked her up from her chair and carried her from the room, up the stairs until they reached her bedchamber.

"What are you doing?" she asked.

"I'm scandalizing you so that you will have no choice save to marry me in the morning."

She laughed at that. "You've already scandalized me, milord."

"How so?"

"Do you have the note I sent you?"

He pulled it from his sleeve.

Rowena opened it up and read it to him. "Knave of hearts and bane to all women, be it known that you must win your tournament for me, otherwise I shall have a most difficult time explaining to my new lord my newest addition."

He scowled at her as if he had no idea what she was talking about. "Your newest addition?"

Rowena took his hand and led it to her stomach, where his words were still written. "Aye, milord. 'Tis early still, but I am rather certain that inside me lives your future heir."

Stryder couldn't breathe as he stared at her in disbelief. "How do you know?"

"I told you 'tis early yet, but my monthly time has passed with no flow. I think we shall be parents to our own child soon, Stryder. But have no fear. I have no intention of making you stay home with us."

"Are you banning me from my home?"

"Nay," she said with a frown. How could he think such a thing? "I would never do such."

"Then I meant what I said below, milady. I never again intend to leave your side. Yea, I will continue to fight for my brothers, but I can't fight without my heart and my heart is you. I love you, Rowena. There is no other lady I would ever have."

She kissed him tenderly. "That is good then, Stryder. Because there will never be another lord I could ever welcome into my heart."

Chapter 18

Rowena paused as Stryder packed the last of her belongings onto one of his wagons. How odd that when she had arrived, the last thing she had ever expected was to leave Hexham with a husband and a child.

Yet here she was, holding Alexander's hand while his father packed them for their trip to their new home.

Most of the nobles were gone already, and on the morrow Eleanor and Henry would leave as well.

Swan was still rather surly with them, but he seemed a little less so today as he sat mounted on his horse between Val and Will with one of his eyes blackened. Raven was holding Alexander's small palfrey and had volunteered to keep the boy out of trouble while they traveled.

It would take a few days to reach Stryder's home where Val and Raven would remain while Swan and Will rode further north to check on Kit and the others.

Her uncle stood beside her with tears in his eyes. Stryder had gladly allowed him to stay on in Sussex as his vassal to oversee the people and lands.

"I shall miss you, sprite," he said before he kissed her cheek.

"And I you, uncle. You will write?"

"Always."

Once the last trunk was packed, Stryder joined her. "We are ready when you are, my countess."

She nodded and gathered her skirts, but before she could take a step, she saw Damien headed toward them.

His long cloak billowed out around him and he was flanked by two looming men. As he approached them, his men fell back.

He stood before them in silence and as with all the other times she had met him, Rowena couldn't tell which one of them he was staring at.

After a long pause, he stepped forward and reached his gloved hand out to ruffle Alexander's hair. An air of supreme sadness engulfed him.

"Take care of your family, Stryder," he said gruffly. "Let no harm ever befall them."

Damien picked Alexander up and placed him on the back of Alexander's palfrey.

Without a word, he turned and left them staring in his wake.

"That was odd," she breathed.

"He's a troubled man," Stryder said quietly. "I only hope that one day he finds peace within himself."

Stryder held his arm out to her uncle. "Take care, my lord. I shall see you anon."

"Aye," her uncle agreed. "I fear without Rowena and her ladies the hall will be far too quiet for my tastes. I shall visit with you very soon."

Rowena said good-bye to him as Stryder scooped her up and carried her to her horse. He set her up high in the saddle, then handed her the reins. "Are you ready, milady?"

"Aye, Lord Knave. Lead me into my future, whatever it may be." Because now that she had her prince, she knew that her future with her husband would never be bleak.

Love really did conquer all—even two headstrong people who were bound to breed even more obstinate children for the future.

But that was all right by her. After all, the world needed heroes who could wield both swords and words with equal skill.

Epilogue

Withernsea, England
Three months later

Christian of Acre sat in the aleroom of the town's only inn, finishing his supper in solitude while the rest of the inn's occupants ate and drank noisily around him.

He'd been here for the last four days, waiting for Pagan and Lochlan MacAllister to meet him. The plan was for them to join forces.

They were all on the trail of Lysander's murderer, who was said to have headed this way with his brothers. If Lysander's killer was anywhere nearby, Christian would find him and he would make him pay for what he had taken from them. And if Lochlan happened to learn anything helpful about his missing brother, then Christian would rejoice even more.

But at the end of the day, the only thing that mattered to him was putting Lysander's soul to rest.

Drinking the last of his ale, Christian left money on the table, then got up to go to his rented room.

Times like this, he almost hated that he traveled alone. Especially since Nassir and Zenobia were newly departed from his company. They had left just the day before, on their way back to Outremer.

But then Christian had chosen to live his life alone.

Besides, he had lived a great deal of his childhood sequestered in a monastery cell where the brothers forbade any chatter at all. They had used their hands to speak to each other. Never their mouths. So silence and solitude were nothing new to him.

Christian reached his room at the end of the hallway and pushed open the door.

He pulled up short as he caught sight of the figure waiting there.

Slight of stature, the unknown person was robed in a long black velvet cloak that gave him no indication of gender or nationality.

"Did you enter the wrong room?" he asked, thinking maybe it was another traveler.

The figure turned toward him.

"That depends," she said, her voice smooth and erotic, and tinged with an accent he couldn't place. "Are you Christian of Acre?"

"Who seeks him?"

The woman moved forward and boldly pulled at the thin gold chain around Christian's neck where his mother's royal emblem had rested since the hour of his birth.

"Aye," she said, letting it fall back to his chest on the outside of his black monk's robes. "You are indeed the one I seek."

"And you are?"

Her elegant hands came out of the dark folds of her cloak to unclasp the catch. Before he could even draw a breath, she let the whole of it fall to the floor with a rush of wind and a heavy thud.

Christian's jaw went slack as he saw her standing there with not a single stitch adorning her dark beauty. Long black hair cascaded over her shoulders, obscuring her breasts as the ends of it tickled the dark triangle at the juncture of her thighs.

"Who am I?" she asked. "I'm your wife, and I'm here to claim you. At least for the night."

Author's Note

There is really no way, in such a short amount of space, to fully describe the conflicts between the East and West that led to the Great Crusades. But for those of you who are unfamiliar with this time in history, I wanted to take a moment and define two terms that you may not be acquainted with.

Outremer is a medieval French word that literally means "over the sea." It was the common term that was used for what we today call the Holy Land. The term *Saracen* was used generically to mean anyone of Arab descent. I prefer to use both terms because they are more authentic to the time period and they are less of a political hot button. The purpose of the Brotherhood books is not to disparage any race or religion.

I firmly believe as Stryder does. History is written by the victors and so long as innocent children suffer, there are no real winners in any conflict. Both sides were wrong, and in the end, the innocent paid. The atrocities of both Saracen and Crusader are aptly recorded for all to read. My heart still weeps for all those who died so needlessly. My only wish is that there really had been an underground Brotherhood that didn't see things divided by politics or religion—men who fought only for those who couldn't fight for themselves. Men committed to freeing anyone who was needlessly suffering.

As T.H. White once penned for King Arthur, "Might shouldn't make right." It is in the grand tradition of the medieval troubadours that I love so much that I offer up a group of heroes who are able to lay aside their cultural and religious differences and fight side by side to make the world a better place for everyone.